By SJD PETERSON

NOVELS
Beyond Duty
Plan B

WHISPERING PINES RANCH
Lorcan's Desire
Quinn's Need
Ty's Obsession
Conner's Courage
Jess's Journey

GUARDS OF FOLSOM
Pup

NOVELLAS
Masters and Boyd

Published by DREAMSPINNER PRESS
http://www.dreamspinnerpress.com

BEYOND
DUTY

SJD Peterson

Dreamspinner Press

Published by
Dreamspinner Press
5032 Capital Circle SW
Ste 2, PMB# 279
Tallahassee, FL 32305-7886
USA
http://www.dreamspinnerpress.com/

Beyond Duty

Cover Art by Paul Richmond
http://www.paulrichmondstudio.com

ISBN: 978-1-62798-002-9
Digital ISBN 978-1-62798-003-6

Printed in the United States of America
First Edition
August 2013

This story is dedicated to Virginia for her amazing inspirational photo and story prompt. Thank you for helping to bring Gunny and Mac to life.

CHAPTER
One

THE short six-block walk from home to Gunny's favorite diner on Main Street was one that he normally enjoyed. Riverview was full of southern small-town charm that was rich in history, and for the most part, the attitude among the residents was relaxed and easygoing. He'd bought the house not long after being promoted to gunnery sergeant, and knew when he retired, he'd be staying. Sure, he'd have much rather owned one of the grander homes closer to the main strip—he'd always had a thing for historical homes but could never figure out how to get rich in the Marine Corps. Besides, his house was perfect for him, tucked back off the street with a large private garden that could be viewed from every room in the place. The gardens were great, but it was the privacy he liked more. The fact that his best friend Mac fell in love with it made the decision to buy an easy one.

Most mornings, Gunny enjoyed the short walk, but he'd woken up in a shitty mood. Not that it was any different from the morning before. In fact, he'd been having a lot of those mornings over the previous couple of months. Whether he woke in the middle of the night or after the sun had risen, it was always the same. His gut would knot up, head filled with static noise, and his whole body would tense. Not just tense, but *holy fuck* tense to the point where he'd wake up with back spasms and cuss and groan in the middle of the night. And didn't those oh-so-fun, twisting-in-agony nightly events make his new, unwanted, best friend insomnia even more irritating. In this irritable mindset, made all the worse because he couldn't figure out what was causing the problem, he grabbed a newspaper and stomped off to the Bonnie Mill Diner.

The Bonnie Mill had been some fancy-ass private home before the turn of the century. From the outside, it was a huge Victorian painted lady with a wraparound porch. Gunny could imagine the typical ladies-in-the-parlor, men-in-the-manlier-rooms kind of house. Cute little chambermaids scurrying around with lace doilies on their heads yelling, "Yes mum, no mum, right away mum." Nowadays, it featured apartments on the upper floors and a kick-ass place to eat Saturday-morning breakfast on the main floor. It wasn't that he couldn't cook his own breakfast. Hell, he'd been a bachelor since eighteen years of age. It had been either learn to cook or suffer the canteen seven days a week. It just seemed pointless to make a big breakfast for a party of one. Besides, the food at the diner was great, the company enjoyable, and it was routine. He liked routine.

Stepping through the door, a lively chorus of "Gunny" from about ten familiar faces filled the air to mingle with the smells of fresh baked pastries, bacon, and freshly brewed coffee.

"Morning." He returned their greeting and waved.

A little of his ire subsided, and a warm smile crossed his face at the early morning welcome reminding him of that old sitcom *Cheers*. Everyone was pretty much regulars, only a couple of the faces unrecognizable. A place where everybody knew your name, although instead of a big wooden bar, the main focus was a soda fountain-style counter, and rather than being a really cool Boston pub, the Bonnie Mill had been converted to a diner back in the nineteen fifties. It still had the original Formica tables and red vinyl chairs set in place back when the diner had been new. So, there really weren't that many similarities between the Bonnie Mill and Cheers, but the greetings were the same.

The only variation came from Bill Klein, who yelled out, "Gunny Gunnery," while he laughed boisterously and slapped the counter with a loud bang.

Not sure what Bill's major malfunction was, but from the moment the guy had found out his nickname was Gunny, short for Gunther, and that he was a gunnery sergeant, the old man had thought it was the funniest joke he'd ever heard. He nodded in Bill's direction and took a seat at the opposite end of the counter as far away from the strange man as he could get. There was just something creepy about a guy who laughed at the same joke nearly every week for a year.

"Mornin', Gunny, what ya in the mood for?" Carrie Anne asked, as she set down a glass of water, then turned over a mug and filled it with coffee.

Carrie Anne was another routine at the diner: more accurately, a weekly annoyance. Every Saturday morning she insisted on waiting on him. She claimed if she had to make sweets all week she was entitled to the man candy—that would be him—on the weekends. And she *was* entitled to whatever she wanted at the Bonnie Mill. Carrie was a twenty-eight-year-old insane bleach blonde with a big mouth and an even bigger, um, set of assets. She had married Carl, the owner of the place, who just so happened to be butt-ass ugly and thirty-something years her senior. She'd tried to convince Gunny she'd married for love, but he didn't believe her, having heard the rumors of her affairs and seeing her leaving the local pub with one of those whom it was rumored she was sleeping with, only a few weeks after the wedding.

"Whatcha bake me fresh this morning, darling?" he asked with a smile.

Carrie Anne leaned in, her assets practically spilling from her two-sizes-too-small white blouse, and licked her brightly red-painted lips before murmuring seductively, "Hot, cherry pie."

After a year of practice, the greasy-looking lips inches from his face and the sickly sweet perfume she wore no longer made his stomach roll. He no longer had to hide the gag behind a coffee cup, having grown used to it or perhaps just become desensitized. There wasn't anything wrong with sweet perfume, just not a complete bottle at one time. Less was definitely more. Even the painted lips—again in moderation—didn't bother him. He'd dated a drag queen once, hot as hell. The things he could do with those pouty and glossy lips— Well, let's just say Carrie Anne was so not sexy. But the woman was a fan-fucking-tastic baker, so he put up with her batting her fake lashes and groping his ass while she walked him to the register each Saturday morning.

"I'll have the three eggs, over easy, bacon, ham, sausage, hash browns, and an extra side of toast, please." He gave her a wink. "And a slice of your cherry pie."

"Coming right up, sugar," she purred, returning the wink.

Gunny shook his head as Carrie swung her hips exaggeratedly as she swished and swayed her way to the kitchen. Gunny couldn't help but wonder as she walked away, trying to be all sexy, what she would say if she knew he was gay and none of her shenanigans did a damn thing for him. Not that he had plans to tell her anytime soon, but sometimes he thought the shit storm that would rain down on him would almost be worth the look on her face. Talk about priceless.

After taking a sip of coffee, Gunny flipped open the newspaper; his eyes nearly bugged out and his breath whooshed out noisily when he read the headlines.

> *BREAKING NEWS: Obama, Pentagon certify*
> *"Don't Ask, Don't Tell" repeal*

Heart hammering in his chest, Gunny wrapped both of his hands around the mug and brought it to his lips, sipping at the steaming brew to cover up the shocked look on his face while he continued to read the article.

> *"Today, we have taken the final major step*
> *toward ending the discriminatory 'Don't Ask,*
> *Don't Tell' law that undermines our military*
> *readiness and violates American principles of*
> *fairness and equality," Obama said in a*
> *statement. "In accordance with the legislation*
> *that I signed into law last December, I have*
> *certified and notified Congress that the*
> *requirements for repeal have been met. 'Don't*
> *Ask, Don't Tell' will end, once and for all, in 60*
> *days—on September 20, 2011."*

Christ! There had been rumors, but just like in civilian life, rumors ran rampant among the troops and more often than not were complete bullshit. Being the government, the bullshit rule was probably even more accurate.

"Fuck me," he grumbled around the mug. Twenty-two years he'd been hiding a big part of himself, and the day before his retirement, DADT was to be repealed? *Are you fucking kidding me?*

"Goddamn shame," John complained to his right.

John Wilson was about a million years old. He still believed women should be barefoot, pregnant, and their place was in the kitchen. John still paid homage to the ancient belief that women should be seen, not heard. Most days John was laughable at best. It was kind of fun to tease the ol' bastard. It didn't take much to get him all flustered and steaming, and Gunny could easily admit he found a perverse pleasure in seeing if he could cause the steam to shoot out of the man's ears before breakfast was over. For the most part the ribbing was in good nature, and he knew John was a dumbass so he didn't take the old man seriously. In that moment, however, with shock causing his heart to beat erratically and him feeling a little off-kilter while his brain tried to figure out if the article was a fact or a joke, he was in no mood for John's antics.

Gunny looked up from the paper and turned to glare at John. "You got a problem with gays in the military, John?"

"Damn straight I do," he spat, pushing his wire-rimmed glasses up on his red, bulbous nose. "This country don't need no damn queers fighting for it. A bunch of nancies running around slapping the enemy? Where is the honor in that? Next they'll be allowing pedophiles and rapists to run our school systems."

Now, for twenty-two years he'd been known as Gunther Duchene, United States Marine. It was the side of himself he presented to the world around him. It wasn't a lie. He was a Marine at the very core of his being. But from the age of ten he'd known two things for a fact. Number one: he would grow up and become a Marine, just as his father and his father's father had, and number two: he was gay. The two things mixed like oil and water, so he kept that private side secret.

He wasn't ashamed of being gay, nor was he a coward by any stretch of the imagination. He was a realist. He'd had to sacrifice one thing for the other and didn't have a single regret. Unlike some people, he didn't need, nor did he ever want, to be one-half of a pair. He had no dreams of meeting Mr. Right, settling down in the 'burbs, and living happily ever after. His vision of a perfect life was combat, technical maneuvers, strategic planning, building a powerful body, and when the opportunity presented, a hot guy to fuck or suck his dick to satisfy his baser desires. Gunny had no wish to be loud, proud, and out. Never felt it his responsibility to be a representative, role model, or any other type of influence for the gay youth. Being a damn good Marine and damn good man defined him, not who his bed partner was.

Having spent over half his life around other Marines, he'd heard every joke and disgusting slur slung at gays and didn't take it personal. They talked the same smack about commanding officers, men, women, straight, gay, bi, black, white, young, and old, it didn't matter; they would eventually get around to disrespecting everyone. Hey, at least they were equal-opportunity dumbasses. He'd wager a good number of them, slinging some of the nastier remarks about gays, would have willingly dropped their fatigues and presented their asses to him. However, this particular morning, John's statement had Gunny clenching the mug and his body literally shaking with anger. How the mug didn't shatter under the pressure, he had no clue. What he really wanted was to wrap his hands around John's thick, judgmental head and squeeze until bones shattered.

Gunny shut his eyes and counted to ten—it didn't work—then twenty, and still the rage swirled around inside him like the coffee he could practically taste in the back of his throat. Somehow, he managed to get control of his body, mainly his hands, and eased the death grip on the cup and set it aside.

"You never served in the military, did you, John?" he hissed.

"No, I had an—"

"Yeah I know, an injury," Gunny interrupted. "I've heard the story." With calm he didn't feel, Gunny folded the newspaper, and tucked it under his arm and pulled a wad of bills from the pocket of his jeans. "Here's the thing, John. I'm having a hard time swallowing your statement this morning." He slammed the bills on the counter with a thunderous slap; every head in the diner turned in their direction. Theatrical, hell yeah, but it got John's attention.

"Don't seem to me a drunken coward who dodged the draft claiming he wasn't physically able to defend this country against the enemy, but physically fit enough to beat on his wife, rightly gets a say in who can and cannot defend this great country of ours."

Gunny didn't wait for a response. A man could only control his rage for so long. Without a word to anyone else, he turned and walked out of the Bonnie Mill to save John Wilson's fool life. *Pretty big of this queer, considering the son of a bitch didn't think I should be defending his country.*

Gunny was still totally pissed off by John's attitude by the time he arrived back at the house. Whether it was because the older he got the less he could tolerate bullshit, the shitty mood he'd woken up in, or if he'd just reached his limit, he didn't know. With a snort, he kicked off his shoes the minute the door slammed behind him and threw himself on the couch. He snatched the remote from the coffee table and angrily clicked through the channels without discerning one channel from another, concentrating more on slowing his panting breath. By the time he made it through the couple hundred channels the second time, his jaw unclenched as the anger slowly drained from him. Giving up on abusing the remote, he picked back up the newspaper he'd thrown on the cushion and was finally calm enough to read more.

HALFWAY through the article, Gunny's cell phone vibrated against his hip, and he snatched it from the clip, flipping it open without glancing at the display screen.

"What?"

"Are you reading this shit?" Mac's voice came though the phone line, sounding as shocked as Gunny had felt earlier.

"Yeah, I'm reading it now," Gunny responded, rubbing a hand across his stubbled jaw as he stared down at the newspaper. "Pretty fucking amazing, huh?"

"Only twenty-two years too late!" Mac huffed. "Do you know how much ass I have been denied because of this stupid fucking law? I was in my prime, Gunny. My prime!"

Macalister Jones had been his best friend since they went through boot camp together twenty-two years ago. Mac was also the only man who had shared Gunny's bed for the last decade, and in turn Gunny was the only one who'd been granted access to Mac's. They'd been fucking each other pretty much since they met, but were honest-to-God best friends and had never been what he would define as a couple.

"Stop your damn whining, you've had the best ass there is," Gunny reminded him.

"Ha! That would be mine; that is why I don't allow you to tap it too often," Mac said pointedly. "It's like a rare work of fine art that has to be adored and stroked lovingly, not slammed into and abused."

"Jones, my bullshit meter is already full for the day." Gunny laughed, feeling better than he had before the phone rang. Mac was a major joker, so it was hard to stay in a pissy mood when under his charm. He was also a big, lovable bastard who'd give you the shirt off his back. As long as you didn't piss him off. Mac was part of the elite scout snipers, a Marine Corps special-forces team, which meant not only was he skilled in reconnaissance but once he found you, he could take your ass out.

"Oh ho! You are nowhere near full," Mac chuckled. "But you will be as soon as I get there," he added in a husky voice.

A rush of arousal went straight to Gunny's groin at the seductive tone of Mac's voice. Gunny started counting the hours down till Mac was home. "You still going to need a ride from the airport?" he asked, distractedly. He'd need to find something to distract him for—eight hours, he groaned silently.

"No, Gunny. I bought a new car and had it shipped to the airport, what the fuck do you think?" Mac asked sarcastically.

"Good, then you won't mind me hanging up on your cocky ass and—"

"Gotta go. See ya at six."

The line went dead.

Gunny flipped his phone shut and threw it on the coffee table, a big goofy grin spreading across his face. He heaved himself up off the couch and went to make breakfast. It had been three months since he'd seen Mac, so with his gruff voice still ringing in Gunny's ears, thoughts of a fine, tight Marine's ass running through his head, all thoughts of John Wilson, DADT, and the rest of the world were pushed out in favor of all the fantasies his little head was spinning. Over the last few months, Mac seemed to be the only thing he could focus on for any length of time. The pissed-off mood gave way to hunger and horniness.

CHAPTER
Two

MAC ended the call, still chuckling, causing the ache in his head to increase. He tossed his cell on the bed and leaned back against the headboard, shut his eyes, and rubbed his temples. The aching wasn't only in his head, but in his chest too. God, he missed Gunny. It had been three months since he'd seen the man, and Mac was going fucking crazy. He'd tried drowning some of his loneliness in more than one bottle of beer the night before, but by the time he gave up and went to bed, he still missed Gunny something fierce.

The feeling wasn't anything new; he missed Gunny whenever they were apart. They were best friends, comrades, lovers, and confidants. However, the absence seemed more extreme this time. Maybe it had to do with the fear that nagged him lately. Everything was changing and he was a little more than worried; in fact, he was scared shitless.

For twenty-plus years his life had been dedicated to the military; for the past ten years—even before that if he were being completely honest—he'd also been dedicated to Gunther Duchene.

Everything about them worked. They didn't put unrealistic demands on the other; each understood his duty to the Marine Corps came first, everything else second. When they were together they took full advantage of their time, laughing, teasing, and fucking like bunnies. When they hooked up, it was always a chance to recharge their batteries even if when they walked away they were both physically exhausted and sporting bruises, but always sated and satisfied.

However, what they had together went way beyond the physical. During times he'd been deployed, thoughts of Gunny had kept Mac sane in an insane world. When he had down time, it was Gunny who assisted him in winding down, made him laugh, and helped ease his soul of some of the horrors combat had forced upon him. Gunny understood like only another Marine could, and that worked both ways. The Marine Corps banded them together, but would the bond between them be as strong once they no longer had a duty to the Corps? Would they tire of each other if they only had each other day in and day out?

You would never tire of him. Mac cocked his head, as the thought sunk in. No, he couldn't imagine ever tiring of Gunny. What he was tired of was leaving the man. The long months, weeks, days, even hours unable to touch Gunny, not being able to see him, feel him wrapped around him while he slept, those were the things he was tired of.

Mac huffed out a breath and heaved himself off the bed. It was the same battle between his heart and head he'd been fighting for months without finding an answer. Knowing change was coming, wanting it, even if the uncertainty of the outcome freaked him out. Yet it was stupid to worry about shit he couldn't change. He was going to retire, as was Gunny, and they'd just have to see where life took them, and if it didn't work— The thought made Mac's gut roll, and he pushed the depressing thought away.

Mac flipped on the bathroom light and grunted at the mess staring back at him in the mirror. Red eyes from too much alcohol and two days' worth of beard growth from pure damn laziness made him look like shit. He brushed his teeth, grabbed his shower kit, and dug around in it until he found his razor and shaving gel. *Time to get presentable for my man*, he smirked at himself.

And Gunny was his man. The only man he wanted in his life. Even before they had become exclusive— The razor came to a halt against his jaw and Mac took a calming breath, before he continued. All these years later, and the thought of anyone touching Gunny made his blood boil. Early on, there had been long periods when they were apart, nearly two years at one point. They'd both sought itch relievers with random hookups. Problem was, for Mac, no matter how hot the guy was, how sexy or wanton, he'd never found anyone who made him feel the way Gunny did. That feeling had never wavered. Twenty-two years since he'd touched Gunny for the first time, and he still tingled when he felt it.

It was going to be hard to walk away from the life he loved, the thrills, missions, strategic planning, the satisfaction of taking out the bad guy. It'd been a good life, and in the end, he still had Gunny at his side, and that was all that mattered. Mac shook his head as the morose feelings made his chest ache. Jesus, he was getting old and sentimental, already mourning the loss of youth.

"Good God, man, listen to yourself," he growled at his reflection. "You're forty-two, not eighty-two."

Mac dropped his razor in his bag, flipped off his reflection, and headed for the shower. In just a few hours he'd be back with Gunny. He'd spend a little time taking out his pent-up frustrations on Gunny's ass, and maybe once he wasn't so damn horny and no longer feeling lonely, he could get a handle on what was really bothering him. For now he focused on getting home, getting his hands on Gunny, and he'd worry about the other shit later.

GUNNY leaned back against the car with his arms crossed. He watched Mac step out of the airport terminal. He was dressed in his fatigues, duffle over his shoulder and a big shit-eating grin on his handsome face. His hazel eyes were hidden behind his shades, but Gunny knew they were dark with hunger and need. They'd been apart three months while Mac was off training his replacement. *Three months without heat, skin, and passion, which was two months, twenty-nine days too long if you ask me.* Gunny's body lit up, nerve endings tingling as Mac stepped closer, and just like that first night in a grungy little hotel in San Diego, Gunny was instantly so fucking hard it hurt.

Gunny recalled the Marine Corps Recruit Depot in San Diego. While waiting for his initial gear to be issued, Gunny had turned his head and met Mac's hazel-green eyes for the first time. He doubted anyone else had noticed the way their eyes had lingered just a fraction longer than necessary, but Gunny had noticed and so had Mac. At twenty, Gunny was one cocky son of a bitch. He knew who he was and where he was going and wouldn't let anyone or anything stand in the way of achieving his goals. Although he was completely selfish and goal-oriented, he still got horny. A lot. It was during their first three-day pass Gunny found out that as cocky as he thought he was, Macalister Jones was just a wee bit cockier, and Gunny ended up getting his cherry ass popped. Twenty-two years later Mac still owned his ass, only he hadn't realized it at the time, or maybe he had but just hadn't admitted it.

"How was your flight?" Gunny asked when Mac was within earshot.

"Good," Mac said nonchalantly.

Years of discretion taught them how to hide their desires to the outside world. If anyone had walked by the car, they wouldn't have seen anything more than two platonic friends. Nor would they have noticed the way the tip of Mac's finger slid along Gunny's thigh as he walked by, arms swinging. But Gunny was acutely aware of the touch that sent a tingling sensation to race down his spine.

Mac nodded, looking over the top of his glasses, meeting Gunny's eyes with a predatory gaze so full of lust, his goddamn breath caught.

No one more than a few paces away would notice the slight touch, and they certainly wouldn't have heard Mac whisper, "Get in the car before I fuck you over the hood," in a husky voice with just a hint of growl.

Gunny heard it, causing the tingling sensation to turn into a full raging fire that settled in his groin. His head was screaming, *Don't you dare fucking move, let him bend your ass over!* but he strolled casually to the driver's side, slid behind the wheel, and slammed the door.

As soon as he had the car in gear and pulled away from the curb, Gunny shot a challenging look in Mac's direction. "One of these days I'm going to drop trou and find out just how fucking cocky you really are."

Mac threw his head back and laughed. When he was in better control of himself, he turned in his seat and lowered his shades. "Two more months and I'll do you in the middle of fucking Main Street. Now hurry up and get us home before I change my mind and do you right fucking now."

And didn't Mac's statement just make Gunny's chest squeeze nice and tight and cause his gut to get all fluttery. That same weird feeling had been battling with another unsettling sensation lately, one of heart palpitations and nausea in equal measures. Gunny didn't have a goddamn clue what was wrong with him, and he was beginning to think he'd stayed in the Marines one term too many. There was a reason most didn't make a career out of the military, because they lost their fucking mind after that many years, and Gunny decided that was what his problem was. Better to concentrate on the sexual aspect and not try to make too much out of it.

Gunny laughed along with Mac and then stole a glance in his direction as he tried to pay attention to the traffic ahead of him. Then he did a double take at the sly grin that curled Mac's full, luscious mouth as his wide, blunt fingers massaged the thick bulge in the front of Mac's fatigue pants. The sight short-circuited Gunny's brain, and the only thing he could think about was the throbbing ache in his groin and getting them to the house, pronto.

"Been a long time, Gunny." Those fingers kept stroking.

Gunny got serious about the heavy rush-hour traffic, doing his damnedest to ignore Mac's deep, husky voice.

Even with his best efforts, he couldn't miss the way Mac pushed the palm of his hand hard against his cock. "Christ, I ache," he groaned.

"Shut up, Mac," Gunny hissed. "Just shut the fuck up. Not another word until we get to the house."

Mac chuckled, the sound deep and gravelly, and Gunny felt it resonate against the pulsing veins of his shaft. He growled low in warning and cranked the radio.

Even with the heavier-than-normal traffic with tourist season in full swing, they made it to the house in record time. Mac set another record by having Gunny slammed up against the closed door, face-first, and his pants around his thighs in seconds flat.

"Fucking missed you, Gunny," Mac rasped against his ear.

He could only nod, his heart hammering, as Mac bit and sucked the side of Gunny's neck. His focus narrowed to the warm, wet mouth, and sharp teeth, and he was reduced to a series of incoherent grunts and growls that meant "*hurry,*" "*Jesus,*" and "*now!*"

Mac didn't tease. The bastard could torment Gunny for hours, fucking days even, without letting him come, teasing that left him a hairsbreadth away from a padded room. Mercifully, Mac never teased their first time together after a long separation, just took Gunny hard and fast, the burn intense, with little more than spit and precum to slick the way.

"Oh, Christ, Mac."

Mac grunted and slammed into him, his hands holding Gunny's hips in a bruising grip, pumping his cock in and out of Gunny with forceful thrusts. Gunny splayed his fingers, trying to get as much purchase on the door as he could. His arms locked, muscles quaking, as he used every bit of strength to keep Mac from fucking him through the door. Raw, carnal power against brute force.

Mac could read Gunny's body better than even he could himself. Mac increased his speed an instant before a knot started to form at the base of Gunny's spine. Mac had his fist wrapped around Gunny's cock. Two strokes with his big, calloused hand and Gunny howled his release; he clenched his ass around Mac's cock and forced him into orgasm along with Gunny.

They were spent, breathing harshly, and Mac wrapped his arms around Gunny's waist, burrowing his face into his neck. Gunny's arms gave out, and Mac collapsed against him, still buried deep in his ass and holding him tightly against a solid chest as they came down from their euphoric high. Yeah, it'd been a long three months of porn and hand jobs, uncertainty and crazy mood swings, but Mac, he could make Gunny forget in an instant that they'd ever been apart.

The rest of the evening was spent in bed—no, not fucking the entire time, although he and Mac had been known to endure some epic fuck-fests in the past. After a quick shower, Mac, coming off a thirty-six-hour stretch of no sleep, crashed in Gunny's arms the minute they fell into bed. Gunny spent most of the evening stroking Mac's head, his muscular shoulders, down his spine, unable to stop touching his warm skin. That irritating battle between the *I'm so happy* chest tightening and the panic-induced palpitations grew fiercer the longer he lay there staring at the man in his arms.

It dawned on Gunny, right into his twisting gut, that this might be the last time Mac would be here. In two short months' time they'd no longer have to hide their sexuality, so why would he want to come home to Gunny? Mac could have guys half his age falling at his feet in worship.

From the neck down, he and Mac could be mirror-image twins. They were six-foot, two-hundred-plus pounds. Their torsos were thick with muscle, and a light pelt of dark hair adorned their chests and abs. They even had the same tattoo. Abstract tribal designs in heavy black lines wove around Gunny's left arm, Mac's on the right, mirror images. About five years ago, they had some rare downtime together and spent a month in Europe. Mac... well, it didn't matter what Mac said about the tattoos binding them together forever. He had been drunk at the time, showing off his new tattoo in a pub, forcing Gunny to show his, and telling the entire place how much he loved his best friend, blah, blah, blah. Mac was a loud, lovable, touchy-feely kind of drunk. It didn't mean anything. At least Gunny hadn't thought it meant anything to Mac at the time. Hell, at the time, Gunny hadn't been sure it meant anything to him. At least he hadn't admitted to himself that the chest tightening meant anything.

The similarities below the neckline sure as hell didn't continue above it. Yeah, they had the same buzz cut and dark stubble, but Gunny's face looked like a growly English bulldog and Mac's face, Christ, his could only be described as statuesque. His brow was gentle with high, perfectly sculpted cheekbones, and while there was nothing refined or stuffy about Mac, his features were regal. He was just fucking gorgeous head to toe.

Lying there some time before the first rays of sunlight streamed through the bedroom window, Gunny finally knew the reason for the shitty mood he'd been in. He was heartbroken. Heartbroken and so fucking scared. He'd never worried about where Mac was or what he was doing; Gunny always knew Mac would come home to him. After the scare with Private Carter, who had threatened to out Mac ten years ago, they'd been an exclusive—well, not a couple but at least exclusive lovers.

Now what? Now that Mac would no longer have to live in fear of being dishonorably discharged, surely he wouldn't be content to just fuck his best friend anymore. He'd want something more, wouldn't he? Why Gunny hadn't thought of this sooner, planned for it, he didn't know. Denial maybe? Contentment?

At forty-two, his hair was thinning, his beard had taken on a silver glow, and he hadn't been on the prowl in over ten years. The thought of hanging out in clubs, looking for random hookups, worrying about safe sex issues, and learning to trust, made his head hurt. Would he ever meet anyone he trusted enough to let him fuck him? Would he have to take on the more dominant role with future lovers?

A small, frustrated sound escaped Gunny, and Mac patted Gunny's chest and murmured, "Shh, I'm here," still fast asleep.

Christ! The man knew what Gunny needed even in his sleep. Gunny tightened his arms around Mac, tears burning the back of his eyes. *How in the hell am I ever going to find anyone like Mac?* Better question was: when had he fallen in love with Mac, beyond friendship?

CHAPTER
Three

AS THE early morning sun streamed through the blinds, Gunny wasn't any closer to finding the answer to the question that wreaked havoc in his head. Careful not to wake Mac, he slipped quietly out of bed, pulled on a pair of fatigue pants, and snuck into the bathroom. After brushing his teeth and splashing cold water on his face, Gunny headed to the kitchen to start a pot of coffee. Only two things cleared his head: Mac—even though he was currently the source of the screwed-up head—and exercise. Probably why he was so muscular—his head was fucked up a lot and Mac was gone a lot. It was how he dealt.

Gunny shoved the coffee table out of the way, dropped down on the living-room floor, and started doing push-ups. Counting each one off, he concentrated on the push and pull of each muscle in his arms. Focused on the way his toes flexed under, keeping his abs clenched, and nothing more. By the time he'd counted off seventy-five, his breathing had sped up; sweat rolled down from his temples and along his spine. The burn with each contraction of muscle radiated up his arms, across his shoulders, and settled as warmth in his lower back. His head was his own once again, the burn and the fatigued muscles his only focus. At one hundred, Gunny rolled onto his back, planted his feet on the floor, and took a deep breath before counting off sit-ups. During these moments, he was in complete control of his body; his mind, and he, and he alone, decided how far he pushed and how hard he drove himself.

At one hundred sit-ups, Gunny began to slow and lose his focus just enough that Mac's face snuck into his head. He pushed the image away and redoubled his efforts, pushed the sinews of his body past their normal limits. "One-twenty-five"—further—"one-fifty."

A CHILL whispered across Mac's back, rousing him from his sleep. He rolled over and reached out, frowning when he encountered cool sheets. "Gunny?"

Blinking against the harsh morning light, Mac's frown deepened when he spotted the empty bed. With a growl, he pulled the covers over his head and tried to snuggle further into the mattress, seeking warmth. Dammit, after three months of sleeping alone, was it too much to ask to wake up against a warm body? Not just any body either. He wanted Gunny's big body wrapped around him, keeping him nice and toasty while he slept.

After ten minutes of tossing and turning and more than a little grumbling and growling, Mac gave up on trying to fall back to sleep. Mac threw off the covers and grudgingly grabbed his fatigues from the floor as he stomped off to the bathroom. He and Gunny were going to have to have a chat. From now on when one of them returned from duty, neither would be allowed out of bed each morning without cuddles and blowjobs.

Mac flipped on the bathroom light and stopped short. He grinned at his reflection when it hit him there wouldn't be any more duty, deployments, or months on end without the other. "I still like the early morning blowjob rule though," he said and winked at himself.

After taking care of his piss hard-on, Mac brushed his teeth and pulled on his fatigues. The smell of fresh coffee brewing called to him, and he flipped off the bathroom light and headed out to find Gunny.

Mac froze when he made it to the end of the hall. On the living room floor, Gunny was in nothing but a pair of camos, bare feet planted on the floor, hands clasped behind his head, as he counted off one sit-up after another. Mac watched, enthralled. Sweat dampened the light pelt of hair on Gunny's chest. His flexing muscles glistened, and the look of concentration on the man's face was sexy as fuck. Warmth rushed to Mac's groin, and he leaned his shoulder against the wall and pressed his palm against his growing erection, enjoying the view and the tingle of arousal.

The longer Mac stood there watching Gunny, the harder he got until he was throbbing with need. Yeah, they definitely needed to chat about their new morning routine. Damn, did they need to talk about it. Like right now, before he exploded.

Mac pushed off the wall and moved into the living room. "Hey! Why didn't you wake me up? I'd have worked out with you."

MAC'S voice stopped him short, and Gunny opened his eyes to find Mac standing over him, dressed in nothing but a pair of fatigue pants with a questioning look on his gorgeous face. It was as if he hadn't done a single rep, the peace he'd found gone as every uncertainty came back in a rush, making his head throb. In defeat, Gunny leaned back on his hands, legs stretched out, and tried to get his harsh, panting breath to slow down as he stared up at Mac. The sight of the man only made it worse, and Gunny closed his eyes and took a deep lungful of air, holding it before he blew it out slowly.

Mac straddled Gunny's right leg and went to his knees. He placed one hand on the back of Gunny's neck, pulling his head back. "Look at me, Gunny."

Gunny took another calming breath and opened his eyes and met Mac's.

Mac rested the other hand on Gunny's rapidly rising and falling lower stomach. "Hey, what is it? What's wrong?" he asked with concern.

They sat there for an immeasurable amount of time—mirrored images, like always—breathing each other in, eyes locked. Gunny wanted so badly to ask him what he felt for him, but was scared shitless of the answer. Gunny held Mac's gaze for a minute longer, neither of them saying a word. In the end, unable to ever get away with lying to Mac, knowing he would see right through it, Gunny sighed and gave him a portion of the truth. "Couldn't sleep, head's all wonked up."

Mac's fingers teased the soft hair on Gunny's stomach as he cocked his head to the side, those expressive hazel eyes searching, looking beyond Gunny's physical form and into the very core of who he was. He felt naked and vulnerable. His biggest fear was that Mac would find the new secret and bring it out before he had time to truly understand it himself.

Whether Mac saw it or not, he knew what Gunny needed. He always knew.

Warm lips pressed against his briefly, a tease of tongue swept across his bottom lip, pulling a moan from him, before he was encouraged to stand. "C'mon, Gunny. Let's go get you out of your head and make you fly."

Fingers entwined, Gunny followed Mac to the basement without a word. His body thrummed with anticipation and excitement. If anyone could help him clear his head, it was Mac. Mac could make him soar out of his body and leave all his worries and other shit behind, leaving in its wake nothing but peace.

Jesus, how he needed some peace.

He and Mac had spent hours together converting the basement into a gym. Every implement or machine was strategically placed to allow for not only workouts but also private feats of endurance. The sturdy hooks in the ceiling and floors were not only for punching bags. The extra-wide weight bench had multiple uses, and the locked cabinet held much more than just hand weights and ointments. So much time and thought had been put into the room; it was a special place for both of them. Normally when he entered the gym with Mac promising to make him fly, Gunny would instantly start clearing his head of all thoughts except pleasing his lover. This time was different. No matter how hard he tried, how badly he needed this, the unease had settled so deeply into his head and heart he couldn't seem to let his fears and worry go. They held him, wrapped around him, enveloped him so tightly, it felt as if he were being suffocated by the weight of them.

One last time, just focus on Mac and enjoy, he thought, but even as he believed it, he couldn't let go of the tension that held his muscles tight. Mac led him to the center of the room, turned, and placed a soft kiss to his lips before he moved to the cabinet. Gunny rolled his neck, closed his eyes, and shook his hands, forcing them to go limp. *Let it all go.* He jumped when he felt a touch to his hand, and willed his body to remain still. He savored the sensation of Mac's warm hands securing the heavy leather cuffs around his wrists. Then Mac stripped him, naked and vulnerable, and Gunny became pliant while Mac secured his arms over his head, allowed Mac to position him in any way he desired. His breath sped up in anticipation as he attached the ankle cuffs to the floor. The feeling of being naked and bound, while his lover was still clothed, just added to the eroticism of the moment.

Every aspect of Gunny's life had been about control. From the way he conducted himself in public and the way he controlled the Marines who had been entrusted to his command to the strength and ability of his body. It seemed odd that he would give up something so ingrained in him to someone his equal in size and strength, much less someone below him in rank. Yet that's exactly what he craved from Mac. To be stripped of all choices, all control, to trust completely. After years of playing, always exploring, experimenting, they found they shared similar needs—kinks, so to speak. Desires unknown to even himself, only brought to the surface by Mac's natural dominance.

Gunny inhaled deeply through his mouth, savoring Mac's spicy flavor on his tongue; Mac's scent filled him, and he held his breath, not wanting to lose that small part of Mac he'd taken. Mac stroked a fingertip down the bony prominences of Gunny's spine, the tickling sensation maddening, but he held still, kept a tight rein on his reactions. It was as if Gunny wanted to pull his scent, Mac's touch, his very essence deep inside him, something to savor when Mac was gone. He was afraid any response on his part would weaken the sensation, or worse, he'd lose part of Mac.

Gunny gasped, and his eyes flew open as sharp, stinging pain radiated out from a pinch to his left nipple. Mac stood within inches of Gunny, a scowl marring his handsome face. "Glad to see you're aware of me. If I wanted you to control your reactions to me, I would have ordered you to be still. Do you wish to make the rules, Gunny?"

Disappointment in displeasing Mac washed over him, and Gunny lowered his eyes, no longer able to meet Mac's questioning hazel gaze. "No."

Mac's other hand snaked out, and his fingers latched on to Gunny's other nipple. The intense pain made him cry out. "Fuck!"

"Yeah, fuck." Mac squeezed harder. "No, what?"

"No, Sir," Gunny rasped. His head fell forward, and he panted, trying to process the pain, move beyond it.

"That's better," Mac praised, releasing one nipple and soothing the sting with the flat of his tongue before doing the same to the other throbbing nub. Mac cupped Gunny's chin in his hand and forced his head up. "Look at me, Gunny."

Gunny lifted his eyes and steeled himself for Mac's questions. Gunny couldn't lie to him, but he wasn't ready to talk about what bothered him. How could he, when he still wasn't sure what to say or how to deal with his feelings? To his surprise, Mac leaned in and brushed his lips against Gunny's. Mac's tongue came out, teasing, encouraging Gunny to open to him, which he did without hesitation. As the kiss deepened, Mac moaned his approval, and Gunny felt the vibration of it down to his toes. The kiss went on and on. A claiming and possessive kiss with tongue, lips, and teeth, and the world stopped turning. In that moment there was only him and Mac, and Gunny let go of everything else. Mac pulled back and Gunny instinctively followed, wanting more, needing that connection to continue, and whimpered when he was denied.

"Shh, I got you," Mac murmured softly. "Close your eyes, Gunny."

Gunny obeyed. Moments later, he felt something silken against his eyes and Mac tying the fabric at the back of his head. Long moments Gunny hung there, waiting. He knew Mac hadn't stepped away; Gunny could hear his slow, even breaths and feel the heat radiating from the man's body. A shudder went through Gunny when a hand landed on his breastbone, the contact of warm skin against his chest all the more acute without his sense of sight.

"Your only job is to feel," Mac whispered.

Gunny's breath caught as Mac's palm slid slowly downward, tickling against the trail of dark hair. Chains rattled as Gunny arched toward a brush of a touch against his erection that stood out proudly from his body, straining toward his stomach.

"And you're not to come unless I command it. Understood?"

"Ye—" Gunny swallowed hard. "Yes, Sir."

Mac grabbed Gunny's cock. His hips instinctively snapped, thrust against that tight grip. "So eager," Mac chuckled. He wrapped a strap snugly around the base of Gunny's straining shaft and snapped it into place. Gunny swallowed down a moan of protest when Mac released him and stepped away.

"I'm going to use the deerskin flogger; any objections, say so now."

That particular flogger was Gunny's favorite. It was a good quality deerskin and so soft. The choice meant Mac had plans for a heavy, sustained flogging, and Gunny's cock twitched in response, a drop of precum dampening the sensitive head in anticipation.

"No objections, Sir," he responded without hesitation.

Mac's steps were measured and sure when he stepped past Gunny. The slapping of the flogger—which Gunny knew was against the cotton of Mac's fatigues, as this was part of Mac's ritual—echoed in the otherwise quiet room.

Gunny jumped when something touched his shoulder, and then immediately relaxed when he recognized familiar fingers massaging his flesh.

"Take a deep breath and relax, going to work all that tension out of you. Make you fly." Mac pressed a kiss against the back of Gunny's neck. "Ready?"

"Yes, Sir." Gunny took a deep breath in and blew it, and the tension, out slowly.

The first strike was against his right shoulder, immediately followed by a strike to the left. There was no pain as Mac moved the flogger in a figure-eight pattern. It was very thuddy but with very little sting. Gunny concentrated on each tiny kiss of the hide, losing himself in the sound and rhythm.

A warm tingle skittered along Gunny's nerve endings from the base of his spine up to the back of his head as the blows continued to rain down, growing in intensity. Gunny swayed to the beat of the erotic dance the flogger demanded. The sound of hide against flesh sang a melody as the hypnotic rhythm moved down his back and across the globes of his ass, the tempo changing only slightly as the flogger made its way down his thigh, to begin its journey upward once more.

"God, you're so beautiful like this, Gunny. So sexy," Mac purred, his voice tight with arousal.

Gunny couldn't speak, only moan his pleasure as he began to float, the chains binding his wrists and ankles the only thing keeping him anchored. All sense of time or place was meaningless as the flogging increased in intensity and then peaked. No thoughts, no physical awareness of his body, even the sound of hide against skin was lost. It was as if a thick blanket of warmth cradled him, and he soared to that special place only Mac could send him.

How long Gunny hung there in a suspended state, his body both the music and the dance, he couldn't swear. He only knew when the cloud around him changed, became heavier, and solid arms wrapped around him, heat against the sensitive flesh of his back.

"Come back to me, Gunny."

"Mmm" was the first sound Gunny could pull from his dry throat.

"That's it," Mac encouraged, his breath warm and sweet against Gunny's ear. Mac's hands slid up Gunny's arms, until their hands met and he entwined their fingers. They embraced skin to skin from head to toe. Gunny had no idea when Mac had lost his pants, but he was very much aware of Mac's hard cock pressing against the crease of his ass.

Mac kissed down Gunny's neck, stopping briefly to suck and nip. He could feel the blood being pulled to the surface, teeth scraping, then wet lips soothing the spot before Mac continued to kiss across Gunny's jaw. Gunny turned his head, met Mac's lips, moaned a soft needy sound, and opened his mouth wide to take Mac's tongue. Fingers teased the hairs of his forearms, sliding downward as Mac continued to kiss him, a complete exploration of Gunny's mouth, demanding, pushing for more, and Gunny gave back as good as he got, loving the way Mac battled, taking control of something as simple as a kiss.

Mac bit Gunny's lower lip, their stubbled jaws rasping against each other as Mac rested his head on Gunny's shoulder. Mac's hands moved from Gunny's arms to his chest, down to his stomach and, thank fuck, wrapped around his weeping cock.

"You're so hard. God, I love your cock," Mac praised; a bit of a growl crept into his voice, causing Gunny to shiver.

Mac's large hand stroked gingerly down Gunny's erection, the soft touch nowhere near what he needed. He needed more, more friction, more, fuck, he just needed more. Gunny's hips thrust of their own accord, and a hiss escaped as the abused flesh of his back slid along the sweat-dampened hairs on Mac's chest. It felt so fucking good.

"Please, Sir," he whimpered, voice rough and low. "Don't you want to fuck me, Sir? God—" He swallowed hard. He sounded needy and wanton, and he didn't care. He was needy, needed Mac in him, filling him. "Sir? Please."

Mac groaned; his slick fingers shook when he swiped them against Mac's crease. One slid into Gunny, teasing, stretching, and he knew he had won.

"My turn to soar," Mac grunted and without warning, pushed his cock deep, stabbing into Gunny's ass in one hard thrust.

He howled from the intensity, the stretch and burn, tossing his head from side to side as the pain mingled with the pleasure in the perfect combination.

"Mine," Mac growled, emphasizing his words with a brutal thrust of his hips.

"Yes! All yours." Gunny's hands curled into fists; he rocked back as hard as he could, needing Mac deeper. Wanting Mac to crawl inside him, touch the very fucking soul that he was the master of. "Yes…. So very much yours."

Gunny trembled with the rightness of his words as they flowed over him, embedded into him, marking him as surely as the tattoos had. How could anyone not see whom he belonged to when they looked at him? Everything he was belonged to, was completely owned by Mac. His very breath. Even if he wasn't going to be Gunny's for much longer.

Mac was pure animalistic power as he plowed into Gunny. Heart slamming, breath harsh and labored, ass, back, and lungs burning, and still Gunny wanted more. Begged with his body, the guttural sounds that poured from him that meant *more, harder, deeper*. One hand tightly wrapped around Gunny's cock, stroking him in perfect sync with Mac's thrusts; Mac's other hand splayed wide across Gunny's stomach.

The room stank of musk and sweat, the air filled with grunts and groans. The sound increased each time Mac changed his angle, hitting that sweet, secret spot deep inside Gunny. Each time Mac pressed deep, his hips rolled, and the short hairs around his cock tickled Gunny's crease. He cried out. Mac pulled all the way out and Gunny's ass clenched, before the thick, flared head split him wide open again. Mac found his rhythm. Gunny's body instinctively followed his lover's lead, as Mac continued the mind-blowing game of thrust and retreat.

Gunny wanted so badly for it to last, the perfect connection between them to never end. But as his balls tightened, a hard knot formed at the base of his spine; he knew it couldn't. The rush of urgent fire that sped like a freight train to his groin had Gunny begging. No matter how he wished otherwise, he couldn't rein it in, couldn't stop it. "Please… can I… Mac… I can't…."

So close to the edge, he could barely form words, but Mac heard them, and just like always, knew exactly what he needed. Mac thrust as deep as he could and tugged at the strap around Gunny's cock until the snap gave way. "Come for me, Gunny. Give it to me, now!"

Gunny's body went rigid for a second, his head thrown back in a silent scream, teetering between pleasure and what lay beyond. One more hard thrust from Mac's powerful hips, and Gunny rushed headlong over the edge; his body convulsed as each wave of pleasure rolled through him, and he shot pulse after pulse of hot spunk, screaming Mac's name. Gunny's eyes rolled back in his head, a rush of heat filled his ass as Mac unloaded deep inside him, and Gunny was flying again.

Finally, no longer able to hold himself upright, Gunny slumped back against Mac's chest, breathing harshly. His entire body trembled with bone-deep satisfaction. Mac kissed the side of Gunny's neck, painted kisses down his body as he released one strap from Gunny's ankle and then the other before once again giving him his full body to lean against. Mac crooned incoherent praises against Gunny's cheek as he removed the blindfold and hit the quick release on the restraints around his wrists. Mac pulled him tighter against him, holding most of Gunny's weight as Mac guided him to the sofa and curled around him. Boneless, sated, and content to let Mac hold him as he basked in the afterglow, Gunny savored Mac.

CHAPTER
Four

THE great thing about Mac was he didn't need to fill each moment with mindless chatter and noise. He let Gunny spend the rest of the day enjoying his blissed-out state with a big goofy grin on his face. They spent time washing each other in the shower, curling up together on the couch watching movies, and just enjoying being in each other's company. However, no matter how peaceful or deep the state of calm Mac could induce in him, it never lasted forever. It couldn't. Reality always snuck back in to fuck with the calm, and doubt was an uneasy and disheartening frame of mind to be in. In fact, it sucked.

While Gunny lay in bed with Mac's head on his chest, listening to Mac's even breaths as Mac drew random patterns with his fingertip along Gunny's stomach, Gunny's mind was a whirlwind of doubt and uncertainty. Why the hell couldn't he just tell Mac what was bothering him? He had shared everything with Mac, had for, well pretty much since they'd met. Early in their military career they'd been deployed together in Operation Desert Storm. At first, they'd been told their company would play a minor role pulling guard duty on POWs, shit of that nature. He and Mac had known it was bullshit. The government didn't send new M1 Abrams tanks for babysitting jobs. It was no surprise to him and Mac when word came down that the first infantry division needed more firepower, so they attached them to their division as their third brigade. It was during that time their bond was truly forged and they learned to trust each other with their lives. So why did he feel he couldn't trust Mac with this secret?

"How do you want to celebrate our retirement? Big party? Vacation?" Mac asked suddenly.

The first thing that came to mind was *I don't*. He didn't want things to change and would gladly enlist for another four years if things could just stay the same between him and Mac. And for a split second, he wished "Don't Ask, Don't Tell" would not be repealed. It was selfish and disgusting, and even as he thought it, he knew it was the panic at the thought of losing Mac that was doing the wishing and not the real Gunny.

"I don't know," he finally admitted honestly.

Mac lifted his head and met Gunny's eyes. "Hey, I know you've been kind of nervous about retiring, but think of it as the next adventure in our lives. It's going to be fun."

Fun wasn't the first word that came to mind. Gunny didn't find the prospect of being middle-aged and single fun. He tried to keep all traces of emotion off his face, but it was difficult with the sea of emotions that raged in him. When Mac leaned up, kissed him, and said, "You'll see," Gunny knew he hadn't hidden those unsettling feelings very well.

Mac's eyes went wide, and he got that sly grin on his face that Gunny loved so much. The one that told him one of Mac's outrageous ideas was being formed. "I got it. I think we should do both!"

"Both?" he asked confused.

"Yeah, party and vacation. It's not just our retirement we're celebrating but the repeal of that bullshit law." Mac's voice got excited; his words faster. "I think when we go to Lejeune for our exit ceremony we should go in full support of the repeal. Oh fuck, Gunny!" Mac hooted. "You and I walking on stage hand in hand. Now that's a hell of a way to leave a lasting impression. Two twenty-plus career Marines, decorated Marines I might add, who served honorably. I think that sends a pretty loud message to the idiots who don't think queers should serve in the military, don't you? C'mon, Gunny, we got to do this." Mac's eyes lit. "We can then combine our retirement celebration with our honeymoon. Kill two birds with one stone." Mac's grin grew brilliant. "And you said I never worry about saving money."

Gunny's lips curled into a wry grin; he was being sucked right into Mac's enthusiasm and infectious smile, but when the word *honeymoon* came out of Mac's mouth, the smile fell and Gunny's heart landed in his gut with a thud. He couldn't fucking breathe. No way had he heard Mac right. He wanted to ask him what he'd said, to clarify, but Gunny's throat had constricted.

"Gunny, you okay?" Mac asked, concerned.

Gunny opened his mouth and closed it a couple of times, trying to push out the words that sat on his tongue, but nothing came out.

"Jesus," Mac growled and sat up in bed, straddled Gunny's hips, and grabbed his face in both of his hands. "What the hell, Gunny? You have a fucking heart attack on me now and I will so kick your ass."

Mac stared at him with a panicked look, which was fine by Gunny because he was panicking the fuck out. *Honeymoon.* Did he dare to hope Mac was serious? Finally, he was able to squeeze out, "Honeymoon?"

"You don't want to marry me?" Mac sounded genuinely hurt, which just confused Gunny all the more.

His heart still flopped around erratically, but at least after a few more seconds, Gunny was able to push through the shock and find his voice. "First of all, you didn't ask me, and second, I am not going to marry you just to flip off the fucking Corps. It's not even legal."

"Neither was being openly gay in the military until now. Shit's changing, Gunny, and for the better. We might not be able to legally marry but that doesn't mean we can't commit our lives to each other and who knows, maybe one day—" An odd expression twisted Mac's face, the hands on Gunny's face tightened, and Mac arched a brow. "Wait a minute. What the hell did you mean, 'just to flip off the Corps'?"

Gunny grabbed Mac's wrists and forced him to ease up. "You can't expect me to say we're married just to send a message, that's just"—*that would just rip out my heart*—"wrong. You can't send a positive message with a lie. And since when are you the poster boy for gay rights?"

Irritation caused Gunny's skin to warm with anger. It wasn't Mac's fault. He wasn't the one who had started to expect more from their relationship. Rationally, Gunny knew that. Yet, even though his head knew it, his heart wasn't playing along. It was holding on to hope.

Mac looked down and frowned, and crossed his arms over his chest defiantly. "Our marriage wouldn't be a lie just because the government doesn't recognize it. We would know it was real," Mac said adamantly. "Why in the hell would we care what they thought of us now? We did our duty. This is about you and me and what *we* want."

"Wait… what…." Oh Christ, Mac looked serious. His jaw was set in defiance, and Gunny couldn't find a trace of humor as he searched Mac's hazel eyes. Head spinning, he tried to get a grasp on the direction the conversation had taken. For months, he'd been setting himself up for Mac to leave. "You don't have to settle for fucking your best friend anymore, you can have anyone you want," he added, still confused as all hell.

Mac continued to stare down at Gunny, a hard glare in his eyes, before his expression softened and he shifted until his legs were stretched out between Gunny's, holding his upper body up on his forearms and his lips inches from Gunny's. "I've been a fucking basket case the last few months, couldn't figure out what the fuck was wrong with me. I mean, how many people can retire at forty-one with a damn good pension, a sweet savings account, and finally do whatever they want, when they want? What was there to be freaking out about, right?" Mac wasn't asking; that he didn't require an answer was evident when he continued on without giving Gunny time to speak.

"Then it hit me, I don't want things to change between us. I mean, I know why we originally stopped fucking with other guys, but it's not like that anymore, Gunny. I'm not settling for my best friend, I'm fucking crazy in love with him." Mac leaned down and brushed his lips against Gunny's. "We never talked about being a couple. Hell, we weren't allowed to be, but we were. Whatever description you put on what we have doesn't matter; we were, and still are, a couple. I've always loved you. Twenty-two years I've loved you and I want to spend the rest of my life with you as my best friend, my boy, my lover, and my husband." He pressed harder against Gunny's lips, demanding entrance, consuming him with the intensity, the desire and need, leaving Gunny breathless when it ended.

"Marry me, Gunny," Mac whispered against his lips.

It was as if a great weight had lifted from Gunny's chest. Months he'd worried about his future, driving himself crazy out of his fool head. Mac was right. They were a couple; Gunny just hadn't allowed himself to believe it or to even hope for it. He was so overcome with emotions he could barely talk. Gunny reached up with a trembling hand and stroked Mac's cheek, pressed a gentle kiss against his lips before saying, "Yes!" Gunny's cheeks heated, embarrassed that he'd become so mushy. "I mean, I'll have to think about it," he deadpanned.

"Oh hell no, you already said yes. I heard it. You can't take it back now," Mac taunted, then leaned down and nipped at Gunny's neck, causing him to jerk.

"Yeah, fine," he moaned, not really thinking about the question anymore as Mac started sucking at his neck.

Mac's smile was brilliant when he pulled back to look down at Gunny, eyes sparkling. "Shall we shake on it?" Mac suggested.

Mac worked Gunny's arms upward till they were above his head, holding his wrists tightly. Gunny glanced over to his right and then to his left, then turned to meet Mac's eyes. "Kind of hard to shake on it in this position," he answered with a small smirk.

Mac started to roll his hips, grinding their cocks together as he pressed a kiss to Gunny's lips, then worked his way across Gunny's jaw, licking and nibbling, causing goose bumps to erupt on Gunny's flesh. "Or we could seal the deal another way," he said against Gunny's ear. "Any suggestions?" Mac emphasized his meaning with a hard thrust of his hips.

"Shit!" Gunny called out at the bite of pain, the curse turning into a moan as Mac's hips began rolling gently again and he continued to tease at Gunny's neck. "I can't think when you do that," he chastised lightly, tilting his head to the side.

"That's okay, I think I know the perfect way to seal the deal," Mac murmured.

"Uh-huh," Gunny replied, not really paying attention to what Mac was saying, his focus now narrowed down to the way Mac held his wrists, the brush of stubble against stubble, chest to chest and cock to cock. But he didn't need to think. Mac set the slow sensual rhythm of their bodies, and Gunny only had to cling to Mac and feel.

This was one of the things he loved most about Mac. How they could come together, no words required, and Mac knew exactly what both Gunny's mind and body needed at any given moment. The doubt and uncertainty gone, the fear of losing the man he loved squelched. And now said man loved him tenderly… softly… unhurriedly.

"Tell me," Mac breathed against Gunny's ear.

"Huh," he moaned. Gunny buried his face in the side of Mac's neck, licking the salt from his skin, Mac's flavor and scent ramping up Gunny's arousal. Everything about the man was pure masculine sexy.

"C'mon, Gunny. Tell me," Mac encouraged softly.

"Yes," he mumbled against Mac's neck.

Mac released Gunny's wrists and ran his hands soothingly down Gunny's arms, then planted his hands on the mattress near Gunny's shoulders and leaned back, ignoring Gunny's small groan of protest. Thankfully, he didn't stop the sweet friction of their shafts sliding along the other.

"Focus, Gunny," Mac chuckled.

Gunny got a glimpse of their damp cock heads, making his pulse speed. "I am," he assured him, now gripping Mac's ass tightly. A droplet of precum seeped from the flared head of Mac's cock, and Gunny's mouth watered with the urge to lick and taste.

"Ow!" Gunny growled, then glared up at Mac when stinging pain radiated from the slap to his shoulder. "What the hell, Mac. What was that for?"

"Just wanted to get your attention," Mac said unapologetically. He leaned down and kissed the abused shoulder; then it was Mac's turn to cry out when Gunny landed a hard slap to Mac's left butt cheek. Laughing, Mac leaned back and shook his head. "Okay, I deserved that."

"Damn right you did," Gunny insisted. "I was in my happy place." His lips twitched, when he glanced back down to their groins. "A very happy place."

"So that's why you said yes? For my dick?" Mac asked with a hint of a pout, which so didn't work for the badass Marine. Gunny fought to hold back the laughter that wanted to break free. This was a very serious matter.

He released Mac's ass with one hand and grabbed the back of his head, pulling him down until their lips were almost touching. "Well, your dick is pretty spectacular." The laughter bubbled up, and he smashed their mouths together before it could burst free or Mac could come up with one of his smart-ass retorts.

Gunny dominated the kiss, pushed his tongue deep, and held Mac firm against him until he pulled a deep moan from his lover. Mac seemed to melt against him. Their bodies picked up the previous slow sensual rhythm but quickly changed to a faster pace to meet the intensity of the demanding kiss.

They went at each other hard and fast, the passion too strong to contain. Seconds after wet heat covered Gunny's stomach, he added to the heat and cried out into Mac's mouth. Gunny held Mac tight, long after the kiss ended and they were both spent, unwilling to lose any contact.

Gunny was in no hurry to move long after his breathing and heart rate had returned to normal, and from the way Mac was totally relaxed where he lay, he didn't appear in any hurry either. Arms wrapped around Mac, and Gunny closed his eyes. The emotional ups and downs combined with the sated feeling and Mac's warmth left him exhausted, and sleep was quickly creeping up on him.

"Tell me," Mac said sleepily, causing Gunny to jerk awake.

"Tell you what," Gunny mumbled, rolling them till they were on their sides facing each other. Frowning at the mess on his chest, Gunny grabbed the sheet and swiped it across his chest and stomach, doing the same to Mac's, before he threw a leg and arm over him.

"Tell me," Mac grumbled.

"I already said yes, I'd marry you, now go to sleep."

"No, tell me you love me."

"Are you serious?" Gunny asked, incredulous. "You woke me up for that?"

"Yup." Mac pushed closer, snuggling. "I haven't heard you tell me you love me."

"I've told you plenty of times," Gunny groaned.

Mac leaned up and looked down at Gunny and sighed dramatically. "Yeah, but that's when you thought we were just best friends. Dammit, Gunny, I told you, you're supposed to say it back, that's the rules," Mac complained.

"The rules, huh?" Gunny reached up and ran the back of his knuckles along Mac's jaw tenderly. "I love you," he said sincerely.

Mac stared at him for a moment, then rolled his eyes and shook his head. "You're such a sap," he chuckled, then lay down and moved in close again. Gunny was about to complain, maybe even slap the teasing bastard upside his head, when he heard Mac whisper, "Thank you. I love you too."

He'd told Mac hundreds of times, had heard Mac say the same to him, but it had never felt this incredible before, like he was hearing it for the first time. Gunny tightened his arms around Mac and kissed the top of his head. "You're welcome."

CHAPTER
Five

"OH NO you don't," Mac grumbled sleepily and tightened his hold on Gunny when he felt him start to pull away. "I am not waking up to a cold empty bed this morning. Now go back to sleep."

"I was going to go start the coffee," Gunny told him, still trying to escape.

"No," Mac growled and threw a leg over the man, effectively pinning him. "I don't want coffee. I want cuddles."

Gunny stilled and was silent for so long Mac finally opened his eyes. Gunny was staring back over his shoulder at him with a strange expression on his face.

"What?" Mac asked grumpily.

"Cuddles? Are you serious?"

"Yes, cuddles." He grunted. "New retirement rules, Gunny. No one is allowed out of this bed in the morning before cuddles and blowjobs."

Gunny's eyes went wide, and then he burst out laughing. "Jones, you are insane, you do know that, right?"

Mac narrowed his eyes and scowled. "I'm serious."

Gunny shook his head. "I don't know; the word just seems almost… obscene coming out of your mouth."

In one deft move, Mac shoved Gunny till he was lying flat on his stomach, and Mac crawled on top of him, burying his face in Gunny's neck. "We could jump right to the blowjobs if you prefer." He wasn't kidding about the cuddling, but he could compromise occasionally.

"Do you remember Private Carter?"

"Who?" Gunny yelled from the bathroom.

"Carter," Mac repeated as he grabbed the two mugs of coffee and headed to the bathroom.

He damn near dropped the hot brew when he spotted Gunny standing in front of the mirror, shaving with just a white towel around his waist; water still dampened his wide back, making his skin glisten. The way he bent slightly at the waist put that magnificent ass on perfect display, caused Mac's pulse to increase and a warm rush of blood to settle pleasingly into his groin. Mac's dick perked up. It was as if he hadn't already gotten off three times in less than twenty-four hours. Anytime he was near Gunny, Mac instantly turned into a randy teenager. He set the mugs down on the counter and moved behind Gunny.

Gunny smiled at him in the mirror. "Sorry, couldn't hear you over the water, who were you asking about?"

The shower-warmed skin was too much of a temptation, and Mac slid his arms around Gunny and placed a kiss to the back of his neck. He loved the way Gunny felt against him, how their similar height and size fit perfectly against each other. "Christ, Gunny, do you have to be such a goddamn tease," Mac groaned, kissing his way across Gunny's shoulders.

"I'm shaving. How the hell is that being a tease?" Gunny asked.

"'Cause you're breathing," Mac crooned, and pressed his cock against the crease of Gunny's ass.

"I'll try to control myself," Gunny snickered. "Now put that thing away. No way in hell am I getting it up again."

"Is that a challenge?" he asked, resting his chin on Gunny's shoulder and meeting his gaze in the mirror.

"Just a fact."

"You don't have to get—"

"You are not fucking me," Gunny said adamantly, pointing the razor at Mac. "Besides, some of us have to work today, and my ass is already sore."

"Pansy," Mac said with a smirk. He wasn't about to admit that while his ass was fine, his nuts ached and it was highly improbable that he'd be able to do much beyond teasing. "Give me that," he said and snatched the razor from Gunny.

"Hey! I was using that."

"Yeah, well, now I'm using it. Turn around," he encouraged.

Gunny turned in Mac's arms and held on to Mac's hips. "It's been a long time since you shaved me."

"Too long," Mac agreed. "Lots of things we haven't done in far too long. I plan on rectifying that problem." He ran the razor carefully over Gunny's jaw.

"Yeah? Like what?" Gunny asked, tilting his head back.

"No talking," Mac chastised as he pressed the blade gently against Gunny's neck. "Don't want you crying like last time."

Gunny waited until Mac moved the razor away to rinse it before responding. "You nicked my nuts," Gunny grumbled. "And I was not crying; I was too busy cussing you out for laughing."

Oh hell, that had been some funny shit. He'd had the razor against Gunny's nut sac when the man got the bright idea to kiss the side of Mac's neck. The kiss hadn't caused the wound, but Gunny's warm breath against his ear had caused him to shudder and—well, a man just doesn't take too kindly to having his balls fileted, even if it was his own damn fault.

"There you go again," Gunny grumbled and shoved at Mac's chest.

Mac bit his lip and tried to get his laughter under control. Gunny continued to glare at him, but the smile curling his mouth ruined the pissed-off effect he was obviously going for.

"Okay, okay, oh grumpy one. I'm sorry."

Gunny grunted in response, but he pulled Mac close again and let him finish shaving him. Gunny watched him the entire time, warmth in his eyes that made Mac's chest tighten. He couldn't wait until they retired. They'd no longer have to miss out on these little moments that really didn't seem all that important until the opportunity was taken away. Sad thing was, most people didn't realize how good they had it. They could start each morning with the one they loved, sharing coffee, a chat, a cuddle, but most people took those things for granted. Lost moments. Months away from Gunny had taught Mac to never take a moment with the man for granted again.

Mac ran a hand over Gunny's face, satisfied it was nice and smooth, and kissed Gunny's jaw. "All done." He held up the razor. "Unless you'd like me to do a little manscaping?" he asked, waggling his brows.

"Not a chance," Gunny chuckled. He took it, dropped it in his bag on the counter, and then wrapped his arms around Mac. "Thank you," Gunny said softly and pressed a tender kiss to Mac's lips. "I've missed this."

"I was just thinking the same thing," he murmured against Gunny's lips.

Mac didn't try to deepen the kiss, taking his time to enjoy the way Gunny felt against him. Gunny's heat, scent—Jesus, everything about the man was intoxicating. He could have spent hours with their lips pressed together, tasting, and their bodies pressed tightly against the other, but Gunny's stomach growled loudly, reminding Mac he hadn't fed the man. One last kiss to Gunny's chin and Mac stepped back. "C'mon, time to feed the beast."

Gunny laughed and grabbed his cup of coffee from the counter and then wrinkled his nose.

"I'll pour us another cup," Mac said. He took the mug and picked up his own. He gave Gunny a pointed look. "You get dressed or you won't be making it to work today."

Mac stopped in the doorway, blatantly ogled up and down Gunny's magnificent body before meeting his gaze. "Or any day for the next week," he said huskily. Mac headed to the kitchen, but not before he saw Gunny visibly shudder. *Twenty-plus years, you still got it,*

Jones. Mac was still grinning like a fool when he poured the cold coffee down the sink.

Just as Mac got the whipped eggs poured into the frying pan, Gunny joined him, dressed in a pair of loose-fitting jeans and a tight navy-blue T-shirt with *Marines* stenciled in yellow across the chest, and grabbed the freshly poured cup of coffee.

"Need any help?" he asked, taking a tentative sip.

"You can butter the toast when it pops up."

They made quick work of preparing breakfast, moving easily around the kitchen together. Gunny playfully bumped into Mac each time he passed, stole a grope of either Mac's ass or crotch, and laughed as he spun away before Mac could grab onto him or swat him. When they sat across from each other at the small breakfast nook, with heaping plates of scrambled eggs, toast, and fresh fruit, Gunny was still chuckling. To Mac, Gunny had always been the most handsome man he'd ever seen, but when Gunny smiled, the kind that reached his eyes as it did now, Gunny was beyond gorgeous; he was stunning.

How was it possible?

As they ate, Mac stole glances at Gunny, in fucking awe. How could he look at this man all these years and his excitement not wane? Not only had it not diminished, his desire seemed to grow each time he looked at his sexy man. Most couples he knew, his parents included, shared a few years of unrestrained passion. Those who lasted longer had love and friendship to sustain them. He and Gunny had both, but they also had…. Mac shook his head. He couldn't even describe what he and Gunny had. Passion was too gentle a word for it. Soon, there would be no more nights sleeping alone, no more missed moments, ever, if he had any say in the matter. *Morning blowjob, don't forget those daily delights.* Mac's body tingled with the thought. Damn, his life was good. In fact, it was going to be fan-fucking-tastic.

"Must be one hell of a daydream."

Mac jerked his head up to find Gunny sitting back in his chair, cup of coffee in his hand and a knowing smirk on his face. He must have been zoned out longer than he'd thought, both his mug and plate empty. Mac dropped his fork and took the same casual position Gunny had. "I was just thinking about how great retirement is going to be."

Gunny studied Mac for a moment, a strange expression crossing his face.

"What? You don't think it's going to be great?" Mac probed.

"Yeah, I'm looking forward to it. It's just—"

When Gunny didn't say anything further, Mac moved to the chair next to him, scooting it close. "Just what?" he asked, stroking his knuckles along Gunny's jaw.

"You're not worried at all?"

"About?" Mac asked in confusion.

"Everything seems to be changing so fast," Gunny said almost inaudibly. He looked down at his plate and scratched the close crop on the side of his head. "I mean, yesterday morning I'm freaking out, worried about leaving the Corps, what I'm going to do with all the time on my hands, how things are going to go between you and me. This morning, I'm sitting here thinking about walking hand in hand with you at the exit ceremony, marrying you." Gunny jumped to his feet and paced.

Mac didn't go after him or say a word, just watched. Sometimes the man needed to work out his thoughts before he shared them. Whatever was running through Gunny's head was causing him to tense, each step jerky. Mac had to force himself to stay seated, wait for Gunny to speak or ask for help. Patience wasn't one of his greatest attributes.

Suddenly, Gunny came to an abrupt halt and spun around; the color had drained from his face, eyes a little wild as he looked at Mac. "Jesus H. Christ! Have you considered what the fuck we're going to say to our parents?" His voice rose in obvious panic. "We have to tell them before we get on that stage." Gunny's eyes went impossibly wider. "Oh, God! I have to tell my ninety-year-old grandfather. I'm going to give the man a heart attack. I'm going to kill my grandfather. And your brother," he said, flailing a hand toward Mac. "What are you going to say to your brother? The man is the biggest homophobe I know. He's going to disown you, Mac. He's going to kill you in your fucking sleep and then disown you." Gunny's chest heaved, nostrils flaring with each breath. The poor man looked as if he was about to explode, or at the very least, shatter the bones in his hands with how hard he had them clenched.

Actually, Mac had thought about telling his family many times over the years. He never did. He figured, why upset them when he couldn't have a true relationship with his lover? Cowardice? Perhaps, but he liked to think it was to not only keep the peace but also to prevent the truth from ruining his career. Mac wouldn't have put it past Ted to try and elevate himself in their parents' eyes by trying to disgrace Mac. It was bullshit; his older brother would do better to improve their parents' opinion of him by putting down the bottle, manning up, and being a dad to his son.

Coming out to his family weighed heavily on his mind as he tried to figure out where his and Gunny's relationship would go in the future. However, not once had he considered he'd been lying to them. They all knew he loved Gunny; the only thing they didn't know was that he and Gunny were fucking each other. What they did in private was none of his family's business. Their sex life wouldn't be his family's business in the future either.

Mac rose and walked over to Gunny, took Gunny's hands in his, and brought them to his lips to kiss the white knuckles. "Hey," Mac said soothingly. "Seems the calm we found you yesterday didn't last very long."

"Yeah, that was before the thought of telling my dad, worse yet, your dad," Gunny shot back. "I don't know about you, but I don't particularly like the thought of telling my mom and dad I've been lying to them all these years."

"And what exactly have you been lying about?"

"Do *not* fucking patronize me, Jones," Gunny barked, pulling his hands free.

Mac snaked his hands out, latched on to Gunny's wrists before he could pull away. Gunny growled, but Mac ignored the warning. "Am I not your best friend?"

"Of course you—"

"I'm the only one you've ever invited to your parents' home for the holidays in over ten years. We've taken our parents on vacation. I stood beside you when your sister passed, you held me as I cried at my grandma's funeral. If I was a woman, your family, or vice versa for that matter, would never have questioned we were a couple. We didn't lie,

Gunny. Hell, it was right in front of their faces, and if they were as stupid as we were not to see it, then that's on them."

Gunny cocked his head to the side and studied Mac. Mac could practically hear the gears turning in that big, beautiful head as Gunny processed Mac's words. After a few moments he said grumpily, "Why do you always have to be the logical one?" His lips twitched as he tried to hold back his smile.

"One of us has to be the brains of this operation," Mac said dryly.

Gunny pulled his hands free once again, but this time instead of trying to step away he wrapped his arms around Mac and tugged him close. "And yet, I outrank you."

"Only because you're a better ass kisser than I am," Mac told him, pressing further still against Gunny, his hands roaming the sinew of muscle along his man's back.

"Oh, really?" Gunny gave him a seductive look Mac felt all the way down to his toes. "I have it from a reliable source that not only do you kiss ass, you're very, *very* good at it."

"Only one ass," Mac clarified. "I'd show you my mad skills if you didn't have to go to work. Any chance you can call off?"

Gunny moaned when Mac squeezed the said ass in question, pushing into Mac's touch. "Wish I could, but can I get a rain check?" he asked hopefully. "Say around four."

"I'll be waiting."

"Thank you," Gunny whispered and pressed a tender kiss to Mac's lips.

Mac knew the thank-you was for more than the offer of ass kissing, but for heading off the panic attack Gunny had been revving up for. How passionate and emotional Gunny could be was only one of the things Mac loved about the man. Another was how Gunny needed him to find his balance. They were a hell of a team.

CHAPTER
Six

THE gleaming eyes and eager faces of potential recruits was a sight Gunny was going to miss. He loved interacting with the young teens who teetered on the edge of manhood, a whole wide world set out before them. Some sought to join the Corps to escape home or as a means to afford college later, but there were some who, like Gunny, dreamed of a career as a Marine. Those were the ones he'd miss. However, recruits, work, or anything not Macalister Jones couldn't hold Gunny's attention, and Gunny resented having to be at the office.

The late-afternoon sun was bright, and Gunny's mood improved the second he stepped out of the recruiting center. Slipping on his shades, he whistled as he made his way to his old truck. He'd left the car for Mac, the man refusing to be seen in the old '74 Chevy. Gunny loved the truck. It reminded him of himself: lots of miles but built solid without the flash. He slid in behind the wheel and slammed the door; Gunny opened his cell and hit the call button. "You want me to pick up anything on the way home?" Gunny asked as soon as Mac picked up the call.

"Well, that depends," Mac drawled. "What are your plans for the night?"

Gunny fired up the engine and turned the air vent to high. The cab of the truck was stifling and he wiped at the sweat on his brow before answering. "I'm thinking shower, home-cooked meal, and an evening of a little ass-kissing fun."

"Sounds good to me. What are you cooking for dinner?"

"I slave away all day long to provide for us. Is it too much to ask that a man have a meal on his table when he gets home? A little respect for my needs would be appreciated here, Mac." Gunny struggled to keep the amusement out of his voice and was thankful he didn't have to hide the wide smile that stretched across his face.

"It's all about you. You. You. You!" Mac wailed. "What about me and my needs? I've been stuck in this house all day long, scrubbing and mopping till my fingers bled. I deserve a little attention as much as you deserve a full belly," Mac complained.

"Oh good God! Nag, nag, nag, that's all you do." Gunny pulled the truck onto the road, biting his lip to keep the laughter from bubbling up.

"That's right," Mac acknowledged. "And until you start showing me a little respect, I'm going to keep riding your ass."

Gunny choked on his laughter. "Not a deterrent, Mac."

Mac was silent for a long drawn-out moment, and then Gunny's words must have hit him, because he roared with laughter. "Yeah, I guess that wouldn't be much of one, is it," Mac conceded, snickering low. "I'll have to withhold riding your ass—"

"Oh hell no! You can't take it back now." Gunny lowered his voice to a husky tone. "You can ride my ass all you want after you kiss it."

"Deal!"

Gunny spotted the food mart sign coming up on his right. "Seriously, I'm passing the market now, do you need anything?"

"Nah, I got beanies and wienies on the stove. And hurry up. I'm bored, lonely, and I need some cuddles, dammit," Mac muttered.

"Christ! Here I think I've agreed to marry a hardcore Marine and I get a fucking cuddle whore. What the hell?"

"Just shows what a lucky bastard you are. Now get home."

Gunny shook his head as the line went dead and he flipped his phone shut. One damn thing was for sure, there would never be a dull moment with Mac around full time, and a hell of a lot of joking and laughter. As he maneuvered through the streets, Gunny felt both excitement, infused with a little dread, and a speck of fear. He'd thought about the conversation he and Mac had over breakfast and what Mac had said made sense. How could their loved ones not know, or at least suspect, he and Mac were lovers? However, Gunny wasn't delusional enough to think telling their families would be as easy as Mac made it sound.

The idea of him and Mac walking up on stage, hand in hand, also weighed heavily on him. Gunny didn't quite understand why Mac wanted to flip off the Corps. Did it mean Mac would have preferred them to be an acknowledged couple; the bigger question, would it have really made any difference at the end of the day? There was nothing to flip off. They had known the facts when they had signed up, known the rules and what they would be giving up. Right or wrong, they had made the decision knowing they would have to hide their sexuality.

What about their friends? How many of them would they lose over this? Gunny pulled into his driveway and turned off the engine. He leaned back against the seat and scrubbed a hand over his face. Their buddy Tom was going to shit a brick when he found out. Tom Nelson, who lived a couple houses down the street, shared the same love of pool and cold beer at the local pub, Jack's. The second time they met him over a pool table, he'd asked if Gunny and Mac were a couple, and they both spit out their auto-response of "Hell, no!" Even as the friendship had grown, neither he nor Mac had told Tom the truth. With a sigh, Gunny stepped out of the truck and slammed the door. He didn't care what Mac said; this whole coming-out thing was going to suck big-time and not in the good, slurpy, wet kind of way.

He took one last calming breath and blew it out slowly. Gunny opened the front door and called out, "Honey, I'm home!"

"In the kitchen."

Gunny pulled off his boots and dropped his keys and wallet on the coffee table as he strolled by. The house was full of yummy scents of oregano, tomato sauce, and fresh baked bread. Gunny's stomach growled loudly. *Hell yeah! No beanies and wienies tonight.* Gunny would recognize that scent anywhere. Mac had made his famous heroically delicious meatball heroes.

He found Mac dressed in nothing but a pair of old threadbare sweats, bent over the oven, his tight ass on perfect display, a temptation Gunny couldn't refuse. He moved close, grabbed the man's hips, and pulled that perfect ass hard against his groin.

"Hey, I'm working with dangerous machinery here," Mac scoffed. He pulled the subs out of the oven and set them on the stove top before he turned and wrapped his arms around Gunny's waist. "I'll take my apologies now," he muttered.

"I'm sorry for molesting your ass while you were operating dangerous machinery," Gunny said. He grabbed it and squeezed. "But in my defense you shouldn't bend over in front of me. It's very hard to resist."

"I wasn't talking about that. Hell, even I find my ass impossible to resist," Mac snorted and rolled his eyes. "I'm talking about nagging me about your dinner being on the table. I'm Suzy fucking Homemaker. I got this shit covered."

"Fine! I'm sorry for doubting you, and I'll call you anything you want as long as you keep cooking like that." Gunny grunted, nodding toward the sandwiches.

Mac released his hold on Gunny and pressed against his chest, forcing him to take a step back. "You just want me for my ass and my heroes," Mac grumbled and moved toward the fridge.

"Yes, that's it," Gunny told him and slapped him on the ass before he could get away. "So either give me that ass or feed me."

Mac gave him a crooked smile over his shoulder. "You ain't getting either until you shower. You've got five minutes."

Gunny thought about going after Mac's ass again as he bent to pull stuff out of the fridge, but a hot shower did sound good. He forced himself to turn away and stripped down as he made his way to the bathroom. After setting the taps, Gunny entered the shower and didn't waste any time washing away the sweat and grime of the day. The disquieting thoughts he'd dealt with all day were blessedly silent, replaced by more pleasurable ones: meatballs, tight Marine ass, and a night wrapped in said soldier's arms. He would not call it cuddling.

After cleaning up, Gunny grabbed a towel and wrapped it around his still-dripping wet body and joined Mac in the kitchen.

Mac stopped dead in his tracks, platter of food in his hand, halfway to the table, when he saw Gunny. Gunny looked down his body and then raised an eyebrow at Mac. "What?"

Mac shook himself and narrowed his eyes. "You know what—" He roamed his eyes up and down Gunny's body; when his gaze landed on Gunny's groin, he licked his lips. Mac continued to stare for another few seconds, and then seemed to get control of himself and set the platter on the table. "C'mon, let's eat. And sit over there," Mac huffed, pointing to a chair at the opposite end of the table, before he spun on his heels and stomped back toward the kitchen.

"Why?" Gunny asked, confused. It was an oversized farm table, with mismatched antique chairs he and Mac had picked up at various estate sales and flea markets. They always sat at one end of the massive piece of furniture, even when they had guests. The head of the table had somehow become Mac's normal spot, and Gunny always sat directly to his right.

"Because I'm hungry dammit and I didn't spend all that time making homemade sauce just to eat my sub cold."

Gunny continued to stand still. He watched Mac grab glasses and a carton of milk and set them on the table, trying to work out what the hell was going on. Finally, Mac picked up one of the empty plates and handed it to Gunny. "Either sit down there"—he nodded toward the far end—"or put some fucking clothes on."

"Give me that," Gunny muttered and took the offered plate. He grabbed a sub, set it on his plate, and plopped his ass down in his usual spot. Ignoring Mac's grumbling, Gunny dug in, savoring the delicious meal, humming as the flavors exploded across his taste buds. Mac steadfastly refused to look toward Gunny, but he couldn't hide his grin. One simply did not talk while devouring heroically delicious meatball heroes. Even Mac's attention shifted, and they inhaled their meals, with only the occasional grunt or groan in true famished caveman fashion. It was a beautiful thing.

Before clearing the table and doing the dishes, Gunny took pity on Mac and slipped on his favorite pair of gray sweats with *USMC* stenciled in navy blue on the hip. In his opinion they were way sexier than the towel, and the exasperated look Mac gave him when he stepped out of the bedroom proved Gunny was right. Probably had something to do with the fact that in some areas, the material was so thin it was practically see-through and the hole in the crotch—which Mac was aware of—added easy access to the fun parts. A hole Mac sought out the moment they were stretched out on the couch.

"Would you stop that," Gunny complained. "I thought you wanted to let your food settle."

Mac lifted his head from where it rested on Gunny's chest and smiled at him. "I do. It is. But that doesn't mean I can't play a little."

Gunny pulled Mac's hand away from his crotch. "You're not playing, you're tickling."

"Whatever. Same diff," Mac huffed and laid his head back down. Luckily for Gunny, Mac didn't return his hand to the hole. Instead, he settled for teasing his fingers through the hair on Gunny's chest.

These quiet times were the ones Gunny missed most when either he or Mac were out of town. Yes, he missed the sex, the conversation, the laughter, but the easy companionable silence went a long way in easing Gunny's head. When Mac was gone, he rarely laid on the couch for any length of time, even to watch TV, or anywhere alone for that matter. His mind rarely slept, always worrying, overanalyzing, and admittedly, oftentimes making mountains out of molehills. His overactive mind had served Gunny well in his career choice, but sometimes made relaxing a bitch. Amazingly, Mac had found the on-and-off switch. One was to take Gunny out of his body and make him fly through his submission; the other was the more curious of the two, the simple repetitive touch of Mac's fingers against his flesh. Mac calmed not only his body but his soul.

After an exhausting day at work, and now with a full belly and Mac wrapped around him, Gunny was about to doze off when Mac's voice startled him, pulling him back from the edge of sleep.

"Hmm?" Gunny asked sleepily.

"I had this crazy dream last night. Do you remember Private Carter?"

Gunny blinked a couple of times, trying to throw off the sleep, and racked his brain for placement of the name. Throughout his career he'd come across a couple men by that name, then it dawned on him. "You mean the guy who threatened to out you?"

"Yeah, well, about that," Mac hedged. He lifted his head and met Gunny's eyes. "I've been thinking about him a lot the last couple of months."

Oh, shit! From what Gunny remembered, Mac had told him Carter was a hot little cherry—a good ten, fifteen years younger than Mac—he had popped ten years ago. Gunny stiffened, not happy with the idea that Mac had been thinking about another man for months.

"Relax," Mac chastised, when Gunny tensed. "It's not what you think." Mac held Gunny's eyes and stroked his cheek.

Under Mac's touch and the sincere expression on his face, Gunny slowly relaxed. Fuck, he hated being like this some days. He was going to give himself an ulcer with the way he always jumped to the worst-case scenario. He huffed out a breath. "Sorry, what about him?" he asked warily.

"He never existed," Mac said matter-of-factly.

"What?"

"I'm serious." Mac shook his head. "No one ever tried to out me. I made it up."

Gunny searched Mac's eyes and waited for the punch line, but the man looked dead serious. After a few more seconds, Gunny finally asked, "Why would you do that?"

"I couldn't stand the idea of you being with someone else and I didn't know how to ask you not to." Mac shrugged.

Gunny's gut rolled at the realization that Mac had lied to him, and an ache settled deep in his chest. He'd have sworn his best friend had always been completely honest with him. Yet even as his heart felt betrayed, Gunny's pride swelled. A smug feeling came over him, easing the sting. Mac hadn't been with him these past ten years out of necessity, but because he wanted to, and he hadn't wanted Gunny with anyone either.

"Gunny?" Mac murmured, interrupting his thoughts.

"Why are you telling me this now? I'd have never known you'd lied. Why now?"

"I'm sorry I lied to you, but I'm not sorry I did it," Mac said unapologetically. "And why now? Well, for one, I'm sick of the psychotic imaginary dude fucking with my dreams for the last couple of months." Mac grabbed Gunny's hand and brought it to his mouth, placing a soft kiss against the back of it. "But more importantly I don't want there to be any secrets between us."

"I hadn't messed with any other dudes for years before Private Carter came along, so I guess it's not a big deal. I can forgive you for that one."

"Really? How long?"

Gunny's cheeks heated. "Five years," he admitted nonchalantly.

"Fuck, I love you," Mac said in an excited tone. He smashed their mouths together in a brief but hard kiss.

"Yeah, well, obviously I've loved you longer."

"Nah, you just figured it out sooner than I did," Mac said.

Gunny arched his brows at Mac. "Any other mistruths you want to get off your chest?" If that's all there was, he could easily forgive Mac for the small falsity.

He hesitated for a long moment and then murmured, "I cheat at cards."

"That's not a secret, you dumbass. Everyone knows you cheat." Gunny laughed.

"Really?" he asked with mock shock. "Damn, and I thought I was pretty good at sneaking in those extra aces."

Gunny rolled his eyes. "Well?" he nudged.

Mac tilted his head back and stared at the ceiling, an expression of concentration on his handsome face. After a few seconds, he looked back down at Gunny. "Remember that butt-ugly purple-and-black shirt you had?"

"Hey! It wasn't ugly, it was trendy." He narrowed his eyes. "What about it?" he asked suspiciously.

"The cleaners didn't lose it. I threw it away."

"You son of a bitch," Gunny roared and surged up, wrapping Mac in a bear hug.

"Hey!" Mac shouted, flailing to get purchase on the couch, but it was to no avail. Gunny rolled, and Mac hit the floor with a loud "oomph."

Gunny landed on top of him, pressing all his weight down on Mac and entwining their legs, effectively pinning the man. "You cut me deep, man," Gunny said, voice dropping dangerously low. "I'm not sure I can forgive you for that one. That was my favorite shirt."

"It was—"

"Don't say it," Gunny growled. "You're in enough trouble as it is."

Mac pursed his lips to keep from smiling, but he couldn't hide the gleam in his eyes.

Relieved there weren't any more secrets or serious lies between them, Gunny went to his feet and pulled Mac up with him. "C'mon, you're going to have to do some serious ass kissing over this one," he told him, pulling Mac along toward their bedroom.

"You're such a big ol' softy," Mac snorted. "I already owed you that."

Gunny stopped and spun around. "You're right, thank you for reminding me." It took all his will to keep from laughing and maintain the glare he shot at his naughty man. He tapped a finger against his chin as if contemplating Mac's punishment.

"It's like a rare work of fine art that has to be adored and stroked lovingly, not slammed into and abused." A wicked grin curled Gunny's lips as he remembered Mac's words from their phone conversation.

Spinning around, he tugged on Mac's wrist forcing him to follow. "You shouldn't have thrown my favorite shirt away, Mac," he told him drolly. "And you *really* shouldn't have called me soft."

Gunny's smile grew wider when he heard Mac mumble, "Me and my big mouth."

Oh yeah, that big mouth was exactly where Gunny was going to start.

CHAPTER
Seven

THROUGH slitted eyes, Gunny watched as Mac slid out of bed and grabbed his sweatpants from the floor. In the early morning light, Gunny saw the man tense as he pulled on his pants and heard the hiss of breath.

"What? No morning cuddle or blowjob?" Gunny complained sleepily.

"I gotta piss," Mac grunted.

"Since when do you need your pants on to piss? Did we have mysterious guests arrive while I slept?" Gunny rolled to his stomach, pulled his pillow close, and bit down on it to keep from laughing as Mac limped toward the bathroom.

"No! And I'm not giving you a cuddle or a blowjob—"

Gunny imitated Mac's southern drawl. "New retirement rules, Gunny. No one is allowed out of this bed in the morning before cuddles and blowjobs."

Mac glared at him from the doorway. "We haven't fucking retired yet," he growled, then entered the bathroom and slammed the door.

Gunny didn't try to hold in the snort of laughter; he let it out, laughing boisterously until tears leaked from his eyes. Poor Mac. His lover had been all hot and horny for Gunny's attentions the night before, screaming and begging for more. And oh God, had the man been tight. It had been not only the three months apart that Mac hadn't had any action; hell, Gunny couldn't remember the last time he'd tapped Mac's ass. Six months? A year?

"Shut up!" Mac yelled from the other room just before the sound of the shower muffled anything else the man might have said.

Gunny laughed harder. Wiping the tears from his eyes, Gunny rolled out of bed and went to join Mac in the shower. The second he opened the door, steam poured out and he could hear the muffled grumblings but couldn't make out what Mac said.

Gunny slid back the shower curtain, stepped in, and yelped as the scorching-hot water came in contact with his skin. "Jesus," he hissed and shielded himself with Mac's body.

Mac was bent slightly at the waist, the hot water pounding down on his lower back, with a scowl on his face. "I've decided I'm not so versatile in my versatility," he griped.

"You seemed pretty damn hot on the idea last night," Gunny reminded him with a smirk.

"Well, I was at the time, but apparently the fire that blazed last night has now settled into a smoldering burn." He gave Gunny an angry glare. "My ass hurts."

"Poor baby," Gunny said with genuine sympathy. He probably should've felt a little bit of guilt for pushing Mac so hard—and riding him hard—but he just couldn't find it in him to regret it. Holy shit, the man was sexy as fuck when he gave up that tight ass, but he could still feel bad for his lover's pain. He reached around Mac and turned down the hot water tap. "That isn't going to help. You'll have it raging again, and not in a good way."

"I like it hot," Mac complained, but didn't try to readjust the temperature.

"That's what got you into this predicament in the first place," Gunny reminded him and grabbed the bar of soap from its holder. "Turn around. I'll wash your back."

Mac eyed him suspiciously, but Gunny just rolled his eyes. "Stop being such a big baby and turn around." He pushed Mac, encouraging him to turn. "I'm not going to mess with you, just wash your back."

Gunny spent a little extra time scrubbing and massaging the grumpy Marine's body; he avoided his ass, and by the time they had finished showering and dried off, Mac was in a little better mood. After making pancakes, bacon, and over-easy eggs for breakfast, Gunny headed to work, leaving behind a smiling Mac, albeit with a hitch in his walk. Gunny, however, walked into the recruiting office whistling with a cocky swagger.

AFTER a light lunch of tuna-salad sandwiches, Mac took his glass of red wine and headed to the bathroom. He filled the tub with hot water, adding a capful of bubble bath. Mac eased down into the sudsy heat and stretched out, laid his head back against the tub, and sighed contently. He'd spent the morning straightening up around the house and washing the sheets on the bed, and he'd thrown some potatoes, carrots, and chunks of chuck roast into the slow cooker. The house now filled with the delicious scents of stewing vegetables and spices. He hadn't lied when he'd told Gunny he had this Suzy Homemaker shit down. House clean, dinner cooking, and nothing to do but wait for his man to get home.

Damn, this is the life. Mac picked up his wine and took a sip. He really did have a great life; the only thing that would have made it better at this moment would be if Gunny were in the tub with him. *Better yet, Gunny dressed in nothing but a smile, feeding me grapes and fanning me with a big tropical leaf.* The image of Gunny as his cabana boy made Mac chuckle.

"Dude, you're losing it," he snorted. Mac downed the rest of his wine, sank deeper into the tub, and closed his eyes. It didn't take long for the combination of the soothing scent of sandalwood bubble bath, the heat, and the wine to take its effect; Mac drifted off.

An hour later, Mac woke with a start, shivering in the now-cool water. He grabbed a towel, wrapped it around his shoulders, and scrambled out of the tub. "That was a bad idea," he muttered. One minute he'd been dreaming of tropical islands, warm breezes, and grapes, the next some giant gnarly hand had plucked him off the beach and dropped him on an iceberg.

After quickly drying off, Mac dressed in a pair of comfortable jeans and T-shirt. Gunny wouldn't be home for at least another hour; now, what the hell was he supposed to do? Work in the garden? Nah! Not enough time and besides, he was clean. The house was clean, dinner done, not enough time to go anywhere or watch a movie.

He plopped down on the couch with a grunt. Two days and already he was bored. Full-time homemaker was so not his thing. Snatching up the controller for the Xbox 360, Mac fired up the console. Time for a little *Call of Duty*. He logged into his account and went in search of inferiors to destroy.

"Alrighty, boys, time to destroy the enemy," Mac said enthusiastically into the microphone.

Loading his silenced weapon, Mac led the way into town, quietly taking out any enemy he encountered. Stopping outside the first building, Mac ran a critical eye around the area. "Clean it out, boys," he ordered. "Leave no survivors."

"Why the hell do I have to go in?" came a staticky voice through his headset. "You're the fucking sharpshooter."

The rest of the team headed into the building without question, leaving one man behind. Mac rolled his eyes at the name choice and the emblem displayed next to it of the little coward. "Well, that explains your screen name, ChrisPMcChicken, and your puny rank as Private. Now get your ass in there before I shoot you myself," Mac growled.

"Asshole."

Mac kept watch outside as his team met their objective. Somehow they only lost one member; surprisingly, it wasn't McChicken. Mac led the way to the second house, taking out the enemies on the way. The rest of the team stormed in and took out the enemy inside. McChicken screamed and cussed the entire time, irritating the hell out of Mac and causing his ears to ring. After meeting their objective, Mac slowly entered the structure, gun at the ready.

"Fuck!" McChicken screeched the fourth time he was killed and had to rejoin the game. "You assholes want to help me out here." He went down again, having taken a headshot. "Jesus Christ, you guys suck."

"How so?" Mac laughed. "I think I'll rename you Private Whiny Pants. You cry more than a little girl."

"Fuck you. If I had a goddamn team to help—"

"Shut up, PWP," another member barked. "Either start shooting the fucking enemy or leave the game."

"Don't shoot, just throw your gun down and go suck on your mama's tit, you big baby," another member chimed in.

Once the house was clear, Mac headed back outside while the others continued to bitch and moan and try to outdo the others with insults. "All of you shut the hell up and focus, we're down in points," Mac said, maneuvering his character out the door. "Shit!" he cursed when he took a hit from a sniper and went down.

"Ha-ha! What's the matter, Brigadier General McAsshole? Not so perfect now, are you?" McChicken spat. His whiny voice dripped with sarcasm.

Mac reentered the game, and just as he caught up with his team, he took a headshot and went down again. "Who the hell keeps shooting me?"

"I wish I could," McChicken said.

High-pitched laughter filled Mac's ears. He reentered the game a third time and again took a head shot. Mac kicked the coffee table, sending it halfway across the room to land on its side. "You little pecker head. Do you have any idea what I do for a living?"

"Hopefully it's not dependent on your gaming skills."

"Incoming enemy helicopters," warned a mechanical voice.

"Take cover," shouted one of Mac's teammates.

Mac ran for the first door. "Goddammit," he growled when he went down again.

"There goes the General again," McChicken howled with laughter. "You sure you should be leading this company?"

"I've had just about enough of you, PWP," Mac snapped and reentered the game. "Keep your shit up, and I will personally hunt you down and kick your ass."

"Would you two shut the hell up? Two minutes left and we're losing," one of the other teammates shouted. "Play the game, ass wipes."

Mac tried ignoring McChicken, who continued to chuckle, and focused on the game. As a team, they played for the next minute or so, closed the gap, and made a push to take over the game. In their excitement they made a mad dash during the last thirty seconds, shooting at everything that moved and even shit that didn't. The enemy, alerted to their position by the random gunfire, doubled back and got behind Mac and his team, and Mac took another head shot and went down.

"Son of a bitch," Mac howled.

"HA-HA," McChicken crowed. "I'm going to start calling you General Brain Splatter. You suck!"

Pissed off, Mac jumped to his feet and threw the controller at the TV. It hit the corner of the stand with a crack, plastic flying, which only enraged him further. "Do you fucking realize who I am?" Mac shouted at the screen. "I am a goddamn Special Forces Marine!"

"Couldn't make it as a Ranger, huh?" McChicken sneered.

"That's it, I'm going to hunt you down and beat some respect into you!" Mac pulled off his headphones and threw them as well.

"Are you kidding me?"

Mac spun around, nostrils flaring as he panted angrily. "I—" He glanced back at the TV, the game having ended—they lost. Groaning, he turned back to Gunny who stood at the door shaking his head. Mac shoved his hands in the pockets of his jeans. "I—"

"Are you tormenting the children again?" Gunny asked wryly.

"He…. It wasn't a kid, it was a devil spawn." Mac pointed toward the TV. "And he started it."

"Seriously?" Gunny cocked his head, his lips twitched in a half grin. "Why don't you stomp your feet? I think your argument would be more effective."

Mac flopped down on the couch and ran a hand over his head, scratching his buzz cut. "Nuh-uh. I don't want to play with him/it anymore." He crossed his arms over his chest and scowled.

"Good thing," Gunny snickered and joined Mac on the couch, giving him a peck on the cheek. "Your toys are all broken."

Mac looked at the scattered pieces of plastic and mangled headset and sighed again. "How was your day?"

Gunny draped an arm over Mac's shoulders and pulled him close. "Much better than yours, I'm guessing."

Moving in closer, Mac buried his face in Gunny's neck. "I got bored," he mumbled.

"You're going to have to find a hobby to keep you from tormenting the youth of the game waves."

"No, you just need to hurry up and quit working and keep me out of trouble." Mac jerked upright. "That reminds me, I talked to my mom and dad today."

Gunny stiffened. "You told them about us?"

Mac gave him an exasperated look. "I'm not that insensitive, Gunny. That's the kind of thing you have to tell someone to their face, not on the phone or in a letter." Although he briefly entertained the letter idea.

Relaxing back against the couch, Gunny laid his hand on Mac's thigh, stroking it. "Sorry," he said meekly. "So what did your parents have to say?"

"You're off this weekend, right?"

"Uh, yeah why?" Gunny asked suspiciously.

"Cool, we're going to see them this weekend. Dad had a load of wood delivered and needs some help cutting and stacking it. And before you ask, Mom told me to tell you she would be making chicken and dumplings."

"Okay, great. Uh—" Gunny shifted nervously. "Are you going to tell them what you want to do at the exit ceremony?" Gunny hedged.

"Yes, *we* are going to tell them."

Some of the color drained from Gunny's face, and his fidgeting increased. "I don't—"

"That," Mac said, pointing toward his nervous lover, "is why we're telling them now. I know you well enough that you'll just worry and stress over it, and the sooner we tell them the sooner you can calm the hell down." He leaned over and pressed a tender kiss to Gunny's lips. "It will be fine. You'll see." Mac kissed him again and then went to his feet. "You go get your shower while I pick up the mess from my temper tantrum, and then we'll have supper."

Gunny stared up at him, still looking a little wary.

Mac grabbed Gunny's hand and pulled him to his feet. "Go." He turned the man around and gave him a little shove toward the bathroom. "I promise it won't be as bad as you're building it up to be in your head."

"Fine." Gunny took a couple steps and looked back over his shoulder. "You sure?"

"Trust me?"

Gunny nodded and went to take his shower. Mac wasn't 100 percent sure his family wasn't going to freak. In fact, he was pretty sure his brother would. However, it still wouldn't be as bad as Gunny would make it if he was left to worry about it too long. The sooner they told their families, the sooner they could concentrate on the plans for their future.

Mac bent and picked up the broken headset and shook his head. But first, he needed to buy some new toys.

CHAPTER
Eight

ZZ TOP rocked out from the speakers, warm summer winds rushed in through the lowered windows, and Mac merged onto the highway to start the three-hour drive to his parents' house. Elbow resting on the open window, he lowered the wraparound shades to protect his eyes from the bright July sun as he sang along to "Sharp Dressed Man." He looked completely at ease, and Gunny envied him that.

Breakfast had been a chore. Mac had made ham-and-onion quiches, one of Gunny's favorite breakfast foods, but the way his gut had flopped around like a fish out of water, he'd had a hard time enjoying it, and an even harder time keeping it down. Regardless of what Mac had said, or his conviction and promises, Gunny knew it was going to totally suck telling Mac's parents they were gay. You just couldn't hide that kind of shit from friends and families for as many years as he and Mac had and not have some fallout. *Major fucking fallout.* Gunny ran a hand across the tense muscles of his neck, rolling his head trying to ease them. Damn right, he was nervous about seeing Theodore and Clare Jones. Gunny loved spending time at their country home. It had a peaceful, laidback feel to it, like its owners. This time was going to be anything but calm. He was worried enough that between the restlessness and the weird dreams, he'd barely slept at all. Which reminded him….

"I had this crazy dream last night," he told Mac, turning down the radio. He wasn't going to tell Mac about the one involving screaming, cussing, and shotguns. No, he was going to try and focus on the one that would keep his mind off the particularly scary one, which included blood and guts.

"Yeah? Was I crazy sexy?" Mac drawled.

"Always," Gunny deadpanned, patting Mac's thigh.

Mac looked over at Gunny and frowned. "Are you mocking me?"

"Yes," he said with a curt nod. Gunny didn't see Mac's hand shoot out till it was too late to protect against the blow. "Ow!" Gunny rubbed the spot where Mac had whacked him in the chest.

Mac glanced at him. "Serves you right," he grumbled. "You're getting slow in your old age," he added with a snort.

Ignoring the taunt, he asked, "Do you want to hear about the dream or not?" Gunny knew what the dream meant; he'd thought about what the dream represented a lot in the past few months, and was curious to hear Mac's opinions.

"Enlighten me," Mac said flippantly.

He shifted in his seat until his back was in the corner, one leg cocked up, knee bent and resting on the seat, so he could watch Mac's expressions as Gunny relived the dream.

"I was dressed in nothing but this—I don't know, leather harness thingy—"

"Ooh, I like this dream already," Mac interrupted with a wide smile on his face.

"Yeah, well, you sure as hell didn't in the dream."

"I didn't?" Mac asked. He stole a brief look at Gunny, shock evident on his face, even with his wraparounds shielding his eyes. "Sounds like something I'd very much like to see you in."

"Oh, you liked me in it just fine. You were the one who picked it out and dressed me in it, even added a little leash to the O-ring in the center of my chest." Mac smiled as he maneuvered in and out of traffic, eyes on the road, but from the expression on his face, he imagined it and liked what he saw. Gunny watched him carefully as he continued. "You weren't happy about your choice once we got to the club."

Mac stared at Gunny for as long as he could before he had to turn his attention back to the road. "I took you out in public dressed like that?"

"Yup, and holy shit were you one crazy son of a bitch." Gunny shook his head and laughed softly as he remembered the very vivid dream. "Before we made it halfway into the club you tried turning yourself into a full-body shield, wrapped yourself around me, and threatened every man that passed you'd gouge their eyes out for laying them on what belonged to you."

"Sounds more like reality than a dream," Mac said confidently. He reached over and took Gunny's hand in his, entwining their fingers. "I would so totally play the jealous lover. Actually"—Mac shook his head—"I would never take you out in public and show off your impressive… assets."

That didn't surprise Gunny in the slightest. Mac had never been comfortable with public displays of affection, even the few times over the years when they'd been free to do so. Mac also didn't share Gunny's kink for exhibitionism. Not that Gunny had ever had the opportunity to play with the lusted fantasy. Mac damn sure had fulfilled many, many of Gunny's other fantasies over the years, many of which were experienced in their gym/playroom, so he relegated the exhibitionism to one he used along with his hand, imagination, and lotion when Mac was out of town.

"What about dressed?" Gunny asked cautiously.

"You mean going to a club?" Mac asked.

"Yeah, I've been thinking; once we sign our official discharge papers, maybe we could go check one out."

"Why?" Mac asked, his voice filled with genuine confusion.

"Never mind," Gunny said, suddenly feeling a little uncomfortable with the whole conversation; he turned and stared out the side window. Gunny hadn't ever understood, nor had he tried to figure out why he had a need to submit to Mac. There was just something about the freedom he experienced, the peace he felt when he turned over control to his lover. It wasn't so much about the pain—that was just a vehicle that allowed him to move out of his body—and he certainly wasn't into humiliation, but the whole idea of submitting to

Mac, belonging to him, and having others know to whom he belonged was something he craved.

Mac tugged at Gunny's hand. "Hey, what's going on in that head of yours?"

Gunny looked back toward Mac, the confusion and concern evident on the man's handsome face. Mac always seemed to know what Gunny needed, what he wanted, so it felt strange asking for something. He rarely had to, and it was one of the aspects of their relationship that he loved most. Why he continued to hesitate when Mac looked at him expectantly, he wasn't sure. Mac had never made him feel less of a man for his kinks. Maybe it was because he'd never really had to ask for them; Mac had simply discovered them.

"C'mon, Gunny. No secrets, remember?"

"I think it would be great checking out one of the leather clubs, hanging out with, and talking to, people who share my kink."

"What am I?" Mac asked with a hint of ire. "I'm the guy doing the tying up and wielding the flogger. Pretty sure I share your kink, Gunny."

"Not exactly," Gunny mumbled.

"What's that supposed to mean?"

"There's one big difference." Gathering up his courage, as his cheeks heated, Gunny admitted, "I like the idea of people seeing us together, knowing I belong to you." He shrugged one shoulder and looked down at their entwined hands before adding, "Kneeling at your feet."

He expected Mac to laugh, but he should have known better. A twinge of guilt poked at Gunny's gut when his lover only asked, "Really?" without a hint of disgust or amusement.

Gunny nodded. "I mean, it's just a fantasy, no big deal really. It would just be nice to talk to someone and figure out why I feel the way I do."

"Does it matter?" Mac asked easily. "I mean, the why of it."

"It does to me. It's weird. I'm a grown man, Mac." Gunny rubbed the ache that had settled at the back of his neck. "Not only a grown man, but a decorated Marine, for fuck sakes. Why does the idea of kneeling at another man's feet like a little bitch turn me on? I mean, it's one thing for you to take control, call me boy, stuff like that when we're in private, but what I don't understand is why I would want other people to see how weak I am?"

"You're not weak," Mac said adamantly. "You're the strongest man I know. It takes a hell of a lot of courage to allow someone to bind you and take control of your body, and a shitload of trust."

"I don't know," Gunny said softly. "Sometimes it feels like I should be able to handle things, but my head gets all wonked, and I need you to help me."

"Nothing wrong in needing someone. I need you all the time." Mac squeezed Gunny's hand and looked at him, a gentle smile on his face, for as long as he could before he had to turn back toward the road. "I think it's a great idea to go check out the clubs, maybe try and find an exclusive, private club which caters to D/s relationships, rather than a leather bar. Give you a chance to see and talk to the submissives."

"You'd go?"

"Of course I would. Don't you know I'd do anything for you?" Mac glanced at him, a small smirk on his face. "Well, almost anything. When we go, you'll be covered from neck to toe. Nobody gets to see that smoking-hot body but me. It's mine. All mine."

"Yes it is, and that works both ways." Gunny leaned over and kissed Mac's check. "I love you."

"I will never get tired of hearing that," Mac said, his voice cracking. "I love you too."

Warmth filled him when he heard the emotion in Mac's voice. "Neither will I." And he wouldn't. He was one lucky son of a bitch to have someone like Mac love him, and he couldn't imagine taking Mac, or his love, for granted.

They spent the rest of the trip talking about clubs, clothes, or lack of them. Most of the time he and Mac laughed, and joked, enjoying each other's company, other times it fell to a companionable silence with the only sound coming from the radio. The trip flew by. Gunny's mind was free of worry over potential problems at their destination.

The panic came back in a rush. Gunny's heartbeat sped up the minute they pulled onto the dirt road that led to Mac's boyhood home.

Resting his head against the window and working to keep his breathing even, Gunny stared out at the landscape. He'd always loved coming to the Shenandoah Valley, the Blue Ridge Mountains to the east and to the west the eastern front of the Ridge-and-Valley Appalachian Mountains. Autumn was his favorite time to visit, the variations of red, gold, brown, and yellow stretched across the thick forest a stunning sight, but the lush green of summer with a cloudless blue sky above was beautiful in its own right. Only Gunny couldn't enjoy the view. He fidgeted in his seat, the sweat on his brow having nothing to do with the bright July sun, and bounced his knee as they pulled into the winding drive. Not even the canopy of trees, with the brilliant rays of light streaming down in small glittery waves, was enough to calm his speeding pulse and rapid breath.

Gunny closed his eyes and took a couple of deep calming breaths, but they did little good; he still felt edgy. When the Envoy came to a halt, Gunny opened his eyes and his gut rolled.

In front of him was a well-kept, colonial-style home constructed of concrete blocks painted a light tan. Two large windows were open, white curtains billowing in the slight breeze, on either side of the bright red entry door. The five white-paned windows on the second floor also appeared to be open. Clare always aired out the upstairs rooms before company arrived, no matter the time of year. A pair of chimneys rose above the pitched tin roof. Gunny had learned on previous visits from Clare that the home had been built prior to the Civil War and had been in her family since being erected. The love and care Theodore and Clare put in their home was evident. Not only was the house beautiful, but also the lawns and gardens.

He'd been here many times in the past, and each time Mac's parents welcomed him, opened their home to him, and made him feel like one of the family. Gunny hoped he'd still be welcome once they found out that not only was their son gay, but planned to marry a man they had thought to be nothing more than their son's best friend.

"You ready?"

Mac's voice jerked Gunny out of his musings. He really wasn't ready for this conversation, would rather put it off or better yet avoid it all together, but he nodded, opened the door, and slid out of the SUV.

Mac followed him and got out as well, and fell in step beside Gunny as they made it up the walkway.

"You keep worrying all the time and you're going to give yourself an ulcer," Mac said with amusement in his voice. It was a tease Mac used often.

Gunny bumped his shoulder against Mac and gave his usual reply. "I think I already have one."

Mac stopped with his hand on the doorknob. "Just think, after tonight I'll no longer have to sneak in your room while we're here, and I'm sure Mom will appreciate not having to make up two rooms each time we visit. She's getting old, ya know," he added with a wink.

Gunny did his best to give Mac a reassuring smile, glad when Mac turned the knob and stepped in the house, since Gunny knew his smile didn't reach his eyes and he felt anything but reassured.

CHAPTER
Nine

STEPPING into the foyer, Mac kept a close eye on his lover. He'd hoped they could spend a quiet day with his parents and wait until tomorrow before telling them of his and Gunny's plans for the future. If Gunny didn't calm the fuck down, Mom would go into crazy mother-hen mode the moment she laid eyes on Gunny. The man was pale, looked like he was about to either run or puke, or both.

"Macalister, is that you?" His mom called from the direction of the kitchen.

"Yeah, it's me and Gunny. Just taking off our boots."

"Lunch is just about ready. You boys go wash up."

"Yes, ma'am," both he and Gunny replied simultaneously.

Mac bent and untied his boots; Gunny, in the same position, was close enough Mac could whisper without being overheard. "Do you remember that time we were here and you had bronchitis?"

"Yeah," Gunny chuckled, shaking his head. "She threatened me with a willow switch if I got out of bed the entire weekend." Gunny shuddered exaggeratedly. "She's tougher and scarier than any Marine I've ever met."

"You look worse right now than you did that time," Mac hissed. He pulled his boots off and set them aside before rising.

Gunny's eyes widened and he stopped in midmotion, hand clutching his boot. "But I'm not sick," he replied quietly, his voice tight with panic.

"You look worse than you did then. I suggest you calm down and start thinking some happy thoughts, or I may just let her torture you." Mac reached down and pulled Gunny's boot off and tossed it aside to land next to its mate, and then encouraged Gunny to straighten. Leaning in close to his ear, Mac whispered, "Or I'll tell her you have some big news you want to share with her and Dad."

Gunny tensed. "You wouldn't," he hissed.

Mac arched a brow at him.

Gunny looked at him speculatively, as if he was trying to figure out if Mac was serious. He obviously came to the right conclusion when he grumbled, "Fuck! You would. That's cold, man," he added and walked stiffly toward the small half bathroom, Mac right on his heels.

"Of course I would," Mac said easily.

Actually, he wouldn't make Gunny tell his parents about the true nature of their relationship; he wanted to be the one to tell them, but watching his mom fuss over Gunny and his big beefy Marine turn into a chastised child would definitely reward Mac with a few laughs.

Mac returned the glare Gunny shot at him in the mirror as he washed his hands with a smug smile and waited his turn. One did not sit at Clare Jones's table without washing his hands. She was fanatical on that point. Growing up, he always knew when dinner was on the table when she hollered "Wash your hands" instead of "Time for dinner" like most moms would do. Mac had always been a stubborn child, so it took many spatula and wooden spoon whacks to his knuckles, but he eventually got it. Now he wouldn't dream of entering the kitchen without washing his hands first. He was a little slow on the uptake sometimes, but he could be taught.

Gunny splashed cool water on his face and patted it dry with a fluffy hand towel before drying his hands. "Better?" he asked, hopeful.

Mac studied him for a second, stole a quick glance to see if his mom or dad had come down the hall, and grabbed Gunny's face in both hands and pressed a soft kiss to his lips. "Much. Now think about the conversation we had on the way here, and that will keep some color in your cheeks."

"Like I said, that's cold, man," Gunny complained.

"No, that's hot as hell." He kissed him again, and then washed his hands.

"Sitting at the table with your parents while I have a raging hard-on is not my idea of a good time, Mac. Your mom is going to know something is up when I can't sit still and I have an agonized look on my face."

"Macalister! Gunther! What's taking you boys so long?"

"Shit!" Mac griped under his breath. *Showtime.* He shut off the taps, grabbed the towel, and dried his hands, smiling at Gunny who was taking deep calming breaths. "Just think about something boring, like golf, or the History Channel." He tossed the towel on the cabinet and pushed his way out the door. "C'mon, before Mom comes and grabs us by the ears," Mac said wryly.

"History Channel is not boring," Gunny grumbled under his breath, as he followed Mac toward the kitchen.

Like Gunny, Mac was a huge fan of history. It was just another thing they had in common, and they enjoyed watching the programs together, or reading books to each other. Mac especially liked ancient weaponry and warfare, but Gunny had a horrible habit of watching the same damn shows over and over and over again. He suspected Gunny could recite word for word the programs and books on Pompeii and Herculaneum from memory. Gunny might have looked all big and macho badass on the outside, but on the inside he was a very sweet, sometimes shy, total geek.

"Hey, beautiful," Mac greeted as he stepped into the kitchen. "All clean," he told his mom, holding up his hands as proof.

"About time you came in to see me," his mom chastised lightly, her smile wide.

"Your fault," Mac said pointedly. "I'd have come in straight away, but you made me wash before I was even allowed a hug." He wrapped her in his arms and hugged her close, kissing her cheek.

"You're too old and too big to be pouting," she told him, her blue eyes sparkling as she reached up and cupped Mac's face in her tiny hands and pulled him down till she could kiss his forehead. "It didn't work on me when you were five, and it doesn't work on me now."

Mac laughed as his mom released him and shoved him out of the way. "C'mere, Gunther. Give me a hug."

"Hi, Clare," Gunny said, bending down and wrapping her into a hug.

Mom was a tiny thing, barely reaching five foot and maybe a hundred and twenty pounds soaking wet, appearing even smaller against Gunny's broad form. Momma might have been slight in stature, but she was tough as nails. She had to be to keep up with him, Dad, and Ted all these years. Her dark auburn hair was now streaked heavily with gray, and many of the silver strands were no doubt a direct result of the shenanigans of her boys when they had been younger and worry now that they were grown.

"Mmm, smells like chicken and dumplings," Mac said, lifting the lid from the large pot on the stove. His stomach growled loudly as the delicious scent filled his nose. "Looks like just enough for me."

"You might want to grab the phone and start dialing nine-one-one, Clare," Gunny growled from behind Mac. "'Cause I'm about to put a beat down on your boy."

"Ow!" Mac protested and dropped the lid with a loud clank when a wooden spoon came down on his knuckles. "Where the hell were you hiding that thing?" he grumbled, rubbing the back of his hand. He glared at a chuckling Gunny, who was taking a seat at the table.

"Serves you right, teasing Gunther like that," she scolded, ignoring Mac's question. "Now go sit down and behave."

"Yes, ma'am," he said and pulled out the chair across from Gunny and kicked the laughing bastard in the shin. Gunny laughed harder. Mac had the sudden urge to stick his tongue out at him, but he resisted it. At least the color was back in the man's cheeks and he didn't look so freaked out.

"Where's Dad?" Mac asked distractedly as he grabbed a big hunk of fresh baked bread and buttered it up.

Mom set a large bowl of dumplings down in front of Gunny, who dug in immediately, grunting his thank-you. "Do you remember Tom Cohen?" his mom asked, moving back to the stove.

Mac chewed on his bread, trying to place the name, and then it hit him. "Dad's old fishing buddy?"

"That's him," his mom said sadly. "He passed away last night, and Louise, bless her heart, doesn't have any children, or much family for that matter, to turn to. Your dad went to help her make the funeral arrangements."

"Thank you," he told her as she set down a heaping bowl of dumplings in front of him.

She paused, her eyes full of sorrow. "You're welcome," she said softly and stroked her hand along Mac's cheek before turning away. "He'll be home by suppertime."

Mac looked at Gunny, who seemed to have lost some of his gusto for his favorite meal. "How's Dad taking the news?" he asked, but his attention was on Gunny. He ran his foot along Gunny's calf, giving him a small smile when he looked up.

"He's heartbroken of course, but you know your dad, he'll put on a brave front." She waved a hand at them, as she returned to the table with a pitcher of sweet tea. "But enough of that, I want to hear how you boys are doing," she said, pouring them each a glass.

"I'm all done working for Uncle Sam," Mac said, thankful for the subject change. "Now I get to sit back with my feet propped up and wait for official unemployed status."

"What about you, Gunther? Are you finished working as well?" Clare asked as she set down the pitcher and returned to the stove.

"No, ma'am. I don't have the pull your son has. I have to work right up until discharge date."

Gunny also appeared to be relieved with the subject change; the tense look of his shoulders visibly eased, and he dug back into his meal with gusto. Mac hadn't needed to worry about Gunny worrying. With a big bowl of his favorite meal in front of him, Gunny looked as happy as a pig in shit.

His mom brought her own filled bowl to the table and sat next to Mac and spread her napkin over her lap before picking up her spoon. "Have you thought about what you're going to do with all your free time?" his mom asked conversationally. "If I know you, and I do," she said, giving him a knowing look, "you'll be climbing the wall and bored out of your mind within a month."

He caught the wary look on Gunny's face. Mac winked at him and finished chewing his mouthful of dumplings before he answered his mom. "I have a few ideas, but I'm going to take some much-needed downtime, maybe do some traveling. That's about it at this point."

"I just don't see you being very happy without a plan, a goal," she said, stirring her stew. "You've never been one who could relax, or even sit for too long. You'll be stone-cold crazy within a month." His mom tilted her head and gave him a knowing look. "Either that or Gunther will strangle you in your sleep."

Mac shot a hard look in Gunny's direction when he made a disgusted noise. Gunny didn't look up from his meal so Mac could shoot some daggers at him through his eyes, the bastard too busy eating and nodding.

"I'm not that bad," Mac complained.

"You were banned from church services, Macalister. I'm pretty sure you were the first and only person to ever be banned from morning prayer by the age of ten," his mom said in exasperation.

Gunny's head snapped up, and his spoon clanked as it hit the bottom of the bowl. "Seriously?"

"No," Mac said.

"Yes," his mom said at the same time. Mac started to protest, but she spoke over him, giving him one of those looks only a mom could give that meant *don't make me beat you*, or maybe, *it will only be more painful if you resist*, and Mac grudgingly snapped his mouth shut.

"The church always had a policy that the families start services with a morning prayer," Mom said to Gunny, ignoring Mac's grunts of protest as he ate. "The children were then excused to the classrooms for Sunday school, or bible study, depending on the age. Macalister did fine as long as he didn't have to sit or keep quiet."

"So how did that prayer time work out for you?" Gunny asked. His lips curled into a smug smile.

"I was given special duties," Mac said defensively. He sighed heavily and dipped his bread into his bowl, sopping up the last of the juice. "Go ahead, Mom. Tell him how special your little boy is."

"I'm fairly certain Gunther already knows," she said with practiced patience.

Mac pushed his empty bowl away and grabbed his glass. "Great, then there is no need to go into details about my specialness." He took a sip of his tea before adding, "What's for dessert?"

"Oh no, please continue, Clare," Gunny encouraged. "You know how much I love hearing about Mac's childhood shenanigans."

Mac was so going to beat Gunny later, and not in the good way. He tried conveying that message to the bastard with a look, but Gunny was having none of it. Instead, he pushed his own empty bowl away and leaned back in his chair.

"As I was starting to say," his mom said gleefully to Gunny, "Macalister had a difficult time sitting still. Theodore threatened to beat the boy within an inch of his life, but his son ignored him. His dad then tried scaring him with the threats of fire and brimstone. Macalister lasted maybe—" The shrill sound of a phone ringing interrupted Mac's embarrassment. "If you boys will excuse me," his mom said, wiping her napkin across her mouth and setting it on the table next to her dish, and went to answer the call.

"Banned from prayer?" Gunny snorted the moment Mac's mom left the room.

Another bowl of chicken and dumplings suddenly sounded really good. Mac grabbed his bowl and went to the stove. "I wasn't actually banned, just given a chore that had to be done each Sunday morning at a specific time," Mac deadpanned.

"Mm hmm," Gunny hummed, amusement evident in his tone. "Why haven't I heard this story before?" he asked, moving to stand next to Mac, bowl in hand.

"It was classified, strictly need-to-know information." He poured a heaping ladle full into Gunny's bowl. "And you don't need to know." Mac handed the ladle to Gunny.

"I'll just get it out of Clare," Gunny told him, as Mac turned away.

Not if I keep you and her sufficiently distracted, Mac thought. Gunny would be the easy part; his mom? He groaned as he plopped down in his chair, knowing Gunny would have the full story of his shame before the weekend was up.

CHAPTER
Ten

A CHILL trickled down Gunny's spine, and he pulled the heavy quilt over him and hugged his pillow tighter against his chest. Through the slightly opened window came the sounds of a dog barking; in the distance a rooster crowed. The open window also allowed for the cool morning breeze, and Gunny snuggled deeper into the soft feather bed. He lay there teetering between drifting back to sleep and wakefulness. The muffled activity in the rooms below and the scent of bacon finally helped him make his choice.

Throwing off the covers, Gunny sat on the edge of the bed, grabbed his T-shirt from the floor, and pulled it on. Yawning as he went to his feet, he stretched his arms behind his back, which protested with a series of snaps and pops. The long car ride and inactivity, at least the weightlifting and stretching kind, had him feeling stiff. He was actually looking forward to a day of splitting logs, stacking wood, and concentrating on the strength of his body rather than the crazy shit his mind was focusing on.

But first, bacon.

Gunny slipped into his jeans, not bothering to button up, and rummaged through his duffle until he found clean clothes and his travel kit. On the way to the bathroom he passed the room Mac had stayed in. Gunny had quietly snuck from the room a couple of hours ago and was sure he'd pulled the door closed, leaving Mac snoring softly. To make sure Mac wasn't still asleep, he pushed the door open and found the room, and the bed, empty.

Not wasting any time, Gunny shaved and showered quickly. After dressing in a pair of tan cargo shorts and a plain white T-shirt, he dropped off his dirty clothes and shower kit in his duffle and headed down to join the others for breakfast. "Good morning," he greeted him as he stepped into the kitchen.

"Good morning, Gunther. Did you sleep well?" Clare asked from where she was flipping pancakes at the stove.

"Yes, ma'am," he said, taking the seat opposite Mac. Mac smiled at him around the slice of bacon he was crunching on. They had already said their good mornings to each other. Mac got his required cuddle and blowjob, so he looked happy and sated this morning. Gunny nodded in acknowledgement.

"Morning, son," Theodore said, sipping from his coffee mug. "Make sure you eat plenty. We have a long day of work ahead of us."

"Yes, sir," Gunny responded. He grabbed the bowl of scrambled eggs, heaping a hearty amount on his plate, and then added a short stack of pancakes and several strips of bacon and covered everything with maple syrup.

Mac was the spitting image of his father, nearly identical in body style and size, same facial structure; even their hazel-green eye color was similar. Gunny only had to look at Theodore to know exactly how his lover would look in twenty years. He could easily admit, his attraction sure the hell wouldn't wane in the slightest; Mac would be just as handsome at sixty-two as he was in his forties.

"So, have you given any more thought to moving closer to home?" Theodore Jones asked his son.

Gunny's forkful of eggs halted halfway to his mouth, and his brows rose in surprise. This was the first Gunny had heard about Mac's family asking him about moving back to his childhood hometown. Mac hadn't lived in Fredericksburg in twenty-two years.

Mac sighed and set his fork down, shifting slightly in his chair to face his dad. "I've told you, I like Riverview. I like the town, the people, and Gunny's there."

"We just thought with you retiring, you'd consider moving closer to home. We'd like to see you more than once or twice a year." Theodore looked up from his plate and added, "You have friends and family here too."

"Dad," Mac said gently, patting his dad's arm. "I won't be traveling or deployed like I have in the past. I'll have plenty of time to spend with you and Mom."

"Theodore, Riverview is only three hours away," Clare said as she set down another platter heaped high with pancakes on the table. "Besides, any closer and you'd drive each other crazy."

Gunny pushed his food around on his plate, watching the interaction between father and son. Mac's dad, while not what Gunny would consider old, was getting up there in years. Gunny could understand the man's desire to have more time with his son; however, Gunny was selfish enough that he wanted Mac home with him.

"You're probably right." Theodore smirked and shook his head. "Pass the eggs, please."

Gunny handed him the bowl.

"Thank you," Theodore said, taking the bowl and adding a pile of them to his plate. "What about you, Gunny?"

"Sir?" he asked, baffled.

"How have you put up with my son all these years and not gone insane?"

"Who says he's not," Mac added, giving his dad a dubious look.

Theodore cocked his head and studied Gunny. Gunny found it unsettling that father and son had the same facial expressions, which seemed to pry into Gunny's mind. He lowered his eyes to his plate, suddenly very interested in his breakfast. It was one thing to have Mac know his thoughts, a completely different story for Theodore to know them.

"Good point." Theodore smiled at his son, and then turned his attentions back to Gunny. "You going to settle down, maybe start a family?"

"Right now I'm just trying to survive this last round of recruits," he sidestepped. "Christ, was I ever that young and eager?"

"I'd say you were," Mac said around a mouthful of food. "I haven't a clue how you didn't get yourself killed in boot camp. I kept waiting for you to get yourself blowed up the way you always ran at everything headfirst with brute instead of brain." Mac pointed his fork at Gunny, but looked to his dad when he said, "He's the only fucking—"

"Macalister!"

"Oh, shit—" Mac held out a hand toward his mom as if to shield a blow. "I mean shoot."

"You're not too old to have your mouth washed out with soap," Clare chastised. "You could take a lesson in manners from Gunther. You never hear him talk with such a potty mouth."

The expression of confusion on Mac's face had Gunny swallowing down a snort of laughter, causing him to choke on the mouthful of bacon. Theodore slapped Gunny on the back, dislodging the unchewed food without ever taking his eyes off his son, nor did his fork hesitate as he continued to eat.

"He's the only what, son?" Theodore asked, efficiently saving his son a good swat upside the head.

Mac glanced at his parents and then winked at Gunny before scooping up a large amount of food and shoving it into his mouth. "I have no idea what I was going to say," he mumbled.

"Maybe Gunther could teach you some table manners as well," Clare said with exasperation.

"C'mon eat up, Mr. Eager Saint," Mac said to Gunny, his tone dripping with sarcasm. "We have a big job ahead of us, and we're going to need our strength. Isn't that right, Dad?"

Gunny wasn't sure if he wanted to kiss Mac or thrash the man; either way, he was glad the subject of their future plans had been averted, at least for the moment.

"Sure do. Eat up, boys," Theodore said with a nod.

"Is Ted coming to join in all the fun?" Mac asked as he sopped up the last of the syrup with a forkful of egg, before dropping his fork and pushing his plate away.

It was only brief, but Gunny saw the warning look Clare gave her husband and the slight shake of her head. Mac must have seen it too because he tensed.

"No, it's going to be just you and Gunther," Clare said, picking up her plate and taking it to the sink. "Your dad and I are going to the funeral home."

Mac's eyes sparked with anger, and he pressed his lips tightly together in an obvious attempt to keep back whatever comment he'd been about to say, before his mom had mentioned the passing of their family friend. There was no love lost between Mac and his brother. Ted had made many choices in his life that had disappointed his parents deeply. Instead of manning up and admitting he was a fuckup, Ted would take every opportunity to disrespect Mac.

"Guess we better get busy, then," Mac said tightly. He took his plate to the sink, handed it to his mom, and then kissed her cheek. "Thank you for breakfast. It was delicious."

"Give my condolences to Mrs. Cohen," Mac said to his dad, giving his shoulder a small squeeze as he passed. To Gunny, he said, "Ready?" as he walked stiffly toward the back door.

With a nod Gunny took his dishes to Clare. "Thank you for breakfast."

She gave him a slight smile. "You're welcome," she responded and patted his arm. "Lunch is in the fridge."

Gunny thanked her again, said his good-byes, and followed Mac out the back door. It was always tense when the subject of Ted was mentioned. Mac assumed the worst of his brother. Mac's parents had learned not to discuss Ted with Mac unless a necessity arose, either to protect Ted or to spare Mac from spending the day in a pissed-off state.

Hopefully, Mac would work off a little of his anger on a stack of wood before the subject was broached again. And Mac *would* bring it up again. Gunny knew Mac wouldn't be able to let it rest until he knew why his brother had once again missed out on the opportunity to actually do something for their parents.

The morning sun was bright, not a single cloud in the sky, nor a whisper of a breeze. It was going to be a hot one. Gunny pulled his shades from the side pocket of his cargo shorts and slipped them on as he tromped down the back steps. "Always the pessimist when it comes to your brother," Gunny said as he hurried to catch up with Mac.

"Yup," Mac responded.

"Maybe he had a good reason for not coming."

Mac flung open the side door to the pole barn. "Look up, Gunny," he ordered, his face flushed with anger as he pointed toward the sky. "Do you see any flying fucking pigs? No? Didn't think so," he growled and stomped into the barn.

Gunny looked upward just to be sure and rolled his eyes. It seemed he'd be the calming presence today. A pissed-off Marine and heavy, sharp objects was a recipe for disaster.

"It was hard to tell if the sky was clear of flying sows, sun got in my eyes," he said jokingly.

Mac snatched an axe from the hooks over the workbench. "I can promise you there wasn't one," he said, irritated. "And don't tell me you didn't see the look Mom gave Dad or feel the instant tension that poured into the room like a thick dark cloud." Mac ran his thumb down the edge of the axe and grabbed a sharpening stone. He took it and the axe to a stool. Mac's movements were jerky, tension obvious in his muscles as he sharpened the axe blade.

Gunny grabbed the other axe, the blade sharp beneath the pad of this thumb. "Yeah, it was pretty hard to ignore the temperature drop in the room when the cloud rushed in," Gunny admitted, resigned.

"I just don't fucking get him, Gunny," Mac said angrily without looking up from his work. "I know he was in town. He's been here all week drinking and causing a ruckus down at the local bar. Bastard is probably shacked up with some local whore, or in jail by now." Mac's hand stilled and he looked up, meeting Gunny's gaze. "Dad just lost a good friend. The last thing he needed was for his son to fucking disappoint him again." He shook his head and went back to work on the tool with a huffed breath.

"Okay, so Ted's an asshole," Gunny conceded. He set his axe on the workbench and stilled Mac's movements by placing a hand on Mac's forearm. When he looked up, Gunny gave him a small grin. "This isn't something new, and as much as you wish things were different, it's not going to happen until your brother pulls his head out of his ass."

Mac gritted his teeth, cutting off the savage sound that started to rumble out of him. He shook his head vigorously. "Just pisses me off. He's forty-five years old, you'd think the selfish bastard would grow the fuck up."

Gunny took the axe from Mac and set it, and the sharpening rock, aside. He cupped Mac's chin in his hand and kissed him until he felt the tension in Mac's jaw go slack as he opened up to accept Gunny's tongue. Gunny explored Mac's mouth in a slow, wet, hungry kiss that went on and on. Gunny's hand slid along Mac's stubbled jaw to the back of Mac's neck, pulling him deeper into the kiss.

Mac moaned a sound of surrender and pleasure; his arms went around Gunny, big hands fisting in the cotton of Gunny's T-shirt, clinging. The kiss morphed from warm and exploring, the gentleness fleeing as the smoldering heat between them began to blaze. Gunny hooked his fingers in the waistband of Mac's shorts and jerked him to his feet, smashing their bodies together. Mac hissed when their hardening cocks came in contact, but he pushed closer still, the electricity between them arcing and flashing.

Gunny snatched the anger from Mac, taking it into himself and returning nothing but pure unadulterated pleasure until Mac was completely focused on Gunny and his desire. Gunny pulled Mac's gray T-shirt from his shorts, humming his approval when his hands came in contact with the warm, furred flesh of Mac's stomach, and it was just enough of a tease that he wanted more. Wanted Mac covering him, surrounding him, inside him.

"I want you," he moaned into the kiss. "So fucking bad." Gunny popped the button on Mac's shorts. The back door slammed.

Gunny and Mac jerked back, Mac nearly falling over his stool. The only thing saving him from falling on his ass was Gunny's quick reflexes. They stood there panting, staring at each other for a brief moment in shock, Gunny gripping Mac's arm. The truck started— obviously Mac's parents were leaving for the funeral home. They both burst out laughing.

Gunny tugged Mac close again. "We're going to have the place to ourselves today," Gunny said against the side of Mac's neck, kissing his warm skin. "Watching you work this gorgeous body, sweat making your muscles gleam." Gunny ran his tongue along the thick muscle, causing Mac to shudder. "We probably should take our lunch down to the pond. Take a swim." He nipped at Mac's skin. "Make sure you don't overheat."

Another shudder went through Mac. "I like the way you think," Mac groaned, tilting his head further to the side. "You going to wash my back?"

"And other things," Gunny promised him. The running engine reminded him they weren't yet alone; Gunny pressed one last kiss to the side of Mac's neck and then released him and picked up his axe. "I'm thinking I owe your brother a debt of gratitude for not showing up," he tossed over his shoulder as he headed out of the barn.

"Well, I'll be damned," Mac sniffed, grabbed his own axe, and fell in step behind Gunny. "Son of a bitch finally did me a favor."

Gunny laughed so hard he snorted. It was going to be an amazing day.

CHAPTER
Eleven

GUNNY sat down on a log and used his T-shirt, long ago removed, to wipe the sweat from his brow and neck. The sun was directly overhead, beating down as the hottest part of the day peaked. Setting his shirt aside, he grabbed the jug of water from the ground and took a big gulp, then poured a small amount over the blister on his left palm, gritting his teeth at the sting.

"What's the matter, old man?" Mac asked with a wry grin. "Can't handle the heat?"

Gunny let his gaze run leisurely down Mac's form, taking in the way the sweat-slick skin glistened in the sun. The fluid movement of Mac's powerful body as he pulled the axe up and over his head, his back arching just slightly before bringing the axe down, splitting the wood easily. Gunny had to take another gulp of water before he was able to speak, the dryness of his throat having nothing to do with the July sun and everything to do with the man before him.

Clearing his throat, he set the jug down and stood. "It is pretty hot," Gunny replied, his voice husky. He moved toward Mac, his need riding him hard.

Mac bent at the waist, set down his axe, putting that perfect ass on display as he picked up the pieces of split wood and tossed them toward the pile for Gunny to stack. Gunny's pulse quickened. The urge to dive in the refreshing pond was alluring, the thought of Mac's naked body against his in the cool water a temptation he simply couldn't resist.

Ignoring the pieces of wood, Gunny grabbed Mac's hand before he could pick the axe up and pulled him along. "C'mon, this old man needs a break."

"Damn, Gunny, I remember when you could put in a full day without needing to take a rest," Mac said facetiously.

"Who said anything about needing to rest?" Gunny challenged.

"Watching my sexy ass work got ya all hot and horny, did it?" Mac teased.

That was an understatement. It didn't take much for Gunny to get turned on by Mac. In Gunny's opinion the bastard was sex on a stick. However, when Mac was working out—all those muscles flexing and bulging, the sweat-damp pelt on Mac's chest and belly, the scent, the look of concentration, the grunts of exertion—Gunny's baser, animalistic needs came to the forefront and he was helpless against them. It was part of the reason they'd spent so much time and money on their home gym and why it was a perfect place for their toys.

Neither of them said a word as they made it to the wooded area that surrounded the pond; both were intent on getting to their destination quickly. The dense trees and brush made it impossible to walk alongside one another, but Gunny was unwilling to lose all contact with Mac. Gunny released Mac's wrist, entwined their fingers, and led them along the small footpath. The temperature beneath the lush trees was noticeably cooler than in the wide-open field they'd just come from, but it did nothing to cool the fire burning in Gunny's gut.

"Christ, I don't remember it being this far," Gunny grumbled.

"The walk is always longer… harder," Mac said wryly. Gunny glanced back at Mac, whose eyes were dark with desire, but his smile smug when he added, "When you get older."

From the tent in Mac's shorts, Gunny wasn't the only one having long and hard difficulties traipsing through the trees. He was about to point it out when he caught a glimpse of the sun sparkling off the water.

"Fuck me," Mac groaned when he too spotted the pond. He started to pull away, but Gunny tightened his grip.

Spinning Mac around, Gunny waggled his brows at him. "This old, soon-to-be retiree can surely accommodate that request."

"Is that a fact?" Mac asked, still trying to move toward the pond. The expression on his face and the gleam in his eyes were like a challenge.

Gunny followed. Stalking.

"You've been awful toppy lately," Mac drawled, and then laughed when Gunny made a growling noise in the back of his throat.

"Still trying to make up for all those months you left me alone." His hand tightened on Mac's. "Left me with nothing but a battered tube of lube and my hand, and I aim to make up for what I lost. You owe me some fucking, Mr. Jones."

Mac looked down at himself and then met Gunny's eyes, a mischievous grin curling his lips. "I do look pretty fuckable, don't I?" He took another step back, teasing. And then another.

Gunny took in Mac's body, his intent to take it all in quickly and then answer in the affirmative, but he got distracted by Mac's hard chest. The nipples, erect under the sweaty dark hair, the perspiration trickling down the golden skin of Mac's sides and his furred belly. "Lickable," he murmured.

They came to a halt near the water's edge, and Mac ran a hand up Gunny's belly, across his chest, pinching at one hard nub. "I'm pretty dirty. Sweaty," he said gruffly. "Think maybe I should rinse off a bit first?"

In answer, Gunny released his hold on Mac's hand, grabbed his hips, and jerked hard, until their sweat-slick bodies were pressed together. Ripped, work-hardened bodies briefly strained against the other until there wasn't a breath of space between them, before melting into one. Two hairy chests, two hard cocks, four hulky legs and strong calloused hands, moving, pressing, until they merged into one massive beast.

Gunny buried his face in the side of Mac's neck, inhaling deeply. He smelled so good. So powerful, like earth and sunshine and something unique that was all Mac, which made Gunny's mouth water. "Goddamn, you smell good." He ran the flat of his tongue up Mac's neck, nipped at his earlobe. "Taste even better."

Mac shuddered against Gunny, dropping his head back in invitation. "And all yours," Mac moaned.

"Damn right you are." He licked and nipped along Mac's jaw, the coarse stubble rough against Gunny's tongue and lips, until he reached the other side of Mac's neck, sucking the salty skin before saying in a desire-thickened voice, "And I'm going to feast on what is mine."

"I don't know, Gunny," Mac said, a little breathy, as Gunny continued to make his way across the man's flesh. "You had a big breakfast and there is a lot of me to eat. Think you can handle it?" he challenged.

Taunting bastard knew Gunny couldn't turn down a challenge. His plans to lick and taste until he was able to get them naked turned into a full smorgasbord of sampling every square inch of Mac's body. Gunny worked his way to Mac's chest, pressed a kiss to his breastbone, and teased the soft hairs with the tip of his tongue. "Gluttony is one of the seven deadly sins," he murmured against Mac's heated flesh. "You're going to send me straight to hell, Macalister Jones."

"Then I'll be in good—fuck!" Mac hissed when Gunny bit down on Mac's right nipple; then he panted as Gunny eased the sting with his tongue and said, "Company."

"You like that? I thought I was the one who liked the kiss of pain." Gunny moved to the other nub, teasing it with his lips. "Quite the role reversal today, wouldn't you say?"

Mac grabbed the back of Gunny's head and pushed his face hard against his chest. "You're talking too much," he growled. "Eat!"

Gunny's dick twitched; a tingling sensation raced down his spine, a direct response to the snap of authority in Mac's voice, and he sucked hard on the delicate morsel, not hesitating to do as Mac commanded. Apparently Mac was done with the teasing. *Works every time,* he thought smugly. Mac may have been the more dominant of them, but that didn't mean Gunny didn't know how to work the man to get exactly what he wanted.

Mac held him there for long moments, Gunny's face pressed so hard against Mac's chest that he could scarcely breathe. No matter—taking Mac's delicious flavor into his mouth, swallowing it down, was his only purpose.

"That's it, Gunny. Fuck yeah. Use your teeth." Mac grunted, his fingers kneading into the flesh at the back of Gunny's skull, encouraging, pressing.

Gunny bit down on the beefy pec, not enough to break the skin, but hard enough Mac would be sporting Gunny's love bite for some time to come.

Mac grabbed Gunny's face and pulled him from Mac's chest. Gunny's teeth scraping along the swollen nub caused Mac to curse under his breath and his back to arch. He barely gave Gunny enough time to catch his breath before he smashed their mouths together and shoved his tongue deep in a hungry kiss. Gunny was forced to open his mouth wide as Mac took what he needed.

Every inch of Gunny vibrated and hummed. His skin sizzled where it came into contact with Mac's, and he could only grip Mac's hips harder, holding on, as the kiss went impossibly deeper, became more brutal. The tips of Mac's fingers dug in behind Gunny's ears, bruising, as he controlled every aspect of the kiss, Gunny's very breath. Gunny's lungs burned, and tears leaked from his eyes, but he couldn't stop, wouldn't stop, until Mac had what he needed.

Suddenly it changed; the all-consuming and demanding kiss morphed into something soft and tender, the fingertips that only seconds before dug into flesh now caressing, soft. Mac languidly sucked on Gunny's tongue, his lips, and the shift from animalistic to gentle left Gunny off-balance and trembling.

"Every fucking inch, boy." Mac's words were harsh but his tone and touch still tender.

"Yes, Sir."

And just like that, their natural inclinations fell smoothly into place. Mac firmly made it known that he was done being teased, and if Gunny submitted to the need riding Mac, the pleasure would be so much more intense if Gunny handed over his control to his lover. He did so without question.

Mac slid a hand into the tight space between their bodies, the back of his knuckles rubbing across Gunny's stomach as Mac fumbled with his shorts, unbuttoning and unzipping and shoving them down his legs, kicking them away.

Mac leaned his shoulder back slightly and tilted Gunny's head down. "You see that?"

Mac's hard cock was pressed between their bodies, the wide, flared head damp with arousal. Saliva pooled in Gunny's mouth, and he swallowed, and then swallowed again, before he could speak. "Yes, Sir," Gunny answered, licking his lips. He couldn't wait to get his lips wrapped around Mac's rigid cock. Christ, he was fucking salivating.

"That's dessert." Mac smirked. "Make sure you save room for it."

"A meal isn't complete without dessert." Gunny kissed Mac's palm and ran his tongue over the salty flesh. "I always clean my plate."

Mac sucked in a harsh breath when Gunny sucked one of Mac's fingers into his mouth, swirling his tongue around the digit, before moving on to the next one. Moving from Mac's fingers, Gunny worked his way up the inside of Mac's arm from wrist to pit. Gunny inhaled deeply as he buried his face in Mac's armpit, his lover's scent stronger, more concentrated, and he took in the musky aroma and taste. He scraped his teeth against the sensitive skin. Mac jerked; a sound, almost like a purr, rumbled in his throat.

"Ah, damn that feels good," Mac groaned and stretched his arm over his head.

Gunny's hands roamed over sweat-slick skin, touching every inch he could reach. Mac made a grunt of protest when Gunny moved from Mac's sensitive underarm to his broad back. "What was that?" he asked, then ran his tongue down Mac's spine as he teased a finger along the crease of Mac's ass. "You want me to quit already?"

"Gunny," Mac said in warning.

"Mmm hmm?" He pressed the tip of his finger farther into Mac's damp, hot crack, nudging his hole. Gunny's other hand found an erect nipple and pinched, as his mouth and tongue sought out the salt of Mac's skin.

Mac's vocabulary skills obviously fled under Gunny's assault. He was reduced to guttural sounds by the time Gunny had made his way up and down both muscular legs and buried his face in Mac's ass.

Dirt and rocks dug painfully into Gunny's knees. The bright sun burning his exposed back and neck and the painfully hard cock bent uncomfortably against the zipper of his shorts were but small annoyances as he teased his tongue against Mac's hole. The way Mac shook, the feel of the hard clenching muscles of Mac's ass in his hands, the dark flavor on his tongue, demanded Gunny's attention. He reveled in being able to reduce Mac to this trembling, moaning, and groaning man of pure need.

"I love eating your ass," Gunny praised. He pressed the tip of one finger inside Mac's ass, still licking at the dark ring and causing Mac to cry out.

"I'm not going to last much longer," Mac panted. "Can't— Gunny!"

An evil idea formed in Gunny's head. He was going to blow Mac's fucking mind. "Open yourself for me."

"I…. Ah… fuck."

"C'mon, Mac," he encouraged, pressing his finger deep and twisting it. "Grab your ass, spread it for me." He pulled his finger out, then shoved it back in hard, Mac going up on tiptoes, body straining. "Show me that ass," Gunny growled. "Do it."

Mac focused on his pleasure as he did as Gunny commanded, bending slightly and pulling his ass cheeks apart wide. "Oh, yeah! Look at that sweet hole," Gunny said, pumping his finger in and out of Mac's ass hard and fast.

"Gu—" Mac took a few harsh breaths; his body tensed as he fought to get control of himself. "I'm…."

"You wanting to cum, Mac?"

"Yes!"

"Can't hold on much longer?" Gunny purred. He pulled his hand back till just the tip of his finger breached Mac's entrance, moving it in a circular motion, stretching.

"No," he bit out.

Mac was vibrating, shaking so hard Gunny worried the man's legs wouldn't be able to hold him up much longer. But he wasn't concerned enough to stop. He pumped his finger in and out a few more times, Mac grunting and cussing between panting breaths.

"One more taste," Gunny said wryly. He pulled his finger free and buried his face in Mac's ass again, his hands gripping Mac's wrists, forcing him to keep his ass cheeks spread, and shoved his tongue deep in tight, wet heat.

"Fuck!" Mac howled. "Goddamn!"

Tightening the hold he had on Mac's wrists, not allowing the man to pull away, Gunny set a hard and fast rhythm, fucking Mac's ass with his tongue. His knees protested, jaw ached, flesh burned, and still he moved his tongue in and out of Mac with single-minded determination, Mac's pleas and cries spurring him on.

"Gunny…. Please, please, please," Mac begged. "I need…."

Gunny fucked him harder.

"Oh, Jesus," Mac moaned pitifully. "Wait, wa—" Mac's entire body went still, no breath, perhaps not even a heartbeat. And then he shouted out his release, body jerking through each contraction, without as much as a breath of touch to his dick. As one last shudder shook Mac's entire frame, Gunny wrapped his arms around Mac's waist and rested his cheek against Mac's ass.

Gunny worked his jaw from side to side, easing the ache before muttering, "Holy fuck that was hot."

Mac shook against him again, and Gunny tipped his head back to look up at his lover as Mac turned to face him. Mac's eyes were gleaming with laughter. "Sorry, Sir," Mac chuckled, reaching down and helping Gunny to his feet. "It would appear the chef has blown your dessert."

Gunny gritted his teeth at the ache in his knees and the more painful one in his groin. "All this feasting talk making you hungry, Mac?" Gunny asked hopefully.

"Famished," he replied, still laughing. Mac popped the button on Gunny's shorts and eased down the zipper. He shook his head as he pushed Gunny's shorts down and then pressed a kiss to Gunny's mouth. "Can't believe you did that," he said against Gunny's lips. "That was incredible and you deserve a proper thank-you," he murmured and slid easily to his knees.

Gunny stepped out of his shorts, kicked them in the same direction as Mac's shorts, and cupped the back of Mac's head in one hand. The other he wrapped around his leaking prick. His pulse raced, the throb in his cock nearly unbearable. "I'm going to warn you right now, I nearly came in my fucking shorts when you blew your load."

Mac stared up at him briefly, his happiness and awe evident on his face. "Guess I'll have to give you a proper thank-you later, then." He shrugged and to Gunny's great delight, leaned forward and sucked Gunny's cock into his mouth.

Thinking of the teasing in the pole barn, the morning spent hard and wanting as he watched Mac work the axe, and his lingering flavor on his tongue, Gunny snapped his hips, pushing his cock deep into that perfect wet heat. Sweat rolled down Gunny's brow and into his eyes. He squeezed them shut and tipped his head back. As the sun heated his face, Mac fanned the fire burning in Gunny's gut, and with a shout, he came deep in Mac's throat. He fed Mac's hungry mouth every drop, until he was spent.

Mac pulled off Gunny's prick with a pop and smacked his lips. "Fucking delicious."

The heat, excessive gluttony, and satiation caused Gunny's head to spin, leaving him woozy. He patted Mac's head as he stumbled toward the pond and dove into the refreshing waters.

CHAPTER
Twelve

GROWING up, Sundays had always been Mac's favorite day of the week. Mom lived firmly by the rule that Sunday was a day of rest, worship, and family. Mac wasn't real big into the whole worshiping thing. Mom and Dad had done a good job instilling morals and values in him; he viewed the Ten Commandments as common sense, and he did believe in a higher power. It was the concept of organized religion he'd never taken a shine to. Now her views on it being a day of rest and family time, he was all on board for. Throw in the pork roast, potatoes, carrots, and homemade bread Mom made every Sunday, top it with a big ol' pan of peach cobbler or apple dumplings, and it easily made up for the couple of hours he'd had to spend in his dress clothes at Woodside Church.

It had been a nearly perfect weekend. The sadness at his dad's friend passing didn't go unnoticed: the only blemish on an otherwise amazing visit. Mac wished he'd gotten to spend more time with his dad, but now that he was no longer traveling or working, he'd make sure to find the time. However, he'd gotten some much-needed quality time with Gunny, amazing food, beautiful weather, and a chance to be back on the land he had loved so much growing up. Now, in true Clare Jones tradition, Mac rested with a belly full of roast dinner and apple dumplings, and he was kicked back on the couch next to his mom while she knitted her newest afghan. Dad went to his room for his nap, and instead of Ted bitching and moaning from his overindulgence headache, Gunny was stretched out in Dad's recliner, lightly snoring.

Yup, just about the best Sunday ever.

Resting his head back against the couch, Mac watched as his mom wrapped the bright green yarn around her needles, making a low clicking sound as she worked. He'd spent hours wrapping balls of yarn for her when he was little, always amazed at the bright colors she'd chosen and the beautiful things she created. In those days, her smooth soft hands had moved much quicker, more fluidly than the arthritic hands did now. Her creations were still just as beautiful.

"What's weighing so heavily on your mind, son?" his mom asked softly.

"What makes you think there's anything on my mind?"

His mom looked up from her knitting and gave him a knowing smile. The look was so smug, Mac was surprised she didn't roll her eyes at him. She set her knitting aside and shifted on the couch till she was leaning back against the armrest, facing Mac. "You've had something on the tip of your tongue all weekend. Spit it out."

Mac returned the smile. He never could hide anything from her, well, most things anyway. "I was going to tell you and Dad about some of my upcoming plans, but with Mr. Cohen's passing and Dad gone most of the weekend, I just didn't feel it was the right time." He shrugged one shoulder. "Now, with us packed and going to be heading out soon, I'm not so sure it's the proper time to be dropping a bombshell on you," he said vaguely.

"A bombshell, huh?" she asked with an arched brow.

"Yeah," he sighed. "It could be taken that way, I guess." He looked down, suddenly interested in a loose thread on his shorts. Damn, this had seemed so much easier in his head. He was suddenly as nervous as a virgin bride, his gut clenching and rolling as proof.

"Hey," his mom said softly, moving to sit next to him and taking Mac's hand in hers. "You know how proud we are of you, right?"

He nodded.

"And how much we love you?" she added.

Mac nodded again.

"There is nothing you could tell me that will ever change either of those things," she said, patting the back of his hand. "You're a good man, Macalister."

"Thank you," he said, kissing her cheek. "I love you too." Mac took a deep breath. "First, I want you to know that I never lied to you. I didn't share everything, but I never lied."

"Okay," she said carefully.

Here goes nothing. "Gunny and I, we've been through a lot together, boot camp, Desert Storm, life. There isn't anyone I trust more than him to have my back; hell, I trust him with my very life." Mac scrubbed a hand over his jaw as he carefully chose his next words. "You know he's been my best friend for a very long time and that I love him. What you don't know is, he's more than just a friend. I'm *in* love with him, have been for years."

"I figured as much," his mom said easily.

"You did?"

She gave him a patient look. "Macalister, I see the way you look at him, the way he looks at you. I swear that man thinks you hung the moon and stars just for him, and you would gladly do it for him if you could."

"I would," he admitted quietly. "I've asked him to marry me."

"And Gunther said yes." It wasn't a question; she already knew the answer.

"The president is signing the repeal of 'Don't Ask, Don't Tell' in September. Gunny and I want to be married before our exit ceremony. You know, show the people who might be afraid of the reversal of the law, that a man, regardless of who he loves or sleeps with, can be a damn fine soldier and an asset to the Corps."

"Told you you're a good man," she said proudly, and then her brow furrowed and she looked at him questioningly. "Is it legal for two men to get married in Pennsylvania?"

Mac shook his head. "The state or church won't recognize it, but for Gunny and I it'll be as real as any other marriage. Our commitment to each other is what matters." He smiled at her, the last of his apprehension seeping from him as she smiled back. "So you'll come?"

His mom touched his face lovingly. "I wouldn't miss it for the world," she said and kissed his cheek. She smiled at him again, her words making his heart sing, but Mac didn't miss the sadness in her eyes.

"What is it?" he asked, concerned.

"It's nothing."

"You have something sitting on the tip of your tongue," he said, using the same words and giving her the same knowing look she'd used on him earlier. "Spit it out."

"It's the expressive eyes, you know," she said with a sniff.

"I got them from you." He winked. "So if you're truly okay knowing Gunny and I are a couple, why the sadness?"

"No matter how old you are, I'm always going to be your mama and want to protect you, and it hurts my heart knowing what you're about to go through," she said with a sigh.

Mac laid his arm along the back of the couch, his mom tucked up close to his side, patting his leg. She was so tiny, and yet just like when he was a little boy and it was he who was snuggled up to her, she was his protector from the big bad world. "What I'm about to do is retire and for the first time in twenty-two years, show off my love for Gunny. Why does that make you sad?"

"Rose-colored glasses," she murmured under her breath.

"I heard that," he said with a soft poke to her ribs. His mom used to tease him when he was little that he always saw the good in everything, no matter how bleak things appeared. "And trust me, I've seen some horrific things, done to and in the name of humanity. Men dying over a dried-up piece of bread or simply out of boredom," he said regretfully. "I no longer see the good in everyone."

"Yet you pull them out from where you tucked them away and wear them now," she said thoughtfully.

"I've heard the derogatory slurs, seen the disgust in people's eyes. Hell, even the Corps didn't want to know, I get it."

"Do you really? It's one thing to hear hate thrown at others while standing behind a façade of heterosexuality. It's a completely different thing to be standing there while the crap is being slung directly at you."

"Oh, great, another pessimist. You sound as bad as Gunny," he complained.

"Gunther's a smart man," his mom reminded him with a smile.

"I know," he said and kissed the top of her head. "He's marrying me, isn't he?"

"That he is," she laughed, and then looked up at Mac and in all seriousness said, "I'm always here to remind you how wonderful you both are, if you ever need a boost."

"Thank—"

They both jumped when the back door slammed and Ted's voice bellowed from the kitchen. "Am I too late for dinner? I'm starving."

"There goes the peaceful Sunday afternoon," Mac grumbled.

"Behave," his mom chastised, and popped him on the leg before she went to her feet and headed toward the kitchen and the asshole who awaited.

"You ready to go?" Gunny asked, the words barely understandable as he yawned at the same time.

"Yes!"

"Car's all packed. I say we make a mad dash for the front door before he comes in." Gunny lowered the leg rest on the recliner and placed his hands on the arms. "Ready?"

He looked between Gunny and the front door, briefly considered all his options, the pros and cons. The last thing he needed was a run-in with his brother, not when escape was so close. Yet even as he contemplated making a mad dash for the car, he simply wasn't about to let the shit bag make him disrespect his parents or worse, make his mom cry. That didn't mean he had to stay long.

"Tempting," he admitted. "C'mon, let's go greet the fucker and say good-bye to Mom and Dad." He slapped Gunny on the back as he stomped past. "Five minutes," he told Gunny over his shoulder. "Ten max." Anything past that and the possibility of punches flying and Mama crying grew exponentially.

MAC stopped at the entrance to the kitchen and leaned against the doorjamb, arms crossed over his chest, Gunny at his flank. He was ready with some witty welcome, but the words caught in his throat when he got a glimpse of his brother leaning against the counter, gulping down a glass of water. He hadn't seen Ted in over a year, and the year hadn't been good to the man.

His dark brown hair was long and stringy, and sweat and God knows what else had matted it to the right side of his head. At one time, they had been comparable in height and size; now, Ted was rail thin, his face gaunt and an ugly shade of gray. An untrimmed beard framed his wrinkled face. Ted no longer looked like the man Mac had known. Instead of the forty-five-year-old brother he had expected to see, he found a stranger who looked twenty years older and frail.

Ted finished his drink, an ugly smile curling his lips when he spotted Mac. "Well, I'll be damned. If it ain't my little brother and his butt buddy," he sneered. He took a step toward Mac, wiped his hand on his dirty green T-shirt, and held it out when he was close enough. "Long time no see."

Not long enough, Mac thought regretfully. One more hour and he'd have been gone. He accepted the offered hand and shook it. "Ted," he drawled with a curt nod.

The mystery of why his brother hadn't shown up the day before was solved as the stench of stale alcohol, cigarette smoke, and piss rolled off the man and filled Mac's nose, which he had to fight not to wrinkle in disgust. Mac shot a look to his mom, who was heaping leftovers on a plate while Ted greeted Gunny. She tried to smile at him, but it was sad, her eyes full of worry and concern.

Mac's disgust shifted lightning fast to rage. Why the hell couldn't the son of a bitch see what he was doing to their mom? Mac's heart broke for her even as the fury sped through his veins. He clenched his hands into tight fists, fighting the urge to knock his brother upside the head, until Ted moved away and took a seat at the table. Mac stayed where he was. He didn't dare move any closer, his control on shaky ground.

"Is that about ready, Mom? I'm starving here," Ted complained and leaned back in his chair like some entitled little boy waiting to be served. He picked up his fork and pointed it at Mac. "I hear you're about to retire. Kinda young to be sitting on your ass all the time, don't ya think?"

"It's one of the perks of being committed and working hard for twenty-two years in a row. They like to give rewards for stuff like that," Mac said sarcastically.

"What about you?" Ted pointed at Gunny and asked, "You too good to work now too?" Ted cocked his head and didn't try to hide his contempt. "Let me guess. You put in to retire too so you could follow my brother around with your nose up his ass like you always have."

Mac started to take a step forward. He was usually good at ignoring his brother's comments, but not so much when they were directed at Gunny. A hand at the small of his back, caressing softly, stopped him, and from the corner of his eye he saw the slight shake of Gunny's head.

"That's enough, Ted," Mom snapped and set a plate down in front of him. "Eat your supper and leave your brother and Gunther alone."

"That's okay, Clare," Gunny said calmly. "I didn't take offense. I always have Mac's back, and to answer your question, Ted, yes I am retiring also."

"Why doesn't that surprise me?" Ted said around a mouthful of food. "Except I'd have thought my cocky brother would be the one behind you."

"Enough," Mom said, slamming a hand down on the table. "I will not have you disrespecting them in my house."

Ted glared at Mac, but didn't say another word. Instead, he shoved a piece of bread in his mouth, a scowl on his face as he chewed it.

Standing there staring at Ted, Mac couldn't help but feel a pang of regret, a sense of loss. How had this man, whom he'd once looked up to and had seen as a superhero when Mac was young, fallen so far from that golden image? Only three years apart, they had been inseparable, spending their time swimming at the pond, building tree forts, hunting, hiding from chores, or staying up at night talking for hours. Everything had changed in their early teens. Mac had joined the ROTC and set his sights on a military career, and Ted had set his sights on women, drinking, drugs, and having a good time. The two paths mixed like oil and water.

Still, he missed what could have been. With a heavy sigh, he pushed off from the wall and stood in front of Ted. He waved a hand toward his mom, conveying everything was okay, and then clutched the top of the chair. "You obviously have an issue with me and Gunny. Why don't we get it all put out on the table and stop these backhanded insults. Are you still mad at me for not bailing you out of jail last time?"

"No!" Ted spat.

"Maybe because the one and only time you called me in the last year was to borrow money and I refused?"

"I don't need your goddamn money," Ted said, visibly shaking with anger.

"Then what is it, Ted?" he asked patiently. "Why do you hate me so much?"

He had to give his brother credit. The man didn't use the protection of a table between them before he started his rant. He got up and made his way around the table, making Mac release the chair and turn to face him. Despite the nearly one-hundred-pound size difference, Ted stood only a foot away and poked Mac in the chest. "I have a big fucking problem with you," Ted sneered.

Mac casually looked down at his chest where Ted poked him one more time. Mac was very much aware of Gunny's moving up behind him when Mac looked at his brother, whose face was red with anger, and smiled. Ted was either one brave son of a bitch, still drunk, or the stupidest. He'd put money on a combination of the latter two.

"Alright. Let's hear it," he encouraged.

"You and… and… it," he said with a nod toward Gunny. "You two have everyone fooled about how you're decorated and celebrated Marines. Have Mom and Dad thinking you're this perfect son. But I know what you are and soon everyone else will too."

"Please," Mac said with a snort of laughter. "Speak your words of wisdom and slay the evil dragon."

"You ain't nothing more than disgusting faggots," Ted scathed, his bloodshot eyes burning with hatred.

Gunny stiffened behind him, and Mac heard the warning in his mama's voice when she said his name, but Mac was focused on his brother and surprisingly wasn't even offended. He might have felt a sense of loss for his childhood hero, but he had lost all respect and care years ago for the man who stood before him now.

"Now I'm not sure I agree with what you deem as disgusting. I'd think an unemployed, drug-addicted drunkard who can't be bothered to care for his kids is a hell of a lot worse than a man who sleeps with another man," he challenged.

Ted puffed up his puny chest and narrowed his eyes. "So you're finally going to admit you're one of those nasty queer boys?"

"If by *nasty queer* you mean am I in love with, and plan to spend the rest of my life with, the most amazing human being I know, then yeah, guilty as charged," he said easily. Mac arched a brow at his brother and added, "If you're just asking because you want to know if we're fucking, that's none of your business."

The room went dead silent for a moment, and it was as if everything around him moved in slow motion. Ted's face twisted into an ugly expression of pure loathing, and he spat as if Mac's words had left a nasty taste on his tongue. Mom took a step forward, her hands coming up. Ted pulled back his arm, and the fist that was intended to connect stopped a mere inch from Mac's nose.

"Don't you ever put your hands on him," Gunny hissed.

Time sped back to normal, and Ted screamed as Gunny spun him around, wrenching his arm up behind his back, and shoved him against the counter. "Get your filthy hands off me," Ted roared. "Nasty faggot pig."

Mac ignored him and turned to their mom, who had tears rolling down her face and a hand clasped over her mouth. "I'm sorry," Mac whispered, his gut clenching at his mom's pain. She shook her head as she continued to stare at her eldest son as he struggled to free himself from Gunny's grip.

"That's enough!" Dad bellowed. "Gunther, turn him loose."

All eyes fell on the man standing in the doorway, his hands curled in tight fists at his sides and his jaw clenched. Theodore stared at Gunny and Ted with an unreadable expression on his face.

No one moved. It was Ted who broke the silence.

"Did you hear that, old man? Your precious boy is nothing more than a disgusting queer," Ted said gleefully.

"I heard it," Theodore said with a detached tone to his voice. "Gunther, let him go," he repeated.

"Dad, I'm—"

"Macalister, it's time you and Gunther head out," his dad interrupted.

Mac's heart fell to his feet, the pain nearly taking his knees out from under him. "Dad?" he asked hesitantly.

"Go home, Macalister." His father steadfastly refused to look at him, his expression emotionless and unreadable.

Mac didn't need to remove the rose-colored glasses his mom had accused him of wearing. They shattered into a million tiny pieces, cutting into his eyes, causing tears to fall. The slivers of glass shredded not only his eyes, but his heart, as the man he respected above all others was sending him away, refusing to acknowledge him. Worse still, he was allowing Ted to remain.

"I'm sorry," he croaked past the lump in his throat, and turned and walked out. The only thing he heard, above the pounding of his heart as he made his way to his truck, was his mother's sobs.

CHAPTER
Thirteen

"I SAID get your fucking hands off me," Ted barked.

Rage. Rage and heartbreak rooted Gunny to the spot, unable to move, barely able to breathe, as the pain in his chest gripped him. The tears that rolled down Clare's face were painful to see, but the anguish he'd seen in Mac's eyes was agonizing. Gunny looked between the stone-faced Theodore and his sobbing wife, trying to get a grasp on what had just taken place. For long moments he stood there torn between thrashing Ted, beating some sense into Theodore, or comforting Clare.

"Hold your tongue," Theodore hissed at Ted, the first emotion the man had shown since he'd walked into the room. Ted stilled. "Let him go, Gunther," Mac's dad said flatly.

Gunny reined in his anger, a nearly impossible feat considering what these men had done to Mac. The urge to thrash both of them was great, yet knowing Mac was hurting and needed him made it feasible to slowly ease the hold he had on the snake and back away warily.

Gunny started toward the door when Clare grabbed him, wrapped her arms around his waist, and buried her face against Gunny's chest. "Take care of my boy," she sobbed.

"I will." Tears burned his eyes and he returned the embrace, awkwardly patting her back. What a horrible thing for this woman to witness. "I'm so sorry," he added regretfully before releasing her and going in search of Mac.

Tromping down the back stairs, Gunny broke into a run as soon as his feet hit the dirt. Rounding the side of the house, he spotted Mac, fists clenched in white-knuckle grips, pacing with heavy steps as evidence of his anger, the dampness on his cheeks of his pain. Gunny didn't even slow his steps until he had Mac in his arms.

"Don't you do it," he said fiercely and pulled Mac hard against his chest.

Mac wasn't sobbing, nor was he cursing like he'd normally do when pissed off. The two conflicting emotions caused Mac to shake, but he was silent, his muscles coiled and stiff against Gunny.

"I know what's going through your head, and don't you even fucking think it!" He gripped Mac tighter, wanting to squeeze the agony out of the man, pull it into himself. *Give me your pain.* "Please."

Mac remained silent; the quiet trembling shredded Gunny's heart. As the minutes stretched out, the feeling of helplessness caused the tatters of his heart to spark, igniting a fire in his belly. "It's not true, Mac. I know what you're thinking and it's not true. That piece of shit is not better than you."

"He wouldn't even look at me," Mac said dejectedly.

The desire for blood filled Gunny, an ugly dark need to punish for what Mac was going through. How dare *anyone* make Mac feel like this? "You listen to me," Gunny bit out furiously and gripped Mac's chin tightly, forcing Mac to meet Gunny's eyes. His heart skipped a beat when he saw the pain there, and the fire roared. "Then he's a fucking fool! I don't know what the hell just happened in there, but I can tell you without a shred of doubt, Ted isn't worthy enough to breathe the same fucking air as you."

"Then why am I out here and he's in there?" Mac pursed his lips and shook his head. "Why am I the one being sent away?"

"I don't know why, Mac. I can't even begin to guess. It's like one minute everything was great and the next everyone had lost their fucking minds."

The scene from the kitchen flashed in Gunny's mind, and he had to close his eyes and take a deep breath as his rage flared brightly again, and the urge to commit violence surged through him. He needed to get his anger under control if he was going to be any good for Mac. *This isn't about you. This is about what Mac needs.*

Gunny opened his eyes to find Mac staring at him questioningly. The vulnerability in his normally cocksure lover's eyes was difficult to see. Gunny smashed their mouths together in a hard, desperate kiss. "I love you so goddamn much," he said against Mac's lips. "Focus on that, Mac."

Mac clung to him a moment, their foreheads pressed together, as they stood there breathing each other in. After a few moments, some of the tension seemed to seep from Mac, and he whispered, "I love you too."

"Let's go home." Keeping a tight hold on Mac, Gunny led him to the passenger side of the truck, opened the door, and waited until Mac slid in, before adding, "And when we get there, I'm going to bottom you so hard."

Mac tilted his head, his brow slightly creased, and then burst out laughing. "Where the hell do you come up with this shit?"

Gunny shrugged, his lips twitching into a grin. "Saw it on a T-shirt."

Gunny closed the door and ran around to the driver's side, feeling better that he'd been able to get Mac to laugh. He slid into the driver's side and held out his hand. "Keys."

"You know it wouldn't kill you to say cuddle," Mac said drolly and handed him the keys.

"I will not. Men do not cuddle, Mac. The word is just—" He started the truck and got them going down the drive, trying his damnedest not to laugh. "Wrong," he finally said. "Besides, I am not a cuddle whore like you."

"Really?" Mac sniffed. "Who was whining the other morning when he didn't get cuddles?"

"I do not cuddle and I most certainly do not whine," Gunny said sullenly. "I grumble."

"And bottom," Mac said and waggled his brows. "Don't forget the bottoming part."

"How could I forget," Gunny snorted. "I'm the grumbling bottom and you're the cocky cuddle whore. Damn, we make a great team."

Mac grabbed Gunny's hand and entwined their fingers. "The fucking best ever," he said with a big happy grin on his face.

Mac situated himself, moved closer to Gunny so he could stretch out his long legs. More of the tension seemed to release its hold on his muscles, and he appeared relaxed. Gunny hit the power button on the radio and tuned it to an easy-rock station.

Gunny kept a periodic eye on Mac as he got them on the highway. Mac was staring out the windshield, eyes toward the sky, his expression one of concentration, but he was humming along to the music, so Gunny stayed silent, not wanting to interrupt the man's thoughts. If there was anything more to say, or if Mac needed to talk, he'd let Gunny know.

A few minutes later, Mac brought their hands to his mouth and kissed the back of Gunny's. "Thank you."

"I'd do anything for you," Gunny told him. And he would; Mac only had to ask. Gunny would have done anything to have been the one in Mac's shoes so his lover wouldn't have to feel the heartache. Had the tables been reversed, he knew without a shadow of a doubt that Mac would know how to make him feel better, how to take him out of his body and mind and help him find peace. All Gunny knew to do was listen and cover up the pain with laughter.

"I know," Mac said confidently. He yawned and rested his head on the back of the seat and closed his eyes.

Gunny looked at Mac for as long as was safe before turning his attention back to the road. Maybe that was all he needed to do right now. Be there for Mac and make him laugh.

Mac didn't say anything else about what had happened until they reached home and were unpacking the truck. "You think I should call him?" he asked thoughtfully.

Gunny pulled out their duffels and handed one to Mac. He didn't need to ask who; Mac hadn't initiated a call to his brother in years and wouldn't. "What are you going to say to him?"

Mac shouldered his bag and pulled out the cooler his mom had packed full of homemade preserves. He gave Gunny a pondering look and then shrugged.

"That conversation will go over well," Gunny said and rolled his eyes.

"Shut up," Mac grumbled and stomped toward the house.

Gunny slammed the rear door closed and followed. "I didn't mean you shouldn't, you stubborn ass," he griped. Gunny pushed past Mac and unlocked the door and pushed it open, allowing Mac to enter first. "I only meant you might want to have some idea what you want to say. Your dad speaks few words on the phone on a good day. What was it he says?" Gunny asked as he dropped his duffel and cooler by the door and shut it. "Phones are for emergencies and making appointments. Conversation is for face-to-face," he said, trying to imitate Theodore's Virginian drawl.

"I hate you." Mac's words were harsh, but his mouth curled up into a teasing grimace.

"No," Gunny corrected, taking the duffel from Mac and dropping it. "You hate it when I'm right." He pressed a chaste kiss to Mac's lips and then slapped him on the ass as he headed to the kitchen.

"That, too."

Gunny went to the fridge and pulled out a beer and held it up. "Want one?"

"God, yes!" Mac sighed and took the beer, popped the top, and took a long pull.

Grabbing another, Gunny made note they were well stocked. They rarely drank at home, preferring to walk down to the pub, but kept beer on hand for company or for when they were doing yard work. Nothing tasted better than an ice-cold beer on a hot summer day. From the blissed-out look on Mac's face as he took another big gulp, a beer after fighting with family ranked right up there.

"You want to talk about it?" Gunny asked hesitantly.

"No. Yes." Mac huffed out a breath, tipped the can up, and drained the rest, then tossed it in the garbage and grabbed another. "I don't know," Mac finally admitted and slumped into a barstool.

Gunny leaned back against the counter from the island and watched Mac carefully, waiting to see if he would say any more. When he didn't, just continued to stare at the beer in his hands without opening it, Gunny finally said, "You've obviously got something on your mind. You've been quietly stewing for three hours."

"I told Mom," Mac said without looking up.

Gunny's belly did a flip, and he took a sip of beer to hide his shock behind his can. "And?"

"Just like I'd told ya, she already knew. They haven't ever seen me date a woman, and I ain't lied and said I had. Ted obviously already knew, or at least suspected. I figured—" Mac popped the top and took a gulp. "I guess I thought he had figured it out too."

"Mac," he said soothingly as he moved closer. "Your first duty has always been to the Corps. They knew that and never questioned that commitment. It took you and I twenty years to figure this shit out and admit we were a couple." Gunny reached across the island and ran his fingers gently across Mac's jaw. "Give your dad some time to come to terms with it."

Mac placed his hand over Gunny's and held it to his cheek. "I'm hating you again," he said gruffly.

"I can live with that," Gunny chuckled. "But can you do it while you cook me some supper while I take a shower?"

Mac's eyes narrowed. "You're kidding me, right?"

Gunny patted Mac on the cheek. "I drove while you snoozed for the last three hours. The least you can do is feed me."

"Hmm. You have a point." Mac dug in his pocket and pulled out his phone and flipped it open. Gunny eyed him suspiciously as he hit only one button, and then pressed it to his ear.

"What are you doing?"

"Ah, ah," Mac tsked and held up one finger to silence Gunny. "Hi. Is this Cory?" After a brief pause he said, "Yeah, it's me. Can you send over my usual?" Another short pause. "Cool! Say thirty minutes?" Mac roamed his eyes over Gunny's body. "Make that an hour." He shut his phone and set it on the counter, a big shit-eating grin on his face.

"Who the hell was that?"

"Cory," Mac said with a shrug.

"And this Cory knows your usual?" Gunny grunted, slowly making his way toward Mac.

Mac saw the movement and eased to his feet. "Yeah, he knows what I like." He took a step back.

Gunny stalked him, following Mac like a predator. "Is that so?"

"Yup, and it's always hot. Spicy." Mac licked his lips. "And so good."

Gunny made a grab for Mac, but he anticipated Gunny easily and stepped out of reach. "This Cory better be a delivery boy."

"Oh he delivers, all right," Mac said huskily.

Gunny growled at him. "Don't make me beat your ass, Jones."

"Not this time," he said, eyes sparkling with laughter. "You promised to bottom me so hard." To Gunny's frustration, Mac spun out of grasp again. "But I might reconsider, if you can catch me," he taunted and made a mad dash for the bathroom, Gunny right on his heels.

Beating the man, bottoming for him, either worked for Gunny. He just better have some food to satisfy his other needs, when he was done. Or Cory was a dead man.

CHAPTER
Fourteen

MAC angrily pressed the buttons on the remote, trying to find something interesting to keep his mind off his dad.

Talk show? *Nope.*

News? *Nope.*

Infomercials? *Oh hell no!*

It had been two days since the blowup with his family and he still hadn't talked to his dad, and Mac was going fucking crazy. Mom had called and apparently they had talked Ted into entering rehab, but she sidestepped questions about Dad. The only thing she'd told Mac was that they both loved him very much and were coming to see him and Gunny on Friday. She told him not to worry; everything would be fine. Well, he *was* worried and everything was *not* fine. How the hell was he going to last three more days without losing it? He needed to get out of the house. Do something, anything, besides stare at the TV.

"Gunny!" Mac yelled, throwing the remote on the coffee table. "I'm going to the pub. You wanna go?"

"I thought we were going to cook hotdogs on the grill?" Gunny called out from the bedroom.

"I want to go out," he yelled agitatedly and snatched his keys from the hook. "Are you going or not?"

Gunny came down the hall tucking his T-shirt into his cargo shorts. "What's the matter?"

"I need to get out of this fucking house," he growled, crossing his arms over his chest. Gunny had been gone all day, playing with his little recruits. Left Mac with nothing but TV and his thoughts. He narrowed his eyes at Gunny. *Bastard.*

"I'm not so sure retirement is going to agree with you," Gunny said with evident exasperation. "It's been less than a week and you've already had a couple tantrums that would put a two-year-old to shame."

"I'm high-strung on a good day," Mac reminded him without guilt. "Boredom does not work for me. When I'm idle for too long I start cleaning my weapons." He cocked a brow at the smirking ass. "Trigger finger gets itchy."

"Guess we better get your toys replaced," Gunny said flatly. "I'm sure fighting with preteens will keep you occupied and your mind off the real weapons." Gunny slipped on his flip-flops and grabbed his shades from the table by the door. "Ready?"

"Private Whiney Pants is thirteen, thank you very much."

"Ah, that makes it better." Gunny's voice dripped with sarcasm as he stepped out into the late afternoon sun and put on his sunglasses.

Mac started to bark out a witty comeback as he locked the front door, but the sight of Gunny standing on the walk grabbed his attention. Gunny wore a pale yellow T-shirt that stretched taut over his muscular chest and highlighted his golden summer-tanned arms. His short hair was still damp from the shower he'd just taken, and his skin still held a slight flush from the hot water. The wraparound shades and cocky swagger made him look all badass. Fuck, his man was gorgeous. "Shut up" was the best retort he could come up with in the face of all that sexy. He pocketed the keys and slid his glasses down over his eyes and grabbed Gunny's hand. "C'mon," he gruffed.

Gunny jerked his hand out of Mac's after just two steps. "What the hell?" Mac demanded.

Gunny scanned the area, a slight panicked look on his face, before meeting Mac's gaze. "What's really going on, Mac?"

"What do you mean?" he snapped.

"You're literally vibrating with anger and you've never once, in all the years I've known you, attempted to hold my hand in public," he said, concerned. "Whatever is going on in your head is a lot more than just boredom."

Anger heated Mac's cheeks, and he glared at Gunny. "You ever think that maybe I didn't hold your hand because I wasn't allowed to?" he hissed.

"And you're still not allowed to," Gunny said calmly. "'Don't Ask, Don't Tell' is still very much a law until the president signs the repeal in September. You really want to take a chance on a possible discharge two months before we retire?"

Mac continued to stare icily at Gunny for a moment until the weight of his words sunk in and Mac's shoulders slumped. "Stupid law," he grouched. "I'll be glad when this shit is all over. It's all this unfamiliarity that is messing my head up."

"C'mon. We can talk about it on the way," Gunny said, indicating the sidewalk with a nod.

They fell in step, walking side by side, and to Mac's irritation, not holding hands. He'd kept such a tight rein on his feelings for Gunny, gotten very good at swallowing down and hiding his attraction for his lover, and he was tired of it. The last year it had become increasingly difficult to keep it under control, and now with retirement imminent, it was nearly impossible.

"You've been a lot different since you've been home this time," Gunny said thoughtfully. "You're always so cocksure and solid. This new Mac—" He shook his head. "I'm used to being the weaker of the two."

"You are not weak," Mac insisted.

"Okay, call it indecisive, unsure, whatever. The point is, I'm used to your cocky attitude. I love that you know what you want, where you're going, and you don't take no shit."

A jogger approached, and Mac waited, nodding as she passed, before responding. "It's easy not to take shit when you know your place, Gunny. I haven't had to make too many decisions outside of strategic planning."

Gunny made an indignant sound, and Mac could tell he was rolling his eyes, even hidden behind the dark wraparound shades. Mac bumped him with his shoulder. "It's true. We've always gotten together in between deployments and I didn't have anything to worry about except dominating you in the bedroom." Gunny made another disgusted grunt, and Mac grinned. "Most of the time. Is that better?"

"Yeah, but I was talking about there being more to me than a good piece of ass."

Mac took a quick glance at their surroundings: the house they walked in front of blocked by hedges, and no one on the streets. He grabbed Gunny's ass and squeezed it briefly but hard. "That's your best feature." Mac yelped, then laughed when Gunny shoved him. "Your brutishness the other one."

"Mmm hmm," Gunny hummed, rubbing at his abused butt cheek.

"Seriously, though," Mac told him sincerely. "I've never really had to plan for much. Uncle Sam has always told me where and when to go, and you take care of my money and make sure I have a place to stay on my downtime."

"So I keep control of your money and home and keep on telling you when and where to go," Gunny said easily with a shrug. "Problem solved."

"If only it were that easy," Mac sighed.

"Why isn't it?"

Mac pulled a leaf from a tree, studied the twisting and entwining veins running through the deep green. It reminded him of his own path, lots of places to go, but getting nowhere. "You've made sure I never have to work again. Beyond an exit ceremony and a honeymoon, we have no plans. How the fuck are you going to keep me out of trouble?" he finally asked, dropping the leaf. "Remember, I'm the one who had to set out snacks while the rest of the kids had family prayer on Sunday mornings. I still haven't learned how to sit still very long."

Gunny pulled open the door to the pub and ushered Mac in with a wave of his arm. "We'll just have to find you a hobby, then, won't we?"

Mac made a point to roam his eyes over Gunny's body as he walked past. "We will indeed."

There was a lot more weighing on Mac's mind. Realizations he'd come to after speaking with his mom and the fallout from Ted. But his head hurt from thinking too much, and there was no chance of finding some of the answers until he spoke to his dad. Right now he'd settle for a little peace in the form of an ice-cold draft and a game of pool.

The blast of cool air caused goose bumps to bloom on Mac's heated flesh as he stepped into O'Toole's. He pushed his glasses on his head and squinted in the dim light until his eyes adjusted. The place was fashioned after a true Irish pub, which Mac found ironic since it was owned by a couple with the surname Chin. Seemed Mrs. Chin had a thing for the Irish actor Peter O'Toole, so much so she insisted the bar be named O'Toole's and set the style of her place as a homage to the actor's heritage. Whatever her reasons or fancy, the place had great atmosphere and even better ale.

The pub was effectively a large wooden cavern of mahogany, walnut, and ebony, softly lit by lamps that hung from the ceiling. The wood-paneled walls set the overall theme, covered as they were by images, reminiscent of the Edwardian era, of men clutching swords, well-toned horses in midflight, and revolutionaries at war. Green leather stools assembled along the bar took up the entire south wall. A dark wooden corridor lined with photographs and emblems led to the pool tables, and Mac headed toward it. Gunny followed behind, and Mac waved at the few recognizable faces. The main bar was a bit subdued, the music low, with a mix of those coming in for a drink after a long work day, and those who came in for a late lunch or early dinner of Irish fare. The back bar was loud, busy, and the overall feeling much more upbeat.

Mac needed the upbeat atmosphere and the ale to subdue his thoughts.

GUNNY looked up from his brew toward a burst of whistles, hoots, and hollering from the pool table in the corner. Mac had his hand raised over his head, slapping a high five against the palm of his current partner, a huge smile on Mac's face. Obviously Mac's unbeaten streak was still going strong. Gunny had tired of the game over an hour ago, relegating his position at the top to a younger shark named Justin who had the same gusto for the game as Mac.

"He's in rare form tonight," Tom said, patting Gunny on the shoulder and taking the stool to his right.

"Yeah, he's definitely eating up the spotlight." Gunny gave his friend a curious look. "They kick you out of Jack's?"

Since his wife died four years previous, Tom had been a regular fixture at Jack's bar. Said he preferred the less fuss of Jack's and the smaller crowds over those of O'Toole's. Tom wasn't one to drink much, oftentimes his glass filled with nothing more than soda, but he knew everyone at Jack's and he loved pool.

"Nah! Jack's trying to drum up new meat. Wednesday night is now the night of cheap beer, hot wings, and drunken college boys." Tom scrunched up his face in disgust. "Too much alcohol and not enough sense ends in nothing but posturing and pissing contests." Tom waved over the bartender.

"Yes, sir?"

"Can I get a Coke, please?" Tom asked and dropped a couple bucks on the bar.

"Complaining about noisy kids and drinking soda," Gunny said with a snort. "Christ, Tom, next you're going to be one of those old cranky men who starts calling everyone whippersnappers and having coffee every morning with the rest of the gray hairs saying shit like, 'In my day.'"

"I had coffee at the diner this morning," Tom said with a chuckle. "Your man doesn't seem like he'll be joining the club anytime soon," he said with a nod in Mac's direction.

Gunny stiffened at the *your man* reference, but forced himself to relax. Mac chalked the end of his cue as he laughed at something his partner whispered in his ear. "Mac is a big noisy kid," Gunny drawled from behind his bottle as he sipped his beer. "I doubt he'll ever change."

"I believe you may be right," Tom snorted and then said, "Thanks, Kirk" when the bartender set a soda down in front of him. He took a drink before asking Gunny, "Getting excited about retirement?"

"Yeah," he answered absently, his attention drawn to the other side of the room. Mac moved to the end of the table and leaned down to take a shot. He looked up and saw Gunny staring at him, and a sly smile curled his lips; he winked before turning his attention back to the game, easily sinking a striped ball in the side pocket.

"Two more months?"

"Technically for Mac, although he's not working anymore," Gunny said, forcing his gaze away from Mac and his tight butt on display as he bent to take another shot. Gunny turned his stool to face the bar. "I've got four more months."

"Exit ceremony in September?"

"Yup." Gunny glanced at Tom, who was looking at him with a strange expression on his face, one Gunny couldn't read.

"I hear Obama is signing a repeal of the DADT law that same month," Tom said. He looked away and started playing with his straw.

"Saw that," Gunny said, keeping his voice neutral as a prickling of unease began to run along his nerve endings. It was beginning to irritate Gunny that the focus of his retirement and future was boiling down to whom he shared his bed with. Instead of looking forward to the next adventure of his life, he worried about family and friend reactions and dealing with a cranky Mac, who was struggling with the same. "Was there a point?" Gunny asked.

"Not really," Tom said, tossed the straw aside, and took a gulp of his Coke. "The coffee crew was talking about you going off on Wilson on the very subject."

"Wilson's an asshole."

"No argument there," Tom chuckled. "But it gave the crew a new subject to ponder with their morning cup of joe."

"Got to love small towns." Gunny finished the beer he'd been nursing for the last hour, wincing at the flavor, and pushed the bottle away. "Kirk, can I get another?"

Kirk waved a hand of acknowledgement at him from where he was drawing a draft.

"Don't matter to me either way, I just thought you'd want to know," Tom said, picking up his glass. "C'mon, looks like Mac has been victorious once again. Shall we go knock him off his throne?"

Gunny studied Tom for a moment. Tom wasn't a big guy, but he was a tough little bastard. He owned a contracting company and wasn't the kind of owner who sat behind a desk and ordered others around. He worked his ass off right along with his guys, and the well-defined muscles of his stocky frame proved it. One of the things Gunny liked most about Tom was his attitude. He didn't talk shit, was laidback and an all-around happy kind of guy. Still, there were times Gunny had gotten a glimpse of the sadness in Tom's eyes, and knew he'd loved his late wife immensely. To hold on to that kind of burden, the kind that would keep one from being truly happy.... *Damn, my obstacles don't seem quite so bad.* At least he had the person he loved in his life. He shook his head. What a fool.

"Hey Kirk, send my beer over to the pool tables." He gave Tom a wide grin and threw an arm around his shoulders. "Let's go claim the throne."

CHAPTER
Fifteen

THERE were two really good reasons why Mac didn't drink hard alcohol in public. One, he got a whiskey dick and horny as hell. Now privately, Gunny enjoyed that excessive liquor made his lover horny and downright ecstatic; whiskey dick doesn't go soft for hours. Publicly, especially with his lover in the same room, not such a good idea, which was the second reason Mac shouldn't, and didn't normally, get drunk with others around. He lost his ability to keep a rein on his control and became very touchy-feely. Needless to say, Mac spent his buzz time trying to seduce Gunny.

When Kirk brought Gunny's beer and yet another Jack Daniel's and Coke for Mac, Gunny should have known then it was going to be an interesting night.

"Rack 'em up," Mac barked in jubilance as he chalked his cue. "Going to show you boys who the top dog is." Mac waggled his brows at Gunny. "I like being a top dog, huh, Gunny?"

Bad. Bad. Bad, screamed a little voice in Gunny's head, but he pushed it away. He stared at the ceiling, eyes unfocused as he thought about what he should do for a split second. *Just one more game, then I'll get him out of here.* Gunny pulled the ball rack from its slot and scooped up the balls. He'd just have to keep some distance between himself and Mac until they left. "That's 'cause you're a Marine. We're always the top dogs," he joked, knowing that had not been what Mac had meant.

"You're a fucking Marine?" Mac's teammate hooted and slapped Mac on the back. "Discharged in '03 after nearly having my nuts shot off in Baghdad."

Gunny shook his head as Mac and Justin bumped chests and yelled, "Oorah! Semper fi!"

"Twenty-two years," Mac said proudly and then pointed at Gunny. "Same for that sexy beast."

"Oh, this could be interesting," Justin crowed. "You a Marine too?" he asked, pointing at Tom.

"Nope," Tom drawled, chalking up his cue stick.

"In that case, no sense in you preparing your stick, you'll be the one on your knees," Justin said crudely. He shrugged one shoulder at Gunny as if to say, *Sorry, man, you're the one stuck with the inferior.*

Gunny smiled and returned the rack to its slot and stepped back next to Tom. He picked up his bottle and took a long pull. "Shit's about to get real," he whispered and wiped a hand across his mouth. "And you came here to avoid posturing and pissing contests," Gunny snorted.

"Well, if you can't avoid them—" Tom picked up his glass and gave Gunny a roguish grin. "—kick their asses. Ready to top these dogs and do a little posturing of our own?"

"Fuck yeah," Gunny replied and clinked his bottle against Tom's glass.

Mac moved to the end of the table, leaned down, and lined up his shot. He pulled back his cue and with a smooth powerful thrust, sent the balls scattering, solids and stripes dropping into the pockets. Mac stood up, hungry eyes locking with Gunny's, and he licked his lips.

Bad. Bad. Bad. The words resounded in his head again, this time as loud as the crack of the balls. Yet even as his mind knew the truth of it, Gunny's body responded with a warm rush of heat as a result of Mac's unerring gaze.

"Solids," Mac called. He moved around to the side of the table to take his next shot, never taking his eyes from Gunny, until he was in position, and then scanned the table.

Gunny sighed in relief when Mac's mesmerizing gaze no longer held his, and he took a large pull from his beer.

While his inhibitions fled with the wind, his pool skills remained tight, and it took Mac less than five minutes to run the table and win the game.

Justin and Mac high fived, and the few people who had been standing around to watch cheered and clapped at Mac's success.

"Go wipe those smug grins off their faces," Gunny encouraged Tom.

"My pleasure."

Gunny took a stool at their high table. *Might as well get comfortable.* He doubted he'd be playing this round. Mac was good, but Tom was a fierce competitor and had been known to have some impressive runs of clearing a table on the break. As Tom racked the balls, Mac headed to the bar. Gunny thought about stopping him—Mac damn sure didn't need any more to drink—but he couldn't bring himself to do it. After the somber Mac he'd had to deal with the last couple of days, at least the man had a smile on his face and seemed happy.

Mac was still smiling when he returned from the bar with a tray of drinks. *Wonder how long that grin will last when he realizes his partner scratched on the break.* Gunny returned the grin warmly. *Top the top and get the man home before things go to hell.*

Mac set the tray down, picked up a bottle of beer and handed it to Gunny, then raised his glass of Jack and Coke. "To us," Mac said, his words slurred, and downed half his drink. His throat worked as he swallowed in long drawn-out gulps. The action was surprisingly arousing, considering Gunny's objection to Mac's excess.

"To us," he echoed and set the bottle back down without taking a drink. "You about ready to head home?"

"Nah, I'm still top dog," Mac said and glanced over to the pool table where Tom was calling out his shot and scowled. "At least I am for now."

"You don't need to win a game to prove anything to me. You'll always be top dog," Gunny assured him.

Mac leaned in close until their cheeks brushed and whispered, "You wanting some topping, baby?"

Baby? Oh yeah, Mac was beyond the feeling good stage and moving headfirst toward sloppy drunk. It was the only time he had ever called Gunny baby. Still, Gunny squirmed a little against his stool when Mac's stubbled jaw prickled across his five o'clock shadow, and Mac's warm breath tickled his ear. "Not till we get home."

Mac straightened, swaying ever so slightly. "There's a lock on the bathroom door."

Gunny pursed his lips and shook his head. "Yeah, not going to happen," he told him adamantly.

"C'mon, baby. Just a quick blowjob," he said huskily and brushed the back of his knuckles along the outer seam along Gunny's thigh. "Remember that time in Key West?"

The image of him on his knees, one of Mac's big paws clutching the white porcelain sink, the other gripping the back of Gunny's head, flashed in his mind. "I remember," he admitted, his voice a little tight. Gunny shifted in his seat, a pleasant ache of arousal settling into his groin from the memory and Mac's nearness. He was about to remind Mac of where they were and who was watching when Tom called out, "Now who's on top?" His boast was followed by cheers and whistles from the spectators.

"What'd you do, cheat?" Mac said goodheartedly, downed the rest of his drink, and to Gunny's great relief, spun around and stomped over to the pool table. "Don't get too comfortable. I'll rack 'em."

Justin flopped in a stool across from Gunny, tucked his hair behind his ears, and pointed at the bottles. "One of these for me?"

"Help yourself."

"Thanks, man," he said and grabbed one and took a long pull. "That Tom is a hell of a player for a civilian." He smirked. "So twenty years, huh? What's your rank?"

Gunny nodded, not bothering to correct the man on his years of service. "Master Gunnery Sergeant."

Justin whistled low. "Nice. I always wanted to make a career of the Corps." Justin stared at his bottle for a moment, an angry expression on his face. "Fucking stray bullets," he said bitterly.

"Sorry to hear that," Gunny said sincerely, as he watched Mac step back from the table to allow Tom to break. How many times had he thanked his lucky stars that he'd never been wounded and Mac had come home whole from a mission?

Justin waved it off with a hand. "It's cool. Got a great job, a wife that don't bitch too much and a second kid on the way." Justin shrugged. "It all worked out. What about you? You got a wife and kids?"

"Nope. Been married to the Corps." Gunny grinned from behind his bottle as he took a small sip. Mac would so not appreciate being called a wife, but he damn sure could be a kid sometimes.

"Sorry about that, man." Justin laughed. "That's got to be hell on the sex life, being married to a bunch of stinky and sweaty Marines."

"That it does," Gunny chuckled. His smile grew wider as he stole a glance at Mac. The lot of them might be hell, but one sweaty Marine was paradise on earth. "Looks like you're about to be bested," Gunny said with a nod toward Tom, effectively steering the conversation away from personal talk.

"No way!" Justin said incredulously and focused his attention on the game.

Tom pointed his cue toward the far right pocket, calling his shot, but Gunny scarcely paid attention, too busy taking in the sight of Mac standing rigid, bulging arms across his muscular chest, and looking so fucking edible. The beer Gunny had consumed was starting to have an effect on his control over his libido, and it was becoming increasingly difficult to come up with a good reason why a bathroom with a locked door was a bad idea. Definitely time to head home and let Mac reclaim his top-dog position.

Tom made the shot easily; the small crowd patted both him and Mac on the back in congratulations, and one spectator handed both men fresh drinks. Gunny cringed when Mac tipped his head back and swallowed the liquid in one big gulp. Mac damn sure would be feeling this night come morning. Mac slammed the empty glass down on the nearest table and stumbled his way to Gunny.

"Did you see that shit?" he slurred. "Bastard took advantage of my drunken state." Mac threw an arm around Gunny's shoulders and squeezed. "I call rematch."

"You might want to wait till next time," Gunny told him and tried to nudge him away a little, but Mac held tight.

"Gunny's right," Tom chuckled. "Be easier when you're not seeing two of everything."

"Gunny is right about everything," Mac garbled. He brought his hand to the back of Gunny's neck, shaking it playfully. "Aren't you, babe?" Mac didn't wait for an answer, instead yelled out, "Hey, waiter, bring us another round."

From the slight crease in Justin's brow and the way his eyes narrowed in on Mac's blunt fingers stroking the side of Gunny's neck, he hadn't missed the term of endearment or the obvious familiarity between him and Mac. *Definitely time to go.*

A petite little brunette who'd come on shift not too long ago showed up at the table. "What can I get you, sir?" she asked, her question directed at Mac.

"Bring us another round," he repeated, with a wave toward the glasses and bottles stacked on the table.

"Sure, no problem," she said pleasantly.

Carla—from what her name tag said—picked up empty glasses and bottles from the table, studying the labels as she placed them on her tray. Mac went back to teasing Tom about being a cheater. Gunny took the opportunity of Mac's distraction to say quietly to Carla, "We don't need another round, but thank you."

Carla nodded, finished picking up the empties, and hurried away.

Gunny's unease grew as Justin sat brooding and continued to stare at Mac's hand caressing Gunny's neck. Gunny nudged the drunken man with his shoulder. "You ready to go?" he asked hopefully.

Mac's grin was wicked when he looked down at Gunny and asked, "You reconsider my offer of a locked door?"

Mac ran his thumb along Gunny's jaw and gently brushed it across his bottom lip. The intimate touch caused alarm to surge through

Gunny, the feeling intensified when Justin's frown deepened. "No," Gunny hissed and shrugged off Mac's arm. "Time to go home."

Mac was either too intoxicated to notice the warning in Gunny's voice or simply ignored it, staring at Gunny and not so discreetly adjusting the bulge in his shorts. "Yeah. Our bed is a better idea." His mouth curled up into a crooked grin.

Gunny gritted his teeth, his muscles tensing when Justin slammed his bottle down on the table. *Here it comes.*

"What the fuck! You're a fucking fag, Mac?" Justin spat.

Mac stiffened next to Gunny; all conversation came to an abrupt halt, and heads turned toward Justin. Tom's eyes narrowed, and he inched closer to Justin as Gunny eased slowly to his feet.

"What did you just call me?" Mac snarled.

"I didn't call you anything. The way you're rubbing on your buddy there like a dog in heat, I *asked* if you were a fucking fag." Justin stood, hands flat on the table, a challenging gleam in his eyes.

"You don't want to do this, son," Gunny cautioned, trying his best to keep his voice calm.

The dumbass didn't back down. "Well?" Justin demanded.

Mac was literally vibrating with anger next to him, and Gunny placed a hand against Mac's lower back and rubbed. "Let's just go home, Mac. We don't want to do this here."

Mac glared at Gunny. "Did you hear what he just asked me?"

"C'mon, let's just go, this guy isn't worth it," Gunny added, keeping his voice even.

"I don't like that word," Mac growled, turning his attention back to Justin. His entire frame tensed and bulged as he appeared to ready himself for a fight. "Someone needs to teach you some fucking manners, boy."

This was the kind of shit they had to look forward to? A night of fun, laughter, and mutual respect shattered because of an affectionate touch? Gunny sighed in resignation and waited to see if Justin was stupid enough to push Mac further or would smarten up and walk away.

"I'll take that as a yes." Justin scrunched up his face in disgust and spat on the table.

Obviously Justin was that stupid.

It never ceased to amaze Gunny how alcohol could make some idiots think they were superheroes. Justin was a good four inches shorter than Mac, easily fifty pounds lighter, and while not fat, definitely not in the best shape. Justin might have been ten years younger, but Mac was still faster and stronger than most men half his age. Mac would snap this punk like a twig, if Gunny stood silently by and allowed it. As much as he'd like to see his lover teach the asshole some manners, they couldn't afford the shit storm that would blow in afterward.

Tom obviously didn't have the same concerns.

"I don't like that word either," Tom hissed and with lightning speed cocked his arm back. Knuckles connected to jaw, sending Justin flying. "Get him out of here," Tom told Gunny with an eager grin on his face and dove on top of Justin.

Gunny wasted no time in wrapping his arms around Mac's chest and pulling him backward through the crowd rushing to see the fight.

"Turn me loose," Mac bellowed as he struggled to free himself.

Gunny tightened his hold. "Not a chance, champ. Tom's got this one."

Mac cursed and struggled all the way through the pub and out the front door. "Sorry, bud, but you're just going to have to save all that aggression for when we get home," Gunny said seductively in Mac's ear once they were out on the front walk alone. He ran his tongue along the outside of Mac's ear and then nipped on his earlobe. "I can handle anything you got to give, baby."

Mac went quiet and stopped struggling and then turned his head to meet Gunny's hungry gaze. He hesitated for a long moment, his big chest heaving, as he tried to decide whether to keep fighting to go back in the pub or take Gunny up on his offer. Gunny ground his hardening cock against Mac's ass, helping him with his decision.

Mac closed his eyes, and he visibly shuddered. When he opened them again, Gunny knew the need of the whiskey dick overpowered the need for blood by the lust sparkling in those hazel eyes. "I'm drunk," Mac said wickedly.

"I know." Gunny smirked.

Mac's anger clearly fled, and he laughed. "Your ass."

Gunny released his hold on Mac and gave him a little shove to get him started toward home. When Mac stumbled, Gunny wrapped his arm around Mac's waist to steady him. Mac started to hum and slung his arm over Gunny's shoulder. As they weaved and swayed their way back down the walk, Gunny couldn't help but think, *Better a sore ass than having to bail Mac out of jail.* He'd have to thank Tom for taking one for Mac and for giving Gunny the opportunity to take one for the team as well.

CHAPTER
Sixteen

MAC winced when the ice pack over his eyes was pulled away, and the bright light of the early afternoon sun caused the throb in his head to intensify. "Please. I beg of you. Just shoot me," he groaned pitifully.

"Here, take these."

"For the love of God, Gunny, lower your voice," Mac begged and pulled the pillow over his face. Even the muffled sound of Gunny's chuckling was too much, and Mac groaned again.

"C'mon. I've got something for your head and you need the fluids," Gunny insisted and tugged at the pillow.

Mac clutched it tighter. "No."

"It will make you feel better," Gunny promised.

"I don't want to feel better. I want you to shoot me and put me out of my misery."

"Fine. Suffer, then," Gunny said in an exasperated tone.

Mac lay there a moment in the darkened silence. The drumbeat banging in his head and the churning of his gut didn't decrease, and now he couldn't breathe. He threw the pillow off and grudgingly sat up. The room spun, and Mac grabbed his head in both hands, moaning until the Tilt-A-Whirl of the room slowed. On the table in front of him was a glass of ice water and two pills. "What are they?" Mac asked, already reaching for them. He popped them in his mouth and chased them down with a sip of water.

"Tylenol."

Mac glared at Gunny as he flopped down on the couch and jostled him. "What is this shit?" he asked and wrinkled his nose in disgust at the funny taste of the water.

"Just drink it, you big baby. It's Pedialyte."

"Pedia what?" Mac asked and sniffed the offending liquid. There was no scent, but whatever was in it had left a rank, metallic taste in his mouth. He smelled it again for good measure.

"Pedialyte. It helps balance the electrolytes you threw out of whack with your bright idea of slamming Jack Daniel's," Gunny told him pointedly. "Now shut up and drink it."

"Aren't you supposed to be at work?" Mac grumbled. He tipped up the glass and tried to drink the entire contents in one big gulp, but the convulsion in his gut advised him against it, and he set the glass down half-full.

"Nope. Stayed home to take care of my sick *baby*," Gunny snorted.

Mac considered the glass again for a moment, but his stomach rolled so badly he thought better of it and slumped over and buried his head in Gunny's lap. "What the hell did I do last night?"

Gunny ran his hand over Mac's head. The caress eased the throb slightly. Mac moaned and drew his legs up, snuggled in closer. "What's the last thing you remember?" Gunny asked softly.

Mac considered the question for a moment. Leaving the house and arriving at O'Toole's were clear memories. Having fun playing pool, drinking, winning, and then only small flashes of the people in the pub, Gunny's ass, blowjobs—Mac tried to put the disconnected images together, but it made his head hurt and he gave up. "I know I was kicking ass on the pool table and having a hell of a good time," he admitted. "I keep getting flashes of you naked and on your hands and knees so I'm pretty sure we had amazing sex." Mac lifted his head and looked up at Gunny. "I'm hoping the hot sex was after we left the bar."

"Yeah, the hot sex came after we got home," Gunny reassured him with a sly grin.

"Thank God," Mac mumbled and laid his head down.

"You did try to get me to blow you in the bathroom, and umm, yeah, you started the touchy-feely thing and called me *baby*."

"Ugh." Mac had the sinking feeling he wasn't going to like what he was about to hear. Fuck! What the hell had he been thinking drinking like that? *Stupid. Stupid. Stupid.* He knew better. "Did anyone notice?"

"Well, I can't be sure if anyone else saw it, but Tom and Justin had a front-row seat," Gunny said cautiously.

Mac cringed as Gunny recounted what had happened with Justin. The churning in his gut and the throb in his head became almost unbearable as the guilt pressed down on him. He closed his eyes and swallowed the bile that rose in his throat.

"Shit! Is he okay?" Mac asked worriedly when Gunny told him what Tom had done.

"Yeah, he's fine. I talked to him this morning. After he dove on top of Justin, he just held him down until some guys in the crowd broke it up. Not a scratch on him."

"And now everyone knows. Fuck! I am so sorry, Gunny," Mac said sincerely and sat up. He swallowed repeatedly as his mouth filled with saliva, fighting to keep the small amount of liquid from coming back up. "If our superiors get wind of this, we are so fucked, Gunny," Mac said miserably and hung his head in his hands.

"Hey," Gunny murmured, rubbing Mac's back. "I don't think it's all that bad. Lots of guys get touchy with their buds when they're drinking, and from what Tom said, he went on an impressive rant when they pulled him and Justin apart. By the end of it, Tom was convinced pretty much everyone thought Justin was a drunken asshole."

"Then I couldn't have been that bad," Mac said. He dropped his hands, and looked at Gunny hopefully.

Gunny pursed his lips and blew out a long breath through his nose. "Maybe to those not within earshot."

"What?" Mac asked in alarm.

"I don't think you touching me looked all that bad by anyone looking on. It was the way you were eating me up with your eyes and a couple of your comments. I'm pretty sure Justin and Tom both know we're more than just friends." Gunny gave him a sympathetic look. "Your comment, 'Our bed is a better idea' was a dead giveaway."

"Goddammit, Gunny. Why the hell didn't you get me out of there? Or at the very least, gag me?"

"That's my kink," Gunny said wryly. "Anyway, I did try to get you out of there." Gunny ran a hand over his buzz cut and sighed. "I should have tried harder. But you were having such a good time. I hadn't seen you smile and laugh like that since you've been home." His shoulders slumped. "I'm sorry."

"Nah, it's not your fault," Mac assured him. He pushed up close and laid his head on Gunny's shoulder. "I know better than to go to the bar when I'm pissed off and bored. It's a dangerous combination."

"You know, I've been thinking about it all morning," Gunny said thoughtfully.

"About?" he prodded.

"Everyone was having such a great time, and the minute Justin suspected we might be fucking, it was like we were less than shit. It didn't matter that only moments before he'd been impressed with our military status, or pool abilities, or the fact that he seemed to really be enjoying himself." Gunny snapped his fingers. "*Poof*! Just like that we're fucking scum of the earth."

"Some people are assholes. Nothing you can do about it. And, hey, it's not like you've never heard that slur before."

"No, but it's the first time I had it directed at me personally and it sucked!"

"Mom said the same thing the other day." Mac rubbed his temple, trying to ease the ache in his head, as he thought back to the conversation. Maybe she had been right; maybe it was worse. He remembered being really pissed off but couldn't recall exactly how it felt when Justin started his shit. "She said it would be a whole lot different. I don't think I paid it much thought."

"I've heard it, read about the bashing and the contempt. Seen it in the news, religious fanatics telling the world God hates fags. She's right. It's—Mac, I was no longer a Marine in that bastard's eyes. I wasn't even a man, nothing more than a fucking faggot who deserved his contempt. And I couldn't even defend myself," he bit out angrily.

"Had to sit there and take it so I don't lose my rank, my pension, respect. Everything I've busted my ass for."

"Only a couple more months," Mac said gently, and massaged the tense muscles along Gunny's chest and abdomen. "We just have to be careful till September; then it don't matter."

"And then what? It's not as if people like Justin are going to go, 'oh look the law's repealed, must mean the queers are cool now,'" Gunny said bitterly.

"No, but at least we can defend ourselves and not have to worry about our pensions and shit."

"And everything will be just hearts and rainbows," Gunny drawled sarcastically. "What the hell ever—" he growled and shoved Mac off him and stomped toward the hall.

"What the hell?" Mac yelled, the stabbing pain in his head reminding him to lower his voice. "Why are you mad at me?" he asked, completely confused at the sudden shift in Gunny's attitude.

Gunny didn't respond.

Mac stayed where he was, trying to figure out what had just happened, his brain still a little foggy from the alcohol. Finally, he stood slowly and stumbled down the hall. He found Gunny in the bathroom setting the taps on the shower. "Why are you mad at me?" Mac repeated.

"I'm not mad at you," Gunny pointed out. "I'm pissed off at the whole fucked-up situation. You've been this crazy man for the last week and now all of a sudden have this *'It don't matter'* attitude."

"I didn't say that. I said after we retire it won't matter if people know." Mac shoved Gunny out of the way, pulled up the lever to shut off the drain and change the flow of the water.

"What the hell are you doing?" Gunny attempted to flip the lever to release the drain, but Mac pushed his hand away. Gunny's face flushed, and he glared at Mac. "I'm trying to take a shower here, do you fucking mind?"

"And I want to take a bath. So either lower your voice and get your ass in the tub with me or wait." He gave Gunny a pointed look. "I'm the sick one here."

"Self-induced," Gunny grumbled, his frustration apparent in his voice. He pulled off his T-shirt and threw it on the floor. "Why are you the one getting to choose? I do believe I was here first." Gunny arched a brow. "And I was gearing up for a hell of a snit—which, I may add, you totally just fucked up with that damn pouty face."

"I don't pout," Mac chafed.

Gunny rolled his eyes and made a growly bear sound, but he shoved his pants off and kicked them haphazardly to the side and stepped into the tub.

"Besides, I knew you would want to take one with me, and you can just as easily have your snit while soaking in a tub with me as you can standing in the shower. Probably easier," Mac added with a smirk. "At least you won't have to hold me up while you're having it." Mac quickly discarded his own clothes and stepped in the tub behind Gunny.

"Hey—"

"My head hurts so I get the bath pillow," he interrupted and sank into the tub. "C'mon, let me hold you while you gripe and groan," Mac encouraged and patted his chest. "Lay your head right here and tell your man all about your woes."

"I seriously don't like you right now," Gunny said with a huff. He eased down between Mac's spread legs and laid his head exactly where Mac had indicated.

"You're so easy," Mac murmured and kissed the side of Gunny's head. "Okay, let me hear it. Dr. Jones is now available."

Gunny hesitated briefly, then chuckled. "I forgot what I was complaining about." He looked up and gave Mac a knowing grin. "This was a way better idea than mine," he admitted.

"My ideas usually are better," Mac teased.

"Like the Jack last night?" Gunny countered.

"Shut up," he complained and slapped Gunny playfully on the chest. "And keep your voice down, my head hurts, ya know."

"Again—"

"Ah, ah." Mac twitched a finger. "I know, I know. You're getting a bit repetitive so knock it the hell off. You're making it worse."

"Sorry," Gunny laughed softly.

Mac wrapped his arms around Gunny's chest as the tub filled. The sound of the rushing water, and Gunny's warm body against his, went a long way in soothing what ailed Mac. Yeah, this was a way better idea than a shower. When the tub was filled, Mac reached up and flipped off the tap with his toes.

"So back to what you were grumbling about earlier, I never said it didn't matter. I know it does and I'll admit that you and Mom were, maybe, quite possibly right."

"Just admit it for once in your life that I'm right and you're wrong," Gunny coaxed.

"I thought I was wrong once, but I was only mistaken," Mac said flippantly.

"Cheeky bastard," Gunny snorted and pinched the inside of Mac's thigh.

Mac yelped and grabbed a handful of hair on Gunny's chest and tugged.

"Okay! Ow!" Gunny hooted and slapped Mac's hand away. "Fine, I give," Gunny muttered and ran his hands along Mac's thighs, massaging the muscles. "So tell me again how I'm right?"

"Yes, Gunny, you were right," Mac said sincerely and laid his head back. "You were right that the whole coming-out thing is going to suck, but honestly that isn't what has been worrying me, or what's been driving me to become a whack job the last few weeks."

"No?" Gunny asked hesitantly.

"Nope. I'm more worried about the whole—" Mac huffed out a breath in frustration, trying to find the right words. "I don't know, Gunny. It's like, I've always known who I was, what was expected of me, and now I have no fucking clue what I'm going to do next." Mac squeezed Gunny. "And before you ask. Yes, the first thing is the whole exit ceremony, wedding, and honeymoon. But then what? I'm not going to spend my retirement fighting with preteens playing *Call of Duty*. I got the short-term agenda covered but long term? Not a fucking clue."

"I thought we would just ride off into the sunset together. All fairy tale and shit," Gunny teased.

"Are you my Prince Charming, Gunny? Going to carry me away on your big white steed?" Mac said seductively.

"Fuck Prince Charming, I want to be your big white steed," Gunny wiggled against him, emphasizing his meaning.

"Deal! I'll be PC and you can be, umm—"

"Hot, wonderful, sexy, smart stallion works just fine for me," Gunny suggested.

Mac laughed and shook his head. He and Gunny never stayed angry when they were around each other. It was as if they always knew what the other was feeling and were able to stave off the uglier emotions. It didn't mean that either of them took the other's feelings lightly or deemed them unimportant. After being together as long as they had, oftentimes only for short visits, they learned not to discuss shit when they were angry. It was a waste of time; nothing got resolved when they had to scream over the other. And now, they were getting too fucking old to be wasting time with such crap.

He kissed Gunny on the temple. "Yes, all those things and more." Mac smirked. "But seriously, I don't like not having a plan."

"We have that in common," Gunny muttered. "Not so much the no-plan thing, I figure we have plenty of time for figuring that out, but the new role in our future, I'm not so sure I'm going to like."

Mac grabbed a bar of soap from the small shelf and lathered his hands while he chewed on Gunny's words. The only thing Mac had been really concentrating on the last few months was his relationship with Gunny. Not the future, nothing but getting home and starting their life together. Maybe that was selfish.

"We don't have to tell anyone else," Mac said sincerely. He continued to wash Gunny as he spoke. "Nothing has to change. Go back to the way it's always been. Just two happy bachelors," he teased lightly.

Gunny shifted, the water sloshing over the side of the tub as he turned and looked at Mac. "Is that what you want?"

Mac thought about it for a moment, choosing his words carefully before he spoke. "No. I'm getting old, Gunny. And to tell you the truth I'm tired of having to watch what I say to you and guard my emotions when others are around. I've been so looking forward to finally being able to relax and let go, but in my excitement, I didn't stop to think about what the fallout from releasing the reins could do to you."

"And you," Gunny reminded him.

Mac's chest ached when he remembered the look on his dad's face as he stared at Ted, refusing to look at his other son. "Yeah, and me," he murmured. "I'll do whatever you want," he said honestly and brushed his thumb along the stubble on Gunny's chin. "I promise not to drink too much when we're in town if you promise to at least go somewhere with me once a year where I can."

Gunny stared at him for a long moment, a strange play of emotions crossing his face, ones Mac was having a difficult time reading. He knew what he wanted, was prepared to deal with the crap, but he couldn't make that same choice for Gunny.

"That's just wrong," Gunny finally responded and shook his head. "You shouldn't have to ask me to take you somewhere and let you get drunk so you can let go and show your feelings for me somewhere other than at home."

"It is what it is," Mac said with a shrug. "You know I'd do anything for you."

"That works both ways." Gunny's brows furrowed, jaw set defiantly. "Why should I care what dumbasses like Justin think of me?" He shook his head vigorously, a gleam sparkling in his eyes. "Fuck him and fuck anyone else who has a problem with me. If you want to get drunk and manhandle me? Do it. You want to grope me in the grocery store? Do it!" Gunny's voice rose as he seemed to become more confident in his conviction. "A couple more months and we can do whatever the fuck we want."

Mac placed a finger over Gunny's lips. "Yes *we* can, but could we please do it a little quieter for today?"

"Sorry," Gunny said lowly.

"And second, don't do this just for me. I'm okay taking it slow. So I'll talk to Dad on Friday, and then we can sit down and figure out how you're going to keep me busy and out of trouble."

"And we need to figure out when we should talk to my family," Gunny added.

"You want to do that now?"

"No," Gunny said with a quirky grin. "But I figure I owe you the same awkward family visit you made me sit through. Fair is fair."

After what had happened with his own family, the thought of enduring it again with Gunny's made Mac's stomach roll, not such a good thing considering the way he'd abused it. But he did owe Gunny, and there was no way in hell he'd ever let Gunny experience it alone. But they would not be doing it today and damn sure not with a hangover. Mac grabbed Gunny's shoulders and pulled him down and wrapped his arms around him. "I'll be there, but can I get through Dad and the hangover first, please?" he asked with a groan.

"No problem. I'm going to need you at your best to deal with Grandpa anyway," Gunny laughed.

Mac groaned again. The crotchety old man already hated Mac. All because he reminded the old bastard of some guy he'd had a fight with forty years ago. At least Mac knew what to expect and knew well enough, when around Grandpa, to stay out of the reach of his cane.

Mac closed his eyes, relaxing further into the tub. He didn't have to worry about Grandpa today. One did not engage crotchety old men with a hangover. A slow reaction time would prove most painful, and with what he and Gunny were going to share with the old man, Mac would definitely need quick reflexes.

CHAPTER
Seventeen

OPENING the Styrofoam container, Mac scowled at the fried chicken as if it were the reason he'd burnt the pork tenderloin. He'd busted his ass since Gunny had left for work. The house was spotless, aired out, candles burning, and he'd planned to make his dad's favorite meal, but that had gone to shit. He grabbed a set of tongs from the drawer and placed the chicken in a covered casserole dish and set it in the oven to keep it warm. At least he hadn't turned the potatoes and corn into black crispy critters like he had the meat. With a sigh, Mac threw the container in the trash can as he headed toward the living room.

"This sucks," he muttered and threw himself on the couch.

Snatch and grab missions, dropping into war zones, hunting some of the most dangerous men on the fucking planet, he'd done them all and never been this nervous. It was going to tear him up if his dad rejected his and Gunny's relationship. No matter the reaction, he and Gunny were going to be together, but it would be nice if his family were there to be a part of that future.

Mac checked his watch and groaned. *Thirty minutes till showtime.* He laid his head back and shut his eyes, doing his best to breathe evenly as his chest tightened and his gut rolled. His attempt to calm himself was foiled when the door burst open, and Mac nearly jumped out of his skin. "Christ, you scared the shit out of me," Mac huffed and put a hand over his speeding heart. "What the hell are you doing here?"

"You didn't actually think I'd let you go through this alone, did you?" Gunny asked with a cheeky grin on his face and a bouquet of wildflowers in his hand.

"Yeah, well, next time you mind calling me? I'm too old to be surprised like that." He grunted but couldn't contain the amusement in his voice.

Gunny chuckled as he moved to the couch and kissed Mac on the cheek. "Sorry, old man."

"Uh-huh. Those for me?" he asked and reached out for the flowers.

"Nope," Gunny said and spun around. "They're to butter up your mom. Figure if it all goes south, three against one, we got a shot against Theodore."

Mac hefted himself up from the couch and followed Gunny into the kitchen. "You're fucking up my living in denial theory." He leaned against the counter next to the sink as Gunny filled a vase with water and began arranging the flowers. "See, in my head, Dad's going to come in, give me a hug, pat me on the head, and apologize. After that, we can all head out for a beer and burger."

"Mmm hmm. Is that why I smell fried chicken?" Gunny inquired mockingly. "Which, come to think of it, is weird since I thought you were making pork?"

"We're not going to talk about that." Mac grunted and pushed off the counter. "I made sweet tea. You want some?"

"Burned it, did you?" Gunny laughed heartily.

Mac grabbed the tea pitcher from the fridge and snagged a couple of glasses, taking them to the island counter. "I said we are *not* going to talk about that," Mac grumbled.

Gunny wrapped his arms around Mac. "I know you're nervous," he said gently, his lips close to Mac's ear. "But it's going to be okay. Either way I'm here," he promised and kissed Mac's earlobe, causing him to shudder.

"Don't get me wrong, I do appreciate it," Mac said thoughtfully. His hands shook as he poured them each a glass of tea. "But you being here isn't going to stop it from ripping my fucking heart out if this goes bad." Mac set the pitcher aside, splayed his hands out on the countertop, and took in a deep breath, holding it briefly before letting it out slowly. He hated this shit. Hated feeling helpless and unsure of himself. The last thing he wanted was to appear weak in front of Gunny, but no matter how hard he tried he just couldn't help being scared shitless. He took one more calming breath.

"I know," Gunny murmured. He stroked his hand soothingly along Mac's stomach. "I'll hold you together if you start to fall apart."

Mac swallowed the lump in his throat and leaned back against Gunny. "Christ, you're turning into such a sappy bastard," he said hoarsely.

Gunny didn't say anything; he didn't need to. Instead he gave Mac what he needed most—Gunny's arms around him—let him lean against his powerful chest, feel Gunny's strength at his back, until Mac was able to get control of his emotions.

"They should be here soon. Better get the table set," Mac said gruffly and straightened.

"I'll get changed and be back to help you." Gunny squeezed him one last time and released his hold on Mac.

Before he could get away, Mac latched on to Gunny's arm and stopped him. "Thank you for coming home early."

"You're welcome," Gunny said sincerely and placed a tender kiss to Mac's lips. "I wouldn't have missed it."

Mac nodded, kissed him back, and went to grab a stack of plates from the cupboard. By the time he had the china and cutlery on the dining room table, Gunny joined him dressed in jeans and a blue button-up shirt. Mac hummed quietly to himself. Gunny had dressed up for the occasion. They quietly finished setting the table, the bouquet of daisies, carnations, and wildflowers in the center.

Mac would have preferred to have had the opportunity to relax, maybe have a beer, or better yet, a stiff drink to take the edge off his nerves before his parents arrived. No such luck. Just as they finished, the doorbell rang. Mac's gut hit his toes with the chiming of the bells, and he looked at Gunny as panic raced through his veins and his breath caught.

"You want me to get it?" Gunny asked.

Mac thought about it for a second. Actually he was debating running to the bathroom to upchuck the tea churning in his gut, versus passing out from the lack of oxygen. In the end, he pulled a deep breath into his lungs and shook his head. "I got it," he said dimly and patted Gunny on the shoulder as he walked by. He could feel Gunny move up close behind him, flanking him as he headed to the door. He stole one last look at Gunny, who gave him a supportive smile, and then turned the knob.

His mom stood on the front stoop dressed in a pale-yellow short set, a wide grin on her face and a covered cake pan in her hand. "I brought your favorite," she said brightly and kissed Mac's cheek as she handed him the cake.

"Chocolate cake?" Mac asked hopefully, steadfastly keeping his eyes on his mom.

"You have another favorite?" she asked sarcastically and swatted him playfully on the arm. "Don't worry, Gunther, I frosted half of it with butter cream," Mom appeased Gunny and hugged him.

"You know what I like, Clare," Gunny told her happily. He snatched the pan from Mac and headed for the kitchen, Mac's mom following.

With trepidation, Mac met his dad's gaze. "Dad," he said, voice cracking. Crap, he hated how weak he sounded. He cleared his throat and in a stronger voice said, "C'mon in."

Mac held his breath, afraid his dad would look at him, more afraid he wouldn't. The last time he'd felt this way, he had been ten, after handing his dad his report card, knowing he'd disappointed him. To Mac's great relief, his dad looked him straight in the eye, gave him a small smile, and patted Mac on the arm as he stepped past him and followed his wife and Gunny into the kitchen. Mac let out the breath he'd been holding and shut the door. His dad wasn't one to discuss his feelings, nor had he ever been affectionate. The small smile and pat were like a balm to Mac's unsteady nerves. It meant his dad wasn't turning away but actually embracing him and Gunny as a couple. Mac stood there for a few precious seconds until his racing heart slowed, and then joined his family in the living room.

Mac's parents were sitting stiffly, side by side on the couch, Gunny standing like a sentry, waiting to see where Mac would sit. His lover meant what he said earlier, had taken it to heart as evident by the way he moved up behind Mac as he took a seat across from his mom and dad.

"Something smells delicious," his mom said conversationally.

"KFC," Mac said sheepishly. "I burned the pork," he admitted.

His mom gave him a small smile. She had always been able to read him, and more than likely, could read his nervousness in the tension of his muscles and the wariness in his eyes. He'd never been able to hide much from her—strike that. Mac thought he had been good at hiding things, but the conversation about his and Gunny's relationship was proof she had read right through his omission.

"I'm sure it will be lovely. Your dad loves KFC, but I rarely allow him to have it." Clare patted her husband's leg lovingly. "His cholesterol has been a bit high as of late."

"Shit… sorry," Mac mumbled. "I mean crap," he corrected. "I can call and order something else, it will only take me a moment." He started to rise, but his father's voice stopped him.

"Don't you dare," he ordered Mac and then turned to his wife with a pleading look. "I won't tell the doctor if you won't?"

"Fine," she conceded. "But that means back to salads and fish next week."

Mac chuckled softly at the look of disgust on his father's face and the incoherent grumbled words. His dad had always been a meat, potatoes, and heavy gravy kind of guy. Rabbit food, as he often called it, had to be pure torture for Theodore.

The silence descended upon them after the chuckling died down. It felt thick, and Mac swore he could feel its weight like that of heavy cloud pressing down on him, surrounding him, making it difficult to breathe. His pulse quickened, and he was itchy. Edgy. As the silence continued to stretch out, no one looked anyone in the eye, and Mac thought he'd crawl out of his skin.

Gunny, bless his big wonderful fucking heart, broke the silence. "Clare, Theodore, can I get either of you something to drink?"

Damn, he could kiss his man. Mac glanced up at his savior, Gunny winking at him with a half smile.

"I'll have a glass of water if it's not too much trouble," Mac's mom said.

"Tea for me, please," his dad added.

"Sure, be right back." Gunny squeezed Mac's shoulder briefly and said, "Mac, why don't you tell your parents about the plans we have to keep you out of trouble?"

Mac looked back at Gunny, his smile falling, and he glared as panic surged through him. His dad might seem okay right now, but Mac doubted that would last long if he told him what he and Gunny had planned to do at the exit ceremony. And he was damn sure his dad wasn't ready to hear about his son's plans to marry another man.

Gunny squeezed Mac's shoulder again. "Mac came up with a great idea to build a small greenhouse in the backyard."

Mac slumped in easement, and once again he wanted to kiss the man. Right after he slapped him of course for freaking him the fuck out. He'd only mentioned the idea to Gunny once about six months ago and was surprised he'd remember it, let alone thought to bring it up.

"What a wonderful idea," his mom squealed. "You are so wonderful with plants, and now you'll be able to enjoy gardening year-round."

The three of them made small talk about the construction of the structure as well as the kinds of flowers and vegetables that would grow best. Gunny took his previous position once he passed out drinks.

The conversation wasn't particularly uncomfortable, but everyone seemed to have a tense edge, no one ready to talk about or broach the subject of the very obvious elephant in the room. It wasn't until they had all moved into the dining room with their plates filled that the subject was finally brought up. Surprisingly, it was Mac's dad who started it.

"Your brother signed himself out of rehab," Dad said sadly. "Only lasted three days."

"Where did he go?" Mac asked carefully.

Theodore shrugged one shoulder and took a sip of his tea. "Don't know. I don't suspect I'll be hearing from him for a while," he said in resignation.

It didn't surprise Mac that Ted had left rehab. It followed his normal pattern, but Mac had hoped this time might be different. Years of discord between the two of them had left Mac with very few warm feelings toward his brother. However, he still didn't wish the man any ill will and hoped one day he would finally get his head out of his ass and man up. Didn't look as if that would be happening anytime soon.

"Sorry to hear that," Mac told him sincerely, staring down at his plate, pushing his corn around with his fork. Mac glanced over at his mom when she made a small hiccupping sound. The worry and sadness crossed her features briefly before she covered it up with a brave smile.

Dad added, "The last time Ted did this, we didn't hear from him for over two months." His dad clenched his jaw and hissed, "I don't know why my sons feel the need to lie to me."

Here we go.

Mac stiffened, even as Gunny's hand came to rest on Mac's thigh. "Sons?" Mac questioned, his voice tight.

His dad looked at him pointedly. "Yes, as in plural. Your brother lies about his drug and alcohol use, and you lie about who you are." He pointed a finger at Gunny. "And so did you," he said with ire.

"And just who do you think we are?" Mac asked defensively. Anger prickled along his skin, but he did his best to keep it under control.

His dad slammed his hand down on the table hard enough for the dishes to rattle and Mom to jump. "Do not mock me."

Mac wasn't intimidated and held his dad's gaze. "I'm serious. Just who in the hell do you think we are?" he repeated, his voice surprisingly calm. "I'm pretty sure I was the same person before Ted started his shit, and I haven't changed since." Mac nudged Gunny with his elbow. "I know for sure Gunny is the same guy I've always known. So I'd love to know your reasoning for calling us liars."

"You're having a relationship with your best friend—male friend, I may add," his dad gruffed. "I think that's a pretty big statement as to who you are."

Mac's fingers curled and tightened around his fork as his irritation increased. He forced himself to relax his hand and set the utensil aside. Apparently the forced relaxation did little to hide the anger since the large hand on his thigh tightened almost to the point of pain. Mac glanced at Gunny, who had a pleading look in his eyes. *Well fuck that.* He'd been worried about this moment all week, and now that it was here, it was as if he could just breathe and deal with the ramifications, good or bad. Had his dad not shown up, spoken to him, it would have hurt like hell, or had his dad been hurt, or disappointed, that would have piled some guilt on him. But to accuse him and Gunny of being liars, well, that just pissed him off to no end.

"So are you saying you've lied to me about being a miner? Tom Cohen's best friend? A father?" His dad's frown deepened with each statement, the confusion in his features evident. Gunny obviously knew exactly where he was going with the line of questioning, because the hand on his thigh went from a grip of warning to a caress of calming.

His dad's face reddened in anger; true to her nature—his mom was to his dad as Gunny was to him—she moved her chair closer and placed her hand gently on her husband's shoulder. "Theodore," she said softly. "Don't—"

"I have never lied to you," his dad snapped, giving Mac a cold stare.

"And I've never lied to you," Mac said, leaning in closer and returning the gaze with a hard one of his own.

They sat for a long moment facing off, no one in the room saying a word. Finally his dad broke eye contact, briefly looking at Gunny, then his wife, before returning his attentions to Mac. "How can you say that?"

Mac grabbed Gunny's hand beneath the table, clutching it, the connection both comforting and empowering. "Because, I am the same person I was before Sunday. I *am* a Marine. I *am* Gunny's best friend. I *am* your son. Who I share my bed with doesn't change those things no more than you sharing your bed with your wife takes away from all the other things you are." Mac sighed and shook his head. "I never lied to you, Dad," he said genuinely. "Yes, Gunny and I are more than just friends—hell, more than best friends—but I swear to you, neither he nor I even considered ourselves a couple until recently. I didn't lie," he said, his voice cracking.

Dad looked thoughtful as he continued to stare at him, the expression on his face hard to read. Mac bounced his leg, the tension increasing as the seconds stretched out; the only thing keeping him grounded was the rhythmic back-and-forth motion of Gunny's thumb along the top of Mac's thigh.

"Sir," Gunny said, his voice calm and sure. "I know this has probably been a shock, and I understand that you may need some time to come to terms with it, but the important thing is that you're here. You're willing to at least hear us out and not turn your back on us."

"I wouldn't ever turn my back on him," Theodore said adamantly. "You either," he added with a curt nod.

"You asked us to leave when you found out." Mac swallowed down the lump of emotion in his throat at the memory. "You refused to even look at me."

His dad ran a hand through his thinning hair, then the back of it over his brow. "I'm real sorry about that. Gunther's right, it was a pretty big shock." He shrugged. "I have to be honest; I'm not real comfortable with the idea. Don't think I'll ever see what attracts you to this big lug," his dad sniffed, pointedly looking at Gunny.

"Hey," Gunny grumbled sullenly. Mac could see the twitch of Gunny's lips as he fought to keep his smile hidden.

Tension drained from Mac in a rush. If his dad could tease or make a joke at Gunny's expense, then everything was going to be okay. Not perfect, nor did he expect his dad to ever totally understand, no more than he could understand his father's preferences. But that was okay; they didn't have to. He'd just have to make sure to prove to his dad that this, this small part of him, was just that, a piece of the whole.

"But seriously, son," his dad said, turning his attention back to him. "I didn't mean to make you think I was sending you away because of your relationship with Gunther. But I was shocked and scrambling to try and figure out how I had missed it and I admit, I settled on the theory that you two had been lying to me—"

"But—" Mac interrupted, but his dad held up a hand to silence him.

"I get what you're saying, and you're right. It was shallow of me to think in those terms, but the only reason I sent you away was because it was the only way to defuse a hostile situation. Do you honestly think anything would have gotten resolved that day had you stayed, given your brother's mood?"

"No," he admitted. "Ted's hard to reason with on a good day."

"Be nice," his mom chastised lightly.

Mac rolled his eyes at her making her smile grow. "Yeah, well, you could have at least explained that to me at the time, saved me the worriment."

"And saved me from dealing with the grumpy bastard," Gunny muttered under his breath.

Mac kicked Gunny under the table, was rewarded with a grunt of pain and a scowl. "Now who's the grumpy bastard," he said quietly out of the side of his mouth.

"Boys," his mom scolded.

Mac dropped his eyes and bit his lip. Funny how this tiny woman had the power to shut down a two-hundred-plus-pound Marine so easily. He stole a quick look at Gunny, who was looking properly chagrined. *Make that two two-hundred-plus-pound Marines*, he thought, amused. Then again, it shouldn't have surprised him; anyone with bionic ears and eyes in the back of her head was someone to be feared. Those were some kick-ass kind of superpowers in Mac's book.

The apologies made and the family set to right, minus the drunken fool, his dad, in typical Theodore Jones fashion, ended the heavy conversation with "So about that dessert?" He rubbed his hands together, a big cheery grin on his face.

Mac released his hold on Gunny's hand and pushed out of his chair. His steps were lighter than they had been in days as he made his way to the kitchen to grab the cake. He was sure there was going to be more on the subject; no doubt, his mom and dad would need time to feel truly comfortable with having a gay son, but they'd deal.

The hardest part was over, and now they could settle into a comfortable peace again. That was, until he and Gunny had to face the Duchenes. However, that wasn't going to happen for at least a fucking week. He needed time to recoup before he stirred another hornet's nest.

CHAPTER
Eighteen

DEATH could either bring a family together or drive it apart.

Ten years after the death of his sister, the disjunction between Gunny and his parents still hadn't been mended. Catherine, eighteen months younger than Gunny, had been such a ray of sunshine within the family that the dark cloud that descended upon them with her passing had never cleared. The fracture between Gunny and his parents was made all the worse by the disagreement over whether to remove Catherine from life support. A skiing accident had left his sister in a vegetative state with no hope for recovery. Where his dad had been indecisive as to whether or not to remove life support, Gunny and his mom were on opposing sides.

It had been two months of living hell.

Gunny knew, in his heart, that Catherine would not have wanted to live like that; in fact, they had discussed it a few times. The conversation had stemmed from his sister's fear for him being deployed to Iraq, and they had discussed death at length. Each of them had expressed their views on life support to the other. He understood his mom's desire to hold on to her only daughter, her belief that having Catherine alive, even as a vegetable, was better than not having her child at all. It was selfish, but understandable. Unfortunately, his mom still held tight to what she viewed as Gunny's betrayal when Dad had taken his side and agreed to respect Catherine's wishes rather than those of his wife.

With pangs of conscience, Gunny dialed his mom's phone number and waited for it to connect.

"Hello?"

"Hi, Mom," he greeted, doing his best to keep his voice cheerful in spite of the morose memories.

"Good to hear from you. How are you, son?" his mom asked; her voice held a surprised tone.

Gunny sat in one of the Adirondack chairs in the shade of a large oak in his backyard and stretched out his legs. "I'm good. And you and Dad?" he inquired.

"We're both doing well."

The formal tone between them made his heart ache, and he had to swallow down the sigh that threatened. He waited briefly to see if his mom would offer anything else. When she didn't he said, "I've been thinking about coming home for a visit."

"Oh? When were you thinking about coming?" she asked hesitantly.

"I'd like to do it soon, within the next couple of weeks?" he asked, hopefully. The sooner he told his parents about his and Gunny's plans, the sooner he could get the weight of it off his shoulders.

"This isn't a good time, Gunny. Your dad and I are leaving for Montreal next week, and we have a lot of things to do to prepare for our trip."

"How long will you be gone? Maybe we can plan something when you return. I'd really like to come see Grandpa." He picked at a damaged section of wood along the arm of his chair; an uneasy feeling seeped into him, making him jittery.

"Two weeks, and I'm not sure what we'll be coming home to when we return. We've been trying to find a nursing home for your grandpa. His dementia has gotten progressively worse over the last few weeks, and he is no longer a candidate for assisted living. He'll be staying with your Aunt Connie until a facility becomes available."

"Why didn't you tell me?" Gunny bit out with irritation.

"And what would that have accomplished? You knew his memory has been fading for years, and now he no longer remembers any of us. It wouldn't have changed anything and only served to worry you," his mom pointed out.

He squeezed his eyes shut and forced himself to calm down before he responded. "Because had you called, I might have had a chance to see him before he no longer remembered who I was," he muttered tightly. Gunny's head began to throb as his irritation grew. He massaged his forehead in an attempt to ease the ache. *It's not worth it.* "Never mind, it was only an idea," he said in resignation. "Have Aunt Connie call me if his condition worsens, and I'll just see you and Dad in October."

"October?" she asked, her tone one of confusion.

Gunny blew out a huffed breath. "For my exit ceremony? We discussed this last time I called."

"Oh, right, right. It will depend on how Grandpa is, but we will try our best to be there," she said blandly.

The throbbing in his head grew. *It's not worth it*, he reminded himself again. If he pressed it any further it would just cause a fight. "Okay, well, just let me know. My love to Dad." He hit the end button before she could respond and slammed the phone down on the small table next to his chair. "Fuck!"

"I take it nothing has changed on the home front?" Mac asked and handed Gunny a beer.

"Only that Grandpa hasn't been doing well and she didn't feel it necessary to tell me," Gunny spat and snatched the offered beer. "Thanks," he grumbled and tipped the bottle up and took a long pull.

Mac took the chair next to him. "Nothing serious, I hope," Mac said gently.

"They are moving him out of assisted living into a nursing home." Gunny took another large swig, his hands clenching the bottle. "He no longer remembers anyone."

"I'm sorry," Mac said gently. "When are we going to go see him?" he inquired, keeping his voice low and even.

"We're not," Gunny muttered.

"Why?"

"Because apparently my parents are going to Montreal while Aunt Connie does the move for Grandpa. Oh, and get this." He laughed bitterly. "She forgot about the ceremony and is not sure if they will make it." He was so done with this shit. If they wanted to talk to him, they could call. Gunny tipped up the bottle and downed the rest of its contents.

"Shit," Mac cursed under his breath.

"My thoughts exactly."

Mac hefted himself out of his chair and held out his hand. "It's too hot out here, let's go stretch out." Gunny glared at the offered hand for a moment, holding on to his irritation. "C'mon," Mac encouraged. "I'll give you a back rub."

Gunny huffed out a breath and allowed Mac to pull him to his feet. "I just don't get her," he said sadly and followed Mac to the house. "It's been ten years for fuck sakes. How long is she going to hold this grudge?"

"I don't know, Gunny," Mac murmured. "Did you talk to your dad?" he asked, opened the back door, and ushered Gunny in.

"No. I was too irritated that I didn't ask to talk to him." He should have called his dad's cell and left a message. Though Lord knows when he would have gotten it. The man rarely had it on, thought mobile phones should be used only for emergencies while traveling.

"We'll call him later. Find out what the hell is going on if you want," Mac offered.

As he passed the kitchen island, Gunny set his empty bottle down and followed Mac into the bedroom. "Nah. I'm not going to worry about it. They know when the ceremony is and if they don't show up, it's on them." Gunny stepped into the bedroom and pulled his sweat-damp T-shirt over his head and threw it to the floor. "I'll call Aunt Connie later in the week and see if I can find out any more on Grandpa."

"That's a good idea," Mac murmured and moved close, his hands landing on Gunny's shoulders. Mac's fingers kneaded the tense muscles, which pulled a deep groan from Gunny. "Damn, you're tight." He placed a chaste kiss against Gunny's lips. "On the bed, I'll go grab the oil."

Gunny nodded, slipped his shorts off, and kicked them in the same general direction as his T-shirt. He crawled up on their bed. Why he still let his mom get to him, he didn't know. It was stupid, but no matter how many times he talked to her, it was always the same. He ended up getting pissed off and tense by her unfeeling and blasé attitude, and she remained *uncaring*, he thought with a shake of his head.

"Which one do you want?" Mac called from the bathroom.

"I don't care." He grabbed Mac's pillow, laying it on top of his own, and stretched out.

Mac poked his head out of the bathroom. "We have sandalwood, musk, or edible cherry," Mac said, holding up three bottles with a sly smile.

Both the sandalwood and musk were full, while the bottle containing the cherry was nearly empty. Gunny arched one brow at him and pursed his lips. "Seriously, why do you ask me this every time?"

"Yeah I know," Mac snorted and stepped out of the bathroom with just the cherry oil.

"We're going to need more of this shit," he said, examining the bottle. Mac's eyes went wide. "Ooh, we should try banana next time," he said excitedly. Mac's gaze then narrowed in on Gunny's groin, and he licked his lips. "I like banana." he teased, waggling his eyebrows.

Gunny shoved the pillows out of the way, flipped over onto his stomach, and rested his cheek on his folded arms. He glared at Mac in exasperation.

"Mmm, even better idea," Mac moaned. "You want my banana, Gunny?"

"This is about me. I want my massage, dammit," he complained.

Mac set the oil on the nightstand and whipped his T-shirt off, popped the button on his cargo shorts, and slowly eased down the zipper. "Inside and out?" he queried huskily.

"Jones," Gunny grunted in warning.

"You really are grumpy, aren't you," Mac muttered. He dropped his shorts, stepped out of them, and climbed on the bed.

Gunny didn't respond. Of course he was grumpy. His mom always brought it out of him—although, with Mac straddling his thighs, his lightly furred calves tickling against the outside of Gunny's legs and Mac's warm, semihard cock pressed against the crack of his ass, the surliness steadily drained from him.

"Just going to have to manhandle it out of you," Mac grumbled and grabbed the oil from the table. The shift caused Mac's cock to press harder against him and Gunny had to clamp his jaw to keep in the moan that threatened to escape.

"What was that?" Mac asked.

Obviously he hadn't been as successful as he thought he'd been at keeping the sound inside, because Mac pressed his groin hard against Gunny's ass and wiggled his hips, pulling another rumbling sound from him. *Bastard.*

"Damn, you're getting heavy," he hissed. Mac wasn't the only one who could be a tease.

"Pure muscle, baby," Mac snorted.

Gunny was about to comment, but slick palms pressed firmly against his lower back and he didn't even try to hold back the moan of pleasure Mac's hands pulled from him. "Ah God, that feels good."

"You're all knotted up," Mac observed and dug his blunt fingers into Gunny's skin, kneading and prodding at the tension. "That call is really bothering you, isn't it?"

Gunny turned a disbelieving scowl on him. "Of course it is!" Mac's sympathetic gaze deflated Gunny's brief flare of anger. "I know it shouldn't," he sighed. "You would think I'd be used to it by now."

"I don't think you'll ever get used to it," Mac said thoughtfully, his fingers still moving, working the tense muscles into submission. "And you'll never stop hoping."

He let Mac's words swirl around in his head for a moment while his body melted into the mattress. On some level, he agreed with Mac. Gunny would never stop hoping his mom would let go of the hurt and pain of Catherine's death. Wished she would one day realize that after she buried her daughter, she caused not only herself but her family more pain by pushing her only surviving child out of her life. Yet, it was neither of those things that weighed so heavily upon him. This time it was more.

Mac massaged the oil along Gunny's spine, helping to ease him further. "What's really bothering me this time is that because of her grudge, she denied me the chance to see Grandpa before his mind went," he said in frustration.

"I wish there was something I could say or do to make you feel better," Mac murmured gently and kissed Gunny's temple.

"Just keep doing that," he told him and lifted his head to brush his lips against Mac's.

"Always," Mac whispered and leaned back to continue the massage.

As Mac's hands continued to move along Gunny's flesh, he did his best to push down the sadness and concentrate on the warm, slick fingers and the press of his lover's hands. The way the rough callouses caught against his skin even with the oil to ease his way. "Maybe I should just go see him next week," Gunny said, more to himself than to Mac.

"Sure *we* can," Mac said.

There was nothing he could do now, and with the way Mac was making him feel boneless, causing a warm buzz to tingle along his nerve endings, Gunny didn't want to do anything but enjoy the touch of his lover. To feel Mac's heat and hardness heavy upon him, the slow rhythmic movement of the bed, the aroma of cherry mingling with Mac's spicier scent, and the sound of his steady breath.

Gunny closed his eyes and cleared his mind of everything but Mac.

CHAPTER
Nineteen

THE thick muscles beneath his palms continued to bulge with tension as Mac worked them hard. He pressed down on knots with enough strength to elicit a grunt of pain from Gunny, which morphed into a moan as Mac caressed the warm skin of Gunny's back, shoulders, and arms. There wasn't anything he wouldn't do for the man. If he could change what had happened between Gunny and his mom, he would. Or, at the very least, erase the pain it caused his lover. He would without hesitation. But no matter how much he wished for things to be different, it was impossible to change what had already been done. The only thing he could do was be there for Gunny, and do his best to help relieve the tension in Gunny's muscular frame and try and ease his mind of things that couldn't be changed.

Mac gripped Gunny's shoulders and set a firm, measured stroke of his thumbs against the base of Gunny's neck. Mac felt the rigidity ease from the man, and his breathing turn slow and even. "That's it," he murmured. "Just let it all go."

"Feels good," Gunny praised quietly. "I love having your hands on me."

Mac moved his palms along Gunny's shoulders to his deltoids, kneading the taut sinew, continuing down to his biceps. Mac loved the way the muscles felt, the smoothness of Gunny's flesh against his fingertips. Mac moved farther down Gunny's arms, until he reached

Gunny's hands. He entwined their fingers. Mac stretched his legs out alongside Gunny's and pressed down upon him.

"My hands the only thing you love having on you?" he whispered against Gunny's ear.

"Mmm. I'm pretty sure I like every inch of you on me."

Mac kissed the shell of Gunny's ear. "My lips?"

Gunny shuddered. "Yes."

He nuzzled Gunny's neck and inhaled deeply, searching for his lover's heady scent beneath the cherry. He ran his tongue along the thick muscle, tasting. "My tongue?" he asked and moaned happily when Gunny's flavor filled his mouth.

"Almost more than your hands," Gunny responded with a husky tone, his breath a little faster.

"That's good." He ran the flat of his tongue along the same path, savoring the saltiness. "Since I love the way you taste."

As Mac licked and nibbled his way across Gunny's jaw, his lover shuddered again beneath him and turned his head to give Mac better access to his lips. "Mmm, I like yours, too."

He licked the corner of Gunny's mouth. "Give it to me," he encouraged.

Gunny opened his mouth, and the second his tongue passed his lips, Mac sucked it into his mouth, sucking hard for a moment before crushing their mouths together. Mac groaned softly. His need heated inside him as the kiss took on a sharp edge.

Reluctantly, Mac forced himself to break the kiss, lips hovered a mere breath apart as he tried to rein in his desire. "Damn!" he rasped and panted harshly. If he had let the kiss go on any longer, the intensity of it would have led to him slamming into Gunny's ass and taking his pleasure. While the thought made his gut flutter and his dick throb, the buildup, the slow journey to orgasm, would be better. Gunny made a sound of protest when Mac released his hands and leaned back.

"Not going anywhere," he assured him and slid his hands beneath Gunny's arms and clutched his shoulders. "What other parts of me do you like touching you?"

"All of you," Gunny moaned.

"Yeah," Mac purred. Chest to back, cock to ass, and legs interlaced, Mac rocked slowly. Mac couldn't help but smile at the sexy rumbling sound Gunny made as Mac's hard length slid along the crack of his ass. "You know what I've been thinking?"

"Hmm?"

Mac continued to rock, loving the way his cock head rubbed along Gunny's ass. The friction was sweet. He pressed a kiss to the back of Gunny's head. "All this worry lately over family." He kissed him again. "Retirement." Another kiss. "Friends and strangers."

He moaned when Gunny pushed his ass up against Mac's hard cock. "I don't want to think about any of that right now," Gunny complained.

"That's my point. At the end of the day none of it matters. This," he said, kissing Gunny's neck. "And this," he emphasized with a small thrust of his hips. "It's all that matters, Gunny. The fact that I'll have you in my arms every night, wake with you every morning, that's what is important, with or without anyone's blessing. You and me," he said fiercely.

"Just you and me, huh?" Gunny groaned.

"Yup."

"What makes us happy?" Gunny questioned further, tilting his head so he could meet Mac's gaze.

Mac grinned slowly and nodded. It was all that truly mattered. Not what his family thought, not Gunny's, not some stupid son of a bitch in a pub, not even the goddamn Corps.

"Good," Gunny ground out and shoved back hard, going up on his hands and knees. With Gunny's skin slick with cherry oil, Mac lost the grip he had on the man's shoulders. He wrapped his arms tightly around Gunny's waist to avoid being slung off the end of the bed.

"Hey!" Mac yelped in surprise. The quick, powerful movement forced him to his knees.

Eyes sparkling with heat and mischief, Gunny looked back over his shoulder. "You said it's about what makes us happy." He thrust his ass back against Mac's groin. "What makes me happy is less talking and more massaging." He quirked a brow. "Unless there is something you can think of that would make us happier right now," he said suggestively, emphasizing his meaning by wiggling his ass.

"You're such a slut, Gunny," Mac growled. He released his hold on the man and slapped one taut butt cheek. Hard.

"Ow," Gunny barked as a perfect impression of Mac's hand flared red on his ass.

"Serves you right," Mac grumbled. "I was going for all romantic and tender." He grabbed Gunny's hips in his hands and pulled him back against Mac's rigid cock. "Is this how you want it, Gunny? Hard and fast?"

"Yeah," he hissed. "Want you to fuck all the thoughts right out of my head."

Mac grabbed the bottle of oil and squeezed out a generous amount into his palm, and tossed the bottle aside. He rubbed his hands together as a thrill ran through him. Romantic, animalistic, slow, fast, he loved fucking Gunny. Even above his own needs, what he loved even more was giving the man what he wanted, what he begged for. "Don't say I never give you what you want," he said playfully.

"That works both ways, Jones. You know you want my ass," Gunny said blatantly.

"Don't make me tie you to this bed and gag you," Mac warned and swiped oil down the length of Gunny's crack.

"Mmm. Don't threaten me with a good—" Mac pushed one slick finger deep in Gunny's ass without warning. "Ah damn," he gasped. Even though it was unexpected, Gunny pushed back against the invasion, his body begging for more.

Mac pulled his finger back until it barely breached Gunny's opening, then plunged it back in, twisting his hand. Gunny's head snapped back, and a low growly sound rumbled from deep within him. "Is this what you need?" Mac asked, repeating the pull and plunge movements at a quick pace. "Or do you need more?"

Gunny panted, the bed frame creaking as he rocked back and forth, following Mac's fingers. "More," he finally bit out.

Mac kneaded the hard muscle of one firm ass cheek, not hampering the man's movements, but rather encouraging him to move.

Curses and pleas spilled from Gunny as Mac continued to let his lover fuck himself on his finger, enjoying the sights and sounds until they grew in volume and became more needy. Only then did Mac slide another finger into the tight, clenching heat.

"Yes! Mac. Harder." Gunny's words were disjointed, his fists clenched in the bedsheets.

Fuck! Seeing Gunny like this, his big body before him, begging for what only Mac could give him, sent his desire soaring. Ignoring his own aching cock, Mac reached between Gunny's legs and wrapped a fist around his prick, pulled it downward, and stroked it in sync with the thrusts of his fingers. Mac brushed his lips across Gunny's lower back and licked the sweet oil from his skin.

"You're so fucking hard," Mac cooed and stroked him firmly. "Already oozing. You want me to fuck you so bad, don't you?"

"God, yes," Gunny groaned, bearing down hard on Mac's hand with each thrust.

Mac ran his tongue along the top of Gunny's crease, then back up his spine. "Gonna give you what you need, Gunny," he whispered against the warm flesh. Releasing Gunny's cock, Mac swiped the mix of oil and Gunny's precum down the length of his own shaft. "I'll always give you what you need," he promised.

"Need you," Gunny said with a shuddering breath. "That's all."

Gunny made a whimpering sound of protest when Mac pulled his fingers free, but he ignored it and grabbed Gunny's hips in both his hands once again. "I'm all yours," he said lowly and pushed his cock along his lover's crease. The flared, ruddy head, slick and glistening, stood out in sharp contrast against the creamy skin of Gunny's ass. Mac bit down on the inside of his cheek and took a couple of harsh breaths in through his nose as he continued to move, pushed away the urge to slam home, deep inside Gunny. He clutched his cock and slapped it against the smooth skin of Gunny's ass before he slid it along his crease again, repeating the cycle over and over and over until his own arousal seeped from the slit.

"Stop teasing and fuck me," Gunny demanded.

Mac shook his head; his smile grew as he realized he'd been in a daze, held transfixed by the sight and sweet friction. He used his thumbs to pull apart Gunny's cheeks to expose that sweet hole and pressed his cock head against it. "Ready?"

"Jones," Gunny growled in frustration. "Would you just shut up and fuck me already!"

Mac's dick twitched at the aggressive tone, and he chuckled. When Gunny was in the mood for power bottoming, Mac could easily admit to himself that he liked it almost as much as he loved dominating the man. *Almost.* Mac laughed silently and pressed forward, meeting resistance. He nudged at Gunny's hole again. "All you have to do is open up for me," he drawled, his voice thick with barely controlled passion, "and it's yours."

Heat flared in Gunny's eyes, and he grinned slyly. The expression that crossed his face as he looked at Mac over his shoulder was cocksure, his voice gravelly and thick when he said, "Mine."

Mac wasn't sure if it was a statement or a question, but the tone of it caused his desire to run rampant. Ratcheting it even higher was the sight of the muscles in Gunny's arms bulging as he gripped the sheets tighter, the way he turned his head slowly and then dropped it between his shoulders, and the flex of the sinew of his back. Mac's eyes rolled back in his head and he cried out when Gunny shoved back hard, impaling himself on Mac's cock.

"Oh, hell," Mac groaned plaintively, instantly going balls deep in Gunny's tight, wet heat.

Gunny stilled, the only movement the rapid rise and fall of his torso as he panted harshly. The muscles of his passage clamped down on Mac's cock, trying to adjust to the sudden and violent intrusion, ripping a needy grunt from Mac.

"Gunny," Mac pleaded. His frame shook with desire. He wanted to pound into Gunny's tight ass, take what he wanted, everything he needed, but he wasn't willing to cause the man unnecessary pain. But God, it was hard holding back. He didn't know how long he would be able to keep the precarious hold he had on his control. "For fuck sakes, Gunny, move," he gritted out.

Without a word, Gunny arched his back and pushed his ass harder against Mac's groin, holding the position and pressure until Mac thought he'd go mad with lust. "Gunny," he repeated in warning. He gripped Gunny's hip with one hand, his shoulder with the other, molding his body along Gunny's back, and spoke against his ear. "Move or so help me I will pound you through this fucking mattress."

Gunny chuckled beneath him, and then, rather than complying with Mac's wishes or taking the warning to heart, he lowered himself to the mattress, arms stretched above his head and legs spread wide.

"Goddammit," Mac cursed when his cock slipped from Gunny's ass.

"Well," Gunny dared, turning his head, a challenging expression on his face.

"Son of a bitch," Mac growled and climbed on Gunny's body, his knees over the man's thighs. He grasped his cock, pressed it against Gunny's crease, and made good on his threat. In one hard lunge Mac buried himself to the hilt. Mac splayed his hands on the widest expanse of Gunny's back, fingers digging in, and set a fast and brutal pace as he plowed in and out of Gunny's ass.

"Is this what you needed?" Mac growled harshly. "A hard and dirty fuck!"

"Yes," Gunny hissed. "Harder," he grunted.

Mac dug his fingers in deeper, finding purchase by balancing on knees and hands. He pulled all the way out of Gunny's ass, and the second his cockhead was free of the tight ring of muscle, he plowed back in.

Gunny cried an animalistic sound that sent a jolt of pleasure through Mac. The power of it settled in his sac, causing it to draw up. It felt so fucking good being buried inside Gunny he could barely stand it. The way Gunny's ass gripped his cock as if it were trying to keep him deep within threatened to strip Mac of his restraint. He gritted his teeth, pushed his desire to the murkiness beneath the haze of lust, and added more force to the snap of his hips.

Incoherent words and grunts poured from Gunny, making him all the more irresistible. Mac squeezed his eyes shut, his belly clenched and he shuddered. *No. No. No.* He silently screamed as he was pushed to the edge of orgasm. *Not yet.*

"Mac," Gunny rasped. "Fuck… harder," he begged in a harsh, gravelly voice. Mac doubted the man knew what he was begging for, or what he needed as he chased his orgasm, closer and closer to release.

The sweat across Gunny's back conspired against Mac, and his slick hands slid and he collapsed, pinning Gunny against the mattress. "Oh, fuck yeah," Mac howled. He wasn't going to last much longer. He couldn't.

"Gunny—" His voice broke, and it was the only warning he gave before he let go and truly fucked the man into the mattress. Each powerful thrust pushed a grunt out of Gunny's chest; the banging of the headboard nearly drowned the sound.

"Now!" Gunny screamed, body going bow-string tight before he convulsed as he came.

Mac rode the edge, hips jerking erratically and without finesse as he pounded Gunny through his orgasm. Only when Gunny gave a long low moan of satiation did Mac fall over the edge and allow Gunny's heat and spasming channel to rip the climax from him.

Mac cried out his release and every muscle in his body tensed. Toes curled. Not only could Gunny handle Mac when he unleashed the full strength of his body, but he reveled in it, begged for more, thus increasing Mac's gratification tenfold.

When the last drop of seed pulsed from his cock, only then did the tension in Mac's body fade, and he melted against Gunny, breathing harshly, heart slamming. Neither of them moved for long moments, letting the quiet settle over them as they both fought to get their breaths and hearts under control.

"Damn," Mac groaned and rolled to his side, keeping one arm and a leg draped over Gunny.

"I couldn't have said it better," Gunny mumbled sleepily.

"I should spank your ass," he told him without true anger. "I was planning on loving you all night long. Nice and slow," he murmured against the flesh of Gunny's bicep.

"Go ahead," Gunny responded.

Mac thought about it for a moment, but in the end he just couldn't muster the strength, or the desire, to punish the man.

"Mmm hmm. Just as I thought," Gunny teased.

"You just keep right on yapping, boy." Mac grunted. "As soon as I catch my breath I'm going to beat you into submission, then spend the rest of the evening with my cock in your ass where it belongs," he teased back crudely.

Gunny shifted slightly until he was lying on his side with a moan. He flopped his arm over Mac's waist and pushed close and kissed his nose. "I look forward to you trying."

Before Gunny had the chance to pull back, Mac grabbed the back of his neck and pressed their lips together in a sweet kiss. He traced around Gunny's lips with his tongue and then sucked his full, lush bottom lip into his mouth, nibbling and tasting before releasing it. "It's a promise, boy," he whispered against Gunny's mouth.

"Nap first?" Gunny said with a smirk.

"You know me too well," Mac chuckled, his eyes closing; he rested his hand on Gunny's hip.

They lay there breathing each other in, Mac's body, mind, and heart content as he gently stroked the soft skin with his thumb. The fog of sleep pressed down on him, and he could feel himself beginning to drift. Before he gave in to its call, he needed to know, and whispered, "Your head clear enough to rest?"

"Yeah," Gunny said quietly.

"I was serious about what I said earlier. Nothing else matters but you and me, and I was a fool to worry about anything else," he told him sincerely.

"Hush and go to sleep," Gunny encouraged and placed another kiss to Mac's lips. "You can prove it later."

Mac smiled, the darkness of sleep beginning to take him. "I might just keep you right here until our retirement is official," he murmured and gave in to slumber.

Gunny's quiet voice said, "I can't think of a better way to pass the time," and followed him.

CHAPTER
Twenty

TO HAVE a retirement ceremony or not was a personal choice. Had the decision been left up to Gunny, it would have been the latter. A nice quiet evening at home, maybe a candlelit dinner for two and his certificate sent via post sounded good to him. While all for tradition and honor within the Corps, he'd never been comfortable being the one in the spotlight.

No, the whole fancy-ass ceremony was Mac's doing.

Gunny glared at his image in the mirror as he buttoned each gold button on his dress blues. He shrugged his shoulders and rolled his neck, the jacket too tight, stuffy. "I should have said no," he told his reflection.

"But you love me," Mac reminded him as he stepped next to Gunny. "Here, let me do it."

Gunny turned and allowed Mac to finish the buttons. "I must or I wouldn't be standing here preparing to wear this damn thing in ninety-degree weather."

"It's only seventy, so quit your bitching," Mac said with a smirk.

"Yeah, well, it's going to feel like ninety," he grumbled. "It's not too late to back out and have that romantic dinner I suggested," he said hopefully and ran his hands along the cool cotton of Mac's dress shirt. While Gunny hated wearing the stuffy uniform, especially how it choked him, Mac looked fucking gorgeous in his.

"Too late," Mac murmured and finished the last button before he ran his hands down the front of Gunny's chest to his waist. "I told you we didn't have to do this if you didn't want to, but changing your mind while a couple hundred people are already gearing up for it—" He arched a brow at Gunny and wrapped his arms around him. "—it's a little late to back out now," he reminded him.

Gunny sighed and rested his forehead against Mac's. He knew how important this was to Mac. Years before, he had thought to make a statement for the repeal of "Don't Ask, Don't Tell" during his exit from the Corps, and Mac had talked about their ceremony at great length. Mac viewed retiring from the military as an honor and one not to be taken lightly. Mac's argument being, he equated the retirement ceremony with a wedding, or a funeral, since they were about the same. It wasn't so much about the person or persons up front on stage, or in the box, but for everyone else to celebrate and show how much they appreciated the people on that stage. Furthermore, not all can, or do, make a career of the Corps, and those who succeed are a very rare and special breed and should be honored accordingly and publicly. Hard to argue with that logic, but Gunny still didn't have to like it.

"I know," Gunny said with resignation. "But did you have to choose the National Museum of the Marine Corps, for fuck sakes?"

Mac laughed and kissed his mouth before taking a step back to inspect Gunny's uniform. He reached up and brushed a finger across the many service medals on Gunny's chest. "I wanted to show you off," he said huskily. "Show everyone what a lucky son of a bitch I am."

Gunny shook his head and gave his lover an incredulous look.

"Okay, okay," Mac chuckled, reading Gunny's look wisely. "But can I at least get credit for choosing the air-conditioned Leatherneck Gallery rather than the scorching sun of Semper Fidelis Memorial Park?"

"Fine," Gunny told him and grabbed his shoulders, turned him around to face the door, and shoved him. "Now let's get this over with."

Over the last few weeks, Mac had settled nicely into retirement life and kept his promise to set aside the worry over not having a *plan*, and they just enjoyed being together. They had been some of the best weeks of Gunny's life, and the sooner they left, the sooner they could put this whole craziness of ceremony and tradition behind them and get back home and back to enjoying life.

THE early afternoon was a gorgeous shade of blue without a cloud in the sky, and Mac slipped his sunshades on and started the car. Gunny slid into the passenger seat and pulled the door closed. He looked good in his blues, damn good, and Mac took a moment to enjoy the sight. Gunny's square jaw was clean-shaven, and Mac could smell the scent of the aftershave. His hair was newly shorn and his skin still golden from his summer tan. Not only was Gunny the sexiest man he'd ever seen, he was also a force of nature, commanding and strong when called upon to be, and yet laid all that strength at Mac's feet and trusted him without hesitation or a shred of doubt. It wasn't a lie what he'd told Gunny in the bathroom as they dressed. Mac was a lucky son of a bitch, and he really did want to show off his man. This gorgeous powerful man was his, and for the first time in his life he was finally able to tell the world. Yes, he wanted to make a statement in favor of the repeal of the bullshit law, but even more so, he simply wanted everyone to know to whom he belonged and who held his heart. *Soon.* No more hiding, and fuck those who took issue with it. It was about his and Gunny's happiness. About being together and enjoying their lives together. They had earned it, deserved it. As he continued to stare at his man, a lump formed in Mac's throat; his chest tightened as the truth of it settled into his soul.

"You okay?" Gunny asked with a concerned voice.

Mac could only nod, as he had to swallow again before he could respond. "Yeah, I'm okay. I was just thinking—" Mac closed his eyes as a wave of emotion stole his voice. When he opened them again, Gunny was staring at him with a concerned expression.

Gunny frowned and grabbed Mac's hand. "What?"

Mac squeezed Gunny's hand and gave him a warm smile. "That I'm very lucky you're going to be at my side today. Thank you."

"No place I'd rather be," Gunny laughed nervously. "Well I'd rather be at your side naked and in our bed, but that's later." He shrugged.

Poor guy really did hate being in the spotlight, and he'd do almost anything to avoid it. The thought of Gunny naked and—

"Ugh, don't even start talking about being naked. I'm having a hard enough time resisting the urge to pull you out of this car and fuck you over the hood as it is," he groaned. "You look so fucking hot."

Gunny pressed his palm against his groin and spread his legs slightly. "You've never fucked me while I wore my blues," Gunny murmured seductively. "Imagine it, Mac, my trousers down around my feet, bare ass on display for you as I lay across the hood of the car. My—"

Mac growled as the image flashed in his mind in vivid color. He ripped his hand out of Gunny's and put the car in gear. "You are so going to pay for this later," he hissed through clenched teeth. Warmth rushed to his groin and bathed his hardening cock in heat.

"Why not now?" Gunny asked, cupping the obvious bulge encased in blue cotton.

Mac forced himself to focus on the road ahead as he pulled into the street. The tingling in his dick made it all the more difficult to keep from giving in to his growing arousal. There was only one way to get Gunny to behave sometimes, and he was forced to use Gunny's submissive side against him or run the very real risk of blowing off the entire ceremony. "Boy," he warned, putting an authoritative snap in his voice, "take your goddamn hand off your dick, it belongs to me. Not another word, do as you're told, and I will blow your fucking mind later. Disappoint me and I will deny you my pleasure for a week."

Gunny stilled; the only sounds were those of the road beneath the tires and the rush of wind, for a long drawn-out moment. *C'mon, Gunny, please behave.* He knew the man was nervous. Hell, Mac was too; his stomach did flip-flops in anticipation of what they were about to do. It would be so easy to show up, listen to the reading of their military biography, say thank you, and accept their certificates. But, this was important. *Why?* Mac thought about it briefly, but he didn't rightly know why. He'd never thought of himself as ever being a role model for gay Marines, or for any service member. Yet now that he was presented with the opportunity, he wanted more than anything to be a positive voice.

After what felt like hours but was only seconds, Gunny bowed his head, folded his hands in his lap, and said, "Yes, Sir."

Mac let out a sigh of relief, and as he maneuvered his way along the streets, he grabbed Gunny's hand and brought it to his lips and kissed the back of it before entwining their fingers and lowering them to the armrest. "Thank you," he said sincerely. "Set your worries aside and just focus on me, please."

Gunny nodded and closed his eyes, no doubt trying to do as Mac asked of him. Blessedly the rest of the drive went quickly and in silence. Gunny looked more relaxed when they pulled into the parking lot. The man had been able to call upon his desire to please, to find peace and a calm headspace.

"You ready?" Mac asked quietly as he put the car in park and cut the engine.

"Yeah," he said with a nod. "I know how important this is to you, so as long as I keep my focus on you, I'll be fine," he said lowly. Gunny lifted his head and met Mac's gaze. "I won't lie, I'm still a little freaked out, and no, I didn't find my headspace. I need you to get me there. But I did spend the time thinking about what we're about to do and—" He shook his head. "I've been acting like an idiot. I let my distaste for public speaking and the spotlight cloud what the bigger issue is here." Gunny's lips curled into a wide grin. "I'm honored to be by your side today and support you in this."

Mac winked at him, returning the smile. "I still plan on rewarding you later," he said slyly.

"You're damn right you are," Gunny laughed, opened the door, and stepped out of the car with hat in hand.

Mac followed Gunny's lead and slid from the car. He adjusted his clothes and set his cover on his head. "Look okay?" he asked.

"You meet inspection," Gunny teased, setting his own cover on his head. "Shall we?" he asked with a formal swipe of his arm toward the walkway.

They fell in step next to each other as they made their way to the side entrance, both walking with their heads high, their steps measured and with purpose. Mac pulled open the door and held it for Gunny and followed him in. Mac discreetly brushed his finger along Gunny's hand as they stood outside the door to the Leatherneck Gallery. Both of them remained silent. Nervousness attacked Mac, making him jittery all over. Gunny's quiet presence next to him made the uneasy feeling bearable. He kept an eye on the clock on the wall next to the double doors.

"I love you," he said barely above a whisper, just as the clock struck the appointed hour.

Gunny's smile was brilliant, and Mac felt the full effect of it in the center of his chest from his low response of "Love you too," which caused it to ache pleasingly.

Mac pulled open the door as together they stepped into the gallery. The core values of the Marine Corps—honor, courage, and commitment—echoed from the marble and glass walls within the Leatherneck Gallery. A gleaming mast stood two hundred and ten feet high, while vintage aircraft flew overhead. The place demanded respect, and Mac straightened his shoulders and walked a little prouder as he made his way to the reception area. Round tables covered in red and blue cloth and set with white china were in front of the helicopter, with two long rectangular tables set directly in front with a podium between them.

A roar of applause went up from their gathered friends, family, and fellow Corps members as he and Gunny made their way to one of the rectangular tables. The schedule of events was already set and known: he and Gunny stopped in front of the commanding officer, acknowledged him, and took their appointed seats.

Mac scanned the crowd before them. His mom and dad sat with proud smiles at one of the round tables directly in front of them, and he acknowledged them with a slight nod and a smile. Unfortunately, he didn't see either Gunny's mom or dad. Mac hadn't expected them, but that hadn't stopped him from hoping they would show up for Gunny's sake. It took a great deal of willpower not to reach over and take Gunny's hand in his beneath the table, sure the man had already looked for them as Mac had. Anger flared briefly in Mac, knowing his lover had to be heartbroken by his parents' snub. Instead he pressed his leg against Gunny's, a gentle reminder that he was there and at his side.

Major Walker stood and made his way to the podium, thanked those in attendance, and asked everyone to rise for the national anthem. Mac removed his cover and stood, and Gunny followed suit. His legs a little unsteady and hands trembling, Mac couldn't help but question if he was about to do the right thing. The room went in and out of focus as his head swam. He still wasn't sure of the answer when the anthem ended and they were told they could once again take their seats. Mac gratefully slumped down into his chair and ran his sweaty palms along his thighs. He stole a quick glance at Gunny; the slight frown and fine sheen of perspiration that dampened the man's brow did little to make Mac feel confident in his decision.

Drinks and hors d'oeuvres were served as Major Walker read from a prepared list of both his and Gunny's biographies. Mac ignored the crepes and stuffed mushrooms that were set in front of him, seriously doubting they would go well with the nausea, but he grabbed the glass of water and took a large gulp, wetting his dry throat.

At last the Major lifted his glass and said, "A toast to Macalister and Gunther, whose service has guaranteed our freedom to celebrate today. They have served so that we may live as we wish in this land of the free. Today we honor Gunther and Macalister and salute their service. May we always remember that serving one's country is the ultimate expression of love for family, friends, and neighbors." He raised his glass higher. "Cheers."

Mac downed the rest of his water and set the empty glass aside and took a deep breath.

"And now Macalister and Gunther would like to say a few words," Major Walker announced and took his seat as the crowd applauded.

"Ready?" Mac murmured lowly.

"Not even a little bit." Gunny grunted in response.

"Good. Let's go," he said and went to his feet.

Mac stood close to Gunny as he stepped to the podium, their shoulders pressed together. Mac could feel the slight tremble in Gunny, which for some odd reason calmed Mac. In the face of Gunny's fear, his uncertainty, Mac's need to comfort his man took the forefront.

Hidden from view by the podium, Mac clutched Gunny's hand and squeezed.

"Major Walker, family, and distinguished guests, thank you for coming," Gunny said.

Crickets.

He and Gunny hadn't discussed what their personal speeches would be. Gunny knew Mac was going to make a statement about the repeal of "Don't Ask, Don't Tell," but he didn't want to know the words. It would have just been one more thing for him to stress over. So it took a few moments for the audience, and Mac, to realize his speech was complete.

Mac gave the man an incredulous look, but Gunny just smiled as those gathered applauded. *Talk about short and sweet.* Mac released his hold on Gunny's hand and reached into the pocket of his trousers and pulled out the speech he'd prepared. "My speech will be a little longer." He gave Gunny a little shove, pulling a burst of laughter from the audience, and spread the paper on the podium.

Pushing aside the last of his nervousness, Mac cleared his voice. "Distinguished guests, fellow Marines, family, and friends: Thank you for honoring us with your presence on this occasion. I joined the Corps twenty-two years ago with pride and wide-eyed wonderment. I wanted to be a part of something bigger than just myself, my family, even my town, and with the naïveté of a child I signed up and headed to boot camp. In the Corps I grew to adulthood, and I have been privileged to become a man while in service to my country and Corps. I have served under great leaders, and I have led great Marines. I am honored to have served side by side with selfless men and women who cared more about Corps and country than they did about themselves. I was told they don't take job applications in the Marines, only commitments. I have stayed true to that commitment and hope I have made a difference, as I carried out my dream."

The audience applauded, and Mac smiled as a couple of the Marines shouted, "Oo-rah!"

"Now, it's time for me to step aside and let younger men and women take over. For those of us who join, the Corps calls to us. We are driven by something almost genetic, to be Marines. We don't choose to join the Marine Corps—we are born to do so. We are brothers and sisters. Our Corps is a family.

"I'm not going to go into the details of my career—Major Walker has already done that, but please know, during the last twenty-two years, I have fought without question for the right to be free. For others to share in that freedom, even though one of my most basic rights was denied me. I have no regrets. However, I do have some parting thoughts."

Mac looked at Gunny, who gave him a slight nod, and he reached for Gunny's hand, entwining their fingers before he continued.

"President Obama has signed into law the repeal of 'Don't Ask, Don't Tell.' This new law arrives as my career in the Corps comes to an end and as such comes too late for Gunny and I to be a part of, but I'd like to say to the leaders I leave behind, remember that your Marines are family. Teach them the family traditions: who we are; what we have done; what makes us different. Communicate. Make sure they get the word. Be open to their ideas. Treat them with respect. Help them to grow into the Marines they want to be. Whether black or white, male or female, active or reserve, gay, bisexual, or straight, we are all Marines. What we share in common goes deeper than any superficial differences.

"To all Marines I leave behind, remember that we are family; our strength lies in teamwork more than individual achievements. Allow no wedge to be driven between you and your fellow Marines.

"To my family, thank you for understanding. And thank you for enduring. And thank you for helping me in so many ways that few ever saw. No matter how great the sacrifice, you always supported me and encouraged me to remain faithful. Any success that I enjoyed, or any good I may have done, was made possible by you. I love you very much.

"Finally, to the one person who truly understands me the most. Who shares my burden and my heart and has made my sacrifice bearable." Mac turned to Gunny and held his gaze, speaking directly to him. "To my best friend, my lover, and my future husband, who is the epitome of strength, honor, and courage. If anyone questions as to whether a gay man can serve and bring honor to the Corps, they only have to look to Gunther Duchene to erase any and all doubt." Tears burned at the back of Mac's eyes, and he blinked them away. Mac gently ran his fingers along Gunny's cheek. "Thank you. I love you very much." Ignoring the gasps, applause, and cheers, Mac leaned in and pressed a gentle kiss to Gunny's warm lips and whispered, "Semper fi."

Mac was still a little unsure of his future, but with Gunny by his side, he knew wherever he went, or whatever he did, Gunny would be there to remind him what was truly important. He couldn't wait to start this next mission.

CHAPTER
Twenty-One

STARING out at the crowd, Mac's arm around his waist, Gunny puffed out his chest just a little more and stood proudly as those there to wish them well on their retirement applauded and cheered. The couple of Marines who stood and yanked their dates from their chairs and stormed out—even the one Marine who flipped them off before he exited—couldn't diminish the swell of excitement that surged through him. He was so proud of Mac. So goddamn honored to be standing next to him, being held by him, and Christ, that kiss. A simple press of lips, yet the meaning behind it, the setting, the message delivered within it, made his heart beat wildly.

Out of the corner of his eye, Gunny spotted Major Walker approach, and he stiffened slightly when he saw the tight set of the man's jaw. He had the utmost respect for the major. He was a tough old son of a bitch, but he had always been fair and a great leader. It wouldn't change the outcome if Walker snubbed them; however, it would suck a whole lot worse to have someone Gunny knew, respected, and genuinely liked look at him with disgust than the Marines he barely knew who had done it before they left. Gunny nudged Mac and discreetly nodded toward Walker. For a tense few seconds he and Mac held perfectly still, waiting to see which way it would go.

"Sergeant Jones, Master Gunnery Sergeant Duchene." Walker paused, studying both Gunny and Mac with circumspection.

The major was an imposing man. He wasn't quite as large as Gunny or Mac, yet for a man in his early fifties his frame was heavy with muscle, a testament to his dedication to the power and strength of his body. His handsome face, with few wrinkles and minimum strands of silver in his dark hair, could only be a result of good genes. Although bigger, and his claim he wasn't intimidated, Gunny shrunk slightly under the man's intense gaze.

Finally, the major jerked, his posture going rigid, shoulders snapping back, chest out, and saluted them.

Gunny let out the breath he'd been holding, and just as Mac did, he saluted in return, lips curling into a relieved smile.

"Hell of a speech, Jones. Shocking, but impressive nonetheless," Walker said and held out his hand.

"Thank you sir," Mac said and shook the offered hand. "I like to leave a lasting impression," he admitted with a wry smile.

Walker shook his head. Gunny thought he saw the man roll his eyes, but he couldn't swear to it since he was doing the same thing at Mac's statement.

"Duchene," Walker chuckled and offered Gunny his hand. "Can't say the same about yours."

He shook the major's hand gratefully. "I leave the shock and awe to Mac, sir."

Walker looked between Gunny and Mac, a thoughtful expression on his face as he seemed to study them for a moment. The coil of tension Gunny had been dealing with all day tightened under Walker's scrutiny. "I've been sitting on the fence with this issue," Walker finally said. "And to be quite honest, I've been leaning more toward the exclusion rather than acceptance."

"I can understand your hesitancy, sir," Mac responded.

Gunny didn't miss the skeptical tone in Mac's voice and stole a glance at him. Mac's expression was neutral, but Gunny knew exactly what that tone in his voice meant: *I'll humor you, be polite, but completely disagree with your opinion.* He'd heard it directed at himself enough times.

"I was wrong," Walker admitted.

"Excuse me, sir?" Gunny asked in surprise.

"You got a problem with your hearing, Marine? I said I was wrong," Walker barked and then softened the harsh tone with a smile. "And that doesn't happen too often. I am a Marine, after all."

"Yes, sir." Mac smirked.

"Good. Just have one question for Duchene," he said with a curt nod toward Mac. "Is he the best you could do?"

"Hey!" Mac bristled.

"He has his moments, sir," Gunny laughed.

"That he does. Mac, give me a call next week. I have a few things I'd like to discuss with you. Now go let your families congratulate you."

"Yes, sir."

Gunny and Mac each acknowledged Major Walker and stepped around the podium. "What did he mean, he has a few things he'd like to discuss with you?" Gunny asked quietly. He didn't think Mac knew Walker all that well, not on a personal level.

"About the speech, I guess," he said with a shrug.

"Call me?" Gunny said derisively.

Mac stopped just before they reached the table where his parents were waiting and cocked his head. "Are you jealous, Gunny?" he asked, keeping his voice low, his eyes sparkling with laughter. "That is so fucking cute," Mac whispered close to Gunny's ear.

He only had the opportunity to growl menacingly as Clare Jones left her husband's side, her tear-streaked face radiant as she threw herself at Mac. "I am so proud of you," she sobbed, burying her face into Mac's chest. "So beautiful."

Mac wrapped her in his arms and kissed the top of her head. "Thank you, Mom." Clare clung to her son for a few moments; her tiny body shook as she silently cried.

Gunny shifted his weight, his chest aching as he watched mother and son embrace. He'd called his mom and dad again to invite them once more to the event, even going as far as to tell them that there was some very important news he wanted to share with them, but as he looked away from Mac and Clare and scanned the room, the ache grew.

Like a child rushing home from school to share news of a good grade or award, only to find the house empty, Gunny was crushed. Forty-two years old and still he was hoping, praying, that his mom would be there to throw her arms around him and tell him how proud she was of him. The burn behind his eyes caused Gunny to squeeze them shut. He would not cry. He was a grown man for fuck sakes. He didn't need mommy's approval. He would not cry.

Small, warm hands gripped his forearm, and Gunny opened his eyes to see Clare looking up at him, her cheeks damp, but there wasn't a shred of sadness in her red-rimmed eyes. "I'm so proud of you too," she whispered, her voice thick with emotion, but her smile warm.

"Thank you." His voice cracked as he pulled her into his arms and hugged her. The ache of loss too painful and his gratitude for this tiny woman who gave him strength so powerful, Gunny was left helpless against the tear that escaped.

Again he was thankful for Clare's support when she continued to hold him until he was able to get his emotions under control and wipe his wet cheek against her soft hair, the evidence of his weak moment dried when she finally pulled back and patted his arm.

The sympathetic look Mac gave him as he hugged his father was proof Gunny hadn't been able to fool Mac, but he didn't comment.

With one arm still draped over his son's shoulders, Theodore held out his hand to Gunny. "Congratulations, son."

Gunny shook Theodore's hand, his throat constricting as it hit him again how truly lucky he was. He had the love of his life by his side and the acceptance of Mac's family. "Thank you, sir," he managed to squeeze out.

MAC had to admit the party ended up being amazingly fun, and he had gotten a lot of positive vibes from those there. Sure, there had been a couple of assholes who hadn't been impressed by Mac's speech, but they left early. Those who stayed had been either supportive or tolerant, but Mac felt the well wishes for his and Gunny's future had overall been sincere. He had no illusions that it was the end of the subject, or there wouldn't be some fallout, but he had other things to worry on.

Although it had done his heart good to see so many show support, he'd been on edge for the last hour and blew out a relieved breath when he finally got Gunny back home. The ride had been quiet. Gunny sat silently tense, staring out the window, his expression thoughtful the entire way home. Mac didn't want to bring up what bothered Gunny until he was able to wrap the man in his arms. Mac knew where the sorrow was rooted, and it took a great deal of restraint not to grab his phone and tell Linda and Carl Duchene exactly what he thought of them for what they had done to their son. Even though he knew it would do no good, nor would it make Gunny feel any better, it would go a long way to make Mac feel better to tell them what fucking idiots they were.

The minute Gunny stepped into the house, Mac kicked the door shut, grabbed Gunny's shoulders, and spun him around to press him up against it. Mac's keys dropped to the floor with a clatter before he cupped Gunny's face in his hands and took his mouth in a deep and bruising kiss. Gunny remained rigid, whether from shock or sadness, Mac couldn't rightly say. Didn't matter. He licked, nibbled, and explored until the man began to respond, a small moan escaping him. Mac swallowed the noise down, taking it deep into himself and feeding his own satisfied sounds to Gunny.

Mac ended the kiss. As he panted, trying to catch his breath, he rested his forehead against Gunny's and rubbed their noses together. "How ya doin', Marine?" Mac asked, speaking against Gunny's lips, but pushed his tongue back in deep before the man could respond.

Gunny's hands went to Mac's back and pulled them closer, his large hands rough, fingers digging in almost painfully, speaking of Gunny's need, his desire, to lose himself in Mac and pleasure rather than where his thoughts had been on the drive home. Mac could almost feel the desperation on Gunny's tongue.

"Doing pretty good now," Gunny said in a husky whisper. His hand dropped to Mac's ass and tugged at the same time he thrust his hips forward.

Mac hissed and squeezed his eyes shut as his arousal swelled. He'd only meant to help Gunny shift his thoughts from dwelling on who hadn't shown up to their party, take the sadness from his eyes, and focus on who had attended. Hadn't planned on doing anything more than kissing, but with the way Gunny was pressing his erection against him, the kneading hands on his ass, Gunny wasn't the only one who needed to take the edge off.

"You're distracting me," Mac murmured against Gunny's neck.

"What?" Gunny asked in amusement as he rolled his hips; the very prominent bulge in his slacks told Mac Gunny knew exactly what he'd meant.

"Bastard," Mac muttered and extracted himself from Gunny's arms. He smiled brightly at Gunny's scowl as he tried to grab him, but Mac anticipated him and spun out of his reach. "I was trying to make you feel better."

"And you were doing a damn fine job of it," Gunny grumbled. "Now c'mere and make me feel real good."

"That's what I'm about to do," Mac called over his shoulder as he headed toward their bedroom.

"Ah, the bed," Gunny said enthusiastically. "Even better."

Mac sped his steps and went directly to the closet, where he'd hidden Gunny's gift. When he stepped out, he froze and sucked in a harsh breath. Gunny had removed his shirt and was bent over unlacing his shoes. The blue fabric of his pants stretched taut, his muscular ass and back flexing. Mac swallowed his moan and clutched the box to keep from grabbing on to that perfect ass and ripping away the material. *With my teeth*, he thought, then rolled his eyes.

"Quit it," Mac growled.

"Wh—" Gunny started and then smirked when he spotted the wrapped box in Mac's hand. "Stop what?" he asked as he straightened.

"Breathing." He shoved the gift into the bastard's sexy bare chest. "You're distracting me again," he grumbled and sat down on the edge of the bed.

Gunny put the box to his ear and shook it. "Can I open it?"

"No, Gunny, I stopped you from taking your clothes off so you could stand there and hold that," he said sarcastically, leaned back on his hands, feet stretched out and ankles crossed. "Give me a show, baby. Shake that box."

"Asshole," Gunny grunted under his breath and set the gift down on the dresser. He pulled the card from beneath the bow and read it aloud, "For our next adventure." Gunny cocked his head and studied Mac. "Our next adventure?" he asked and set the card aside. He pulled the ribbon free. "Sounds ominous."

Mac watched Gunny's face closely as he lifted the lid and frowned when he pushed aside the tissue paper and pulled out the gift. He brought the folded pair of black leather pants to his nose and inhaled deeply. His smile was crooked when he lowered the pants and looked at Mac. "Next adventure?"

"You said you wanted to start exploring the leather daddy clubs," Mac said easily. "Figure you'd need to be dressed appropriately."

"In just leather pants?" Gunny teased.

"Keep digging," he said and pointed toward the box. His voice had a bit of a growl in it at the thought of Gunny going in one of those clubs in nothing but a pair of leather pants. Mac would be up on charges of assault soon after arrival.

Gunny folded the pants and set them on the dresser next to the box. He ran a hand lovingly over the leather before he rummaged in the box. He pulled away more tissue paper and took out another folded garment. He carefully unfolded it and held the long-sleeve, black leather shirt up to his chest. Arching a brow at Mac, Gunny tilted his head. "Um, Mac. The subs usually wear a harness."

"And you'll be wearing that," Mac pointed out resolutely. "And it will be buttoned to the top."

"But—"

"This is not open for discussion, Gunny. Keep digging," Mac growled and crossed his arms over his chest.

"And you thought I was cute when I'm jealous," Gunny chuckled lowly.

Mac grunted in response as he watched Gunny fold the shirt in the same careful manner and set it on top of the pants.

Gunny pulled out the last gift and unwrapped it. Gunny held the collar in both hands, the tissue paper fluttering to the floor. He ran his thumb over the leather, flicked the large silver O-ring. The look on

Gunny's face was hard to read. Mac had expected what? Turned-on? Excitement? But what he saw looked like reverence, confusion, tenderness. Mac hadn't expected those emotions.

Mac hefted himself off the bed and ran his hand down Gunny's back. "You okay?"

"I sometimes have these dreams," Gunny said softly, still looking at the collar. "I'm in this club and there is this huge crowd standing around me, all trying to get my attention. I'm not sure whom to pick. They are all screaming and it's this jumble of noise so I can't understand them. I'm so fucking confused, but I know I can't be there without someone." Gunny turned over the collar in his hand and shook his head. "Then you push your way through the crowd, walk right up to me and put a collar around my neck, and everyone knows who I belong to."

"That's why I'd never let you in one of those clubs alone." Mac wrapped his arms around Gunny's waist and kissed the back of his neck. "Everyone would try to take you from me."

Gunny set the collar aside and turned in Mac's arms. "They could try," he said and pulled Mac in closer. "What you did today—" Gunny swallowed hard and squeezed his eyes shut briefly. When he opened them again, the sincerity and warmth in them made Mac's chest tighten. "That was better than any dream. Thank you," Gunny said, voice thick with emotion.

"I didn't do—"

"Shut up and take a compliment," Gunny chastised lightly. "You announced to all our peers, friends, and family that I belonged to you." His voice cracked, and he laughed to cover it up. "Yeah, yeah, I know I'm a major sap."

"Yup you are," Mac said and kissed the man until he was breathless. "But you're my sap." Mac nuzzled Gunny's neck as he caught his breath. Between the thought of Gunny being vulnerable, along with the images Gunny's dream inspired running on a loop in Mac's head and the warm naked torso pressed against him, Mac couldn't help but smile. He was a lucky son of a bitch.

"You know," Mac added, still nuzzling. "You may belong to me, but you own me."

Gunny shook with laughter. "Yeah, now who's the sap?"

"Shut up," he grumbled and nipped at the thick muscle.

"Ow! Bastard!" Gunny shoved him; Mac stumbled back. "Vampire is not going to be one of your new hobbies." Gunny grunted and rubbed his abused neck.

"I don't know," Mac said with a grin. "Might be a good plan to keep me out of trouble. I'm really, really good at sucking."

"It's the biting part that worries me," Gunny tossed over his shoulder as he headed out the door.

"Hey! Where the hell you going?" he asked, following Gunny down the hall. "And I won't bite too hard, maybe just nibble a little."

"You're not the only one who thought about retirement activities," Gunny replied and stepped into the guest room.

Mac leaned against the doorframe as Gunny rummaged around in the closet. "If it's a stake and hammer, I won't be impressed," he warned him.

Gunny brought a large cardboard box out and set it on the bed. "Damn! Why didn't I think of that?"

"'Cause you like the biting and the sucking too much," he reminded him and pushed away from the door. "Nice wrapping paper."

"Thanks. Did it myself," Gunny said proudly.

Mac rolled his eyes and pulled the clear tape from the seam of the box, opened it, and burst out laughing. He grabbed one of the new headsets for his Xbox and held it up. "You bought me toys! I love you," he snorted.

"A full dozen. That should keep you busy for a while," Gunny chuckled. "Can't have a boy without his toys." Mac arched a brow. "Okay." Gunny laughed harder, holding up his hands in defense. "My *man* can't be without his toys."

Mac dropped the headset back in the box and wrapped his arms around Gunny's waist. "That's right, 'cause a happy man with toys takes damn good care of his boy," Mac said and pressed their mouths together. "I love it, thank you."

"Mmm. I like being your boy." Gunny slid his hands under Mac's arms and around him, and pulled him in tighter. "You're welcome," he murmured against Mac's lips.

Mac's pulse sped, his arousal warming as his hands roamed along Gunny's back. He kissed him passionately, feeling Gunny's erection renew and press against his own rigid length. "Can we please have sex now," Mac groaned. He dropped both hands to Gunny's ass and ground their groins together. "I've had enough sentiment and pleasantries and parties, and I just really want to show you my appreciation by fucking you silly."

"I love you fucking me," Gunny said in a harsh whisper and humped hard against Mac.

"Good, 'cause I love me fucking you." He started to pull Gunny toward the door, keeping their lips pressed together.

It had been an amazing day, even with the blemish of Gunny's missing parents. He was proud of the speech he'd made. Telling everyone Gunny belonged to him, and he to Gunny, had been an even prouder moment. But none of it could compare to the way Gunny made him feel when they were wrapped around and in each other. They had a whole lifetime to explore beyond duty activities.

CHAPTER
Twenty-Two

Dear Mom and Dad,

I hope this letter finds you both well. I've picked up the phone a half a dozen times to call, but I couldn't seem to get my thoughts together, so I'm writing my feelings down. I ask you to forgive me this, but I felt it was the easiest way to say what I need to without losing my nerve, getting angry or upset. So here goes.

I've learned a lot throughout my life, but I think the best lesson I've learned is to never regret the things I've done, only the things I haven't. You see, I can admit that I've made many mistakes in my life, but I wouldn't change a single one of them. While I may not be proud of every decision I've made, I'm glad I made them. I've learned from both the good and the bad choices. Had I not made mistakes, I would not have learned from them, and without those life lessons, I wouldn't be the man I am today.

A good man.

Do you know how I know I'm a good man? Because an honest, hardworking, loyal, and good man loves me. Mac knows every mistake

*I've ever made, knows what scares me, what my
weaknesses are, who I am at the very core of my
being, and he still wants to spend the rest of his
life with me. I must have done something right
in my life, learned my lessons and atoned for my
mistakes, because had I not, if I'm not a good
man, then someone like Macalister Jones would
not have asked me to marry him.*

*I love you both very much and nothing
would make me happier than to have you there
as Mac and I commit ourselves to each other.
I've attached the details and directions as well
as a video from our retirement ceremony.*

Love Always,

Gunny

The letter went unanswered.

GUNNY looked around his backyard, the last of the leaves hanging on precariously in the cool fall wind. Mac's greenhouse, nearly complete with its peaked glass roof, stood as the backyard's centerpiece. Winter would settle in soon and bring with it the holidays and the New Year. He smiled when he thought of bringing in 2012 with Mac as his husband.

To say there hadn't been any fallout from Mac's speech during their retirement ceremony would be a lie. A couple of the guys Gunny had known, served beside, and had considered friends had the same reaction the asshole Justin had, but for the most part he had to admit Mac had been right. Everything was going to be okay. Would he ever get used to the disgusted looks on the faces of strangers when they saw him and Mac holding hands? No. Would such derogatory words like faggot forever bother him? Yup. However, he didn't dwell on them. He had an amazing life with Mac, and he wouldn't change that for anything or anyone.

"There you are," Mac called out.

Gunny turned to see Mac tromp down the back stairs, dressed in black trousers and a white tailored dress shirt, the same as Gunny wore. Mac had been letting his dark hair grow out, the silver streaks shining in the early afternoon sun, and he looked so damn good it caused Gunny's breath to catch.

"Hey," he said.

"Car's all packed," Mac informed him as he came up to stand next to Gunny and wrapped an arm around his waist. "You about ready to go?" he asked, his lips brushing softly along Gunny's cheek.

"Almost." He turned and took Mac into his arms. "I was just thinking about the New Year," he admitted lightheartedly.

"Yeah?" Mac ran his hands up and down Gunny's back, pressing them closer. "What about it?"

A shudder went through Gunny as Mac's warm breath and soft lips tickled along his jaw. "I was just thinking how amazing it's going to be to bring in the New Year with you."

"This year and every year," Mac promised still kissing and nibbling. "We better go if you plan on bringing it in as my husband," he whispered against Gunny's ear, making him shudder again.

"Husband," he echoed. "I like that word," Gunny hummed happily.

"Mmm, me too," Mac murmured and took Gunny's mouth in a blistering kiss that bathed him in warmth, despite the cool temperatures. "Now, I'm ready," Mac said breathlessly when the kiss ended.

Gunny could only nod, a goofy grin on his face as he followed Mac to the car. Mac held the passenger-side door open for him and waited until Gunny slid in and buckled up before he shut the door and ran around to the driver's side.

"It's weird," he told Mac once they were on the road. "Nothing will be different between us this afternoon, it's not even legal, but why the hell am I so giddy over the word husband?" he asked thoughtfully. "I mean seriously, what changes between us?"

Mac shrugged. "I don't know. Maybe because it sounds better introducing you as my husband rather than 'this is the dumbass who shares my bed every night and puts up with my bullshit'?"

"You are such an ass," Gunny laughed.

"Yeah, but you're the dumbass who puts up with me," Mac said wryly.

Mac cocked his head and looked at Gunny for a second, a thoughtful expression on his handsome face, before turning his attentions back to the road. "Honestly, I think it's because it's a way of fitting in to what society deems normal. Not that I've ever considered myself as such." He arched a brow and chuckled. "But why can't we be viewed as the same? There is absolutely no difference between what we have and what our parents have other than you and I are the same gender."

"Good point," Gunny said with a curt nod. "Although, I was thinking more along the lines of, introducing you as my husband lets people know we're committed, and that I'll rip their fucking arms off if they try to wrestle you from mine. But yeah, your explanation is pretty good too," he conceded.

"Dammit, why the hell didn't I think of that? Your reasoning sounded more like something I would have said," Mac grumbled.

"I think you're finally rubbing off on me," Gunny said seriously.

"I'd like to rub off on you," Mac said with a seductive tone. He glanced down at his watch. "I think we have time for a premarriage celebratory orgasm."

"I am not standing up in front of your parents and chaplain smelling like sex," Gunny told him adamantly. "Your dad may be coming around to the idea his son is marrying another dude, but that doesn't mean he's real comfortable with it yet." He shook his head. "This close to Christmas I am not messing up my shot at a great gift."

"Mom does the shopping. But you're right, probably not a good idea." Mac held out his fist. "Mile high club?"

Gunny bumped his knuckles against Mac's. "Deal!" It would definitely keep his mind off the four-hour flight to Key West. *I hate flying.* A shiver ran through Gunny. Anything to keep his mind off the fact that he'd be thirty thousand feet above the ground worked for him, and if it included an orgasm, all the better.

Mac maneuvered the SUV into the parking lot of the Community Center. A friend of Tom's who was a minister had agreed to preside over the ceremony. Neither Gunny nor Mac was very religious, but Mac's mom had thought their union should be blessed, and who was he to fight with Clare Jones?

"Last chance to back out?" Mac said, putting the car in park and shutting off the engine. "Once you say 'I do,' I own your ass for the rest of your life."

"You already own me, Macalister Jones, this is just details," he said and leaned over and placed a soft kiss on Mac's cheek.

"Ditto," Mac said, his voice a little hoarse, and stepped out of the car.

As they made their way up the sidewalk, Gunny checked his pocket for the one-hundredth time and felt the outline of the gold band and smiled. His smile grew even wider as he stepped into the foyer of the Community Center and spotted their good friend Tom chatting with Mac's parents.

"Hi," Gunny said with a wave.

The three of them waved back. Clare stepped up first and wrapped her arms around Gunny. "Hi, Gunther. You look wonderful."

"Thank you, Clare," he said and returned the hug briefly. She moved on to give her son a hug, and Gunny shook hands with both Theodore and Tom, and thanked them for coming.

Since their retirement ceremony had been such an elaborate affair, he and Mac had decided that the only ones they really wanted at their commitment ceremony were their parents; Tom had insisted on coming, and well... Gunny's mom and dad? It still hurt his heart that they hadn't spoken to him since he had told them about him and Mac. He rubbed at the ache in his chest and did his best to push the morose feelings aside. He'd invited them; it was all he could do. Besides, it wasn't as if he and his mom were on the best of terms anyway.

Mac slung an arm over his mom's shoulder and asked, "Are we ready?" He looked at Gunny pointedly and winked.

Gunny nodded and followed him to a large office that belonged to the director of the center. The room was sparse, plain white walls, devoid of any personal touches. The man who occupied the room was either just moving in or boring as hell. The minister, John Russell, whom they'd met only once before, smiled at them from where he sat behind a metal desk, and closed the book he'd been reading. Gunny suspected it was a bible, but from where he stood he couldn't be sure. John was anything but boring and definitely brought color to the room. He was a good ten years younger than Gunny, had a head full of shaggy brown hair, and looked more like a hipster than he did a minister in his blue plaid vest, cream jacket, and gold scarf. But Gunny had liked him instantly, and he was pretty hip.

"Ah, the special couple has arrived," John said in greeting, pushing his bangs from his eyes, and stood. "Are we ready to proceed?"

"Yes," he and Mac replied in unison.

"Great!" John surveyed the room briefly. "How about we stand over there by the window. This office is so—" He wrinkled his nose. "Boring."

Gunny shrugged and moved to where he'd been instructed.

"Do you have the rings?"

Gunny reached in his pocket and pulled out the gold band and started to hand it to John; Mac did the same. "No. No. You can hold on to them. I was just making sure you had them." After a brief silence he added, "Not very talkative, are you?" and scanned back and forth between Gunny and Mac.

"I don't know about him," Mac said, thrusting his thumb toward Gunny. "But I'm kind of in a hurry to get the honeymoon started," he said flippantly.

Everyone in the room laughed, including the minister. If more men of God looked like John and had the same disposition, Gunny might not have minded going to church.

Gunny nudged Mac with an elbow and whispered, "Behave, your mom is listening."

Mac laughed harder and draped his arm around Gunny's shoulders. "I'm pretty sure she already knows the honeymoon is the best part of the celebration. Don't you, Mom?"

"Behave," Clare said, echoing Gunny, and whopped Mac on the back of the head playfully as she moved to stand close to him. Theodore chuckled and came to stand on the other side of her.

Mac, properly chastised, dropped his arms to his sides and did as his mom ordered, but the mischievous smirk remained.

Tom, who stood to Gunny's right, shook his head, but Gunny could see him biting his lip. No doubt to keep from commenting, or in an attempt to get his laughter under control.

"Okay. Okay. Settle down and we'll get you two on your way in no time," John said and opened his book. "We are here today to celebrate the love between Macalister and Gunther. They have chosen to stand before you to make this declaration of commitment and loyalty. As we gather to share this most important moment in their lives, let us surround them with our love and best wishes for them, their wedding day, and their journey in their new life together.

"Macalister and Gunther, you have chosen to be married, and this ceremony serves to symbolize your love and commitment to each other. It speaks of passion and fire, of hearth and home, and creates a new light and space within which you both will live. This light burns bright and hot much like a flame, and is imbued with a unique spirit which characterizes both of you, and when fused together shines twice as bright. May the eternal flame of your love continue to burn brightly for as long as you both shall live. You are about to make promises to each other. No other vow is more important than those you are about to pledge. As you take this life journey as one, always remember the true magic of love is the ability to stay the course."

Although they stood next to each other, Gunny brushed his pinkie along Mac's hand, needing the connection between them. Mac grabbed Gunny's hand and squeezed. The trembling in Gunny's legs stopped with the connection.

"Macalister, do you take this man to be your partner, to share your life openly with him, to love, honor, and comfort him, in sickness and in health for all time?"

"I do," Mac said without hesitation.

"Macalister, please repeat after me. I, Macalister Jones, take you, Gunther Duchene, to be my partner, to stand beside you always, in celebration and sadness, for richer, for poorer, to love and to cherish, for now and forevermore."

Mac repeated the declaration, his voice clear and confident, and Gunny's heart swelled until he thought it would burst from his chest.

John asked Gunny to repeat the same. He did so without hesitation, although his voice caught with the surge of emotion halfway through. Mac moved his thumb over the back of Gunny's hand in a caress; the simple touch grounded him enough that Gunny was able to repeat the rest of his vows with a stronger voice.

"If you'll face each other please, place the ring on the other's finger, and repeat after me," John instructed. "With this ring I wed you and pledge my faithful love. I take you to be my partner and promise to share my life with you, to speak the truth to you in love. I promise to honor and tenderly care for you forever."

With shaking hands, Gunny carefully slid the gold band on Mac's finger and allowed Mac to slip a ring on his as they repeated what John said. Gunny kept his eyes low, focusing on the ring. His heart raced, and his eyes burned with unshed tears; he knew if he met Mac's gaze, he'd lose it.

John placed his hand over Mac and Gunny's. "These are the hands of your best friend, strong and full of love for you, that are holding yours on your special day as you promise to love each other today, tomorrow, and forever. May God watch over you both, and bless you with passionate love, and through that love, may the slightest touch from these hands comfort you like no other."

John released their hands and with his book clutched to his chest said, "You have expressed your love and commitment through the vows you have taken today and with the exchanging of rings. It now gives me great pleasure to pronounce you joined in this sacred union. Please share your happiness with each other now with a kiss."

His throat dry, Gunny swallowed hard and leaned in to meet Mac halfway and pressed their mouths together. "I love you," Gunny whispered against Mac's lips.

He felt Mac's mouth curl up into a smile against his, and he said lowly, for Gunny's ears only, "I love you, too."

"Ladies and gentlemen, please join me in congratulating the happy couple."

Gunny kissed Mac one more time, and with their hands still joined they turned around. Clare was sniffling into a tissue, Theodore and Tom both had large smiles on their faces, and Gunny was now forever committed to his best friend, his husband. But what made the tears he'd been holding back stream down Gunny's face and his heart feel complete, was the sight of his mom and dad standing next to the door with big smiles on their faces.

Gunny brought Mac's hand to his mouth and kissed the back of it before releasing it. He made his way on shaking legs to his parents. "Thank you for—" He choked on the words, unable to continue. His dad smiled and patted him on the back before his mom wrapped her arms around Gunny and hugged him tight. He fought to stop his tears. Mac was right—he was a sap.

When he released his hold on his mom, she reached up and cupped his face in her hands and looked up at him with tear-filled eyes.

"Do you know how I know Mac is a good man?" she asked.

Gunny couldn't speak, his heart in his throat, and could only shake his head.

"Because you want to spend the rest of your life with him," she said on a sob and hugged him again.

The tears he'd tried so valiantly to hold back fell as the three of them stood there hugging and crying. Gunny didn't know what their coming meant for their relationship, but they were here, he was married to Mac, and his future looked beyond amazing.

SJD PETERSON, better known as Jo, hails from Michigan. Not the best place to live for someone who hates the cold and snow. When not reading or writing, Jo can be found close to the heater checking out NHL stats and watching the Red Wings kick a little butt. Can't cook, misses the clothes hamper nine out of ten tries, but is handy with power tools.

Visit Jo at http://www.facebook.com/SJD.Peterson;

http://sjdpeterson.blogspot.com/; https://twitter.com/SJDPeterson; and http://www.goodreads.com/author/show/4563849.S_J_D_Peterson. Contact Jo at sjdpeterson@gmail.com.

Also from SJD PETERSON

A WHISPERING PINES RANCH NOVEL

LORCAN'S
DESIRE

SJD PETERSON

http://www.dreamspinnerpress.com

WHISPERING PINES RANCH from SJD PETERSON

http://www.dreamspinnerpress.com

PUP

A GUARDS OF FOLSOM NOVEL

SJD PETERSON

http://www.dreamspinnerpress.com

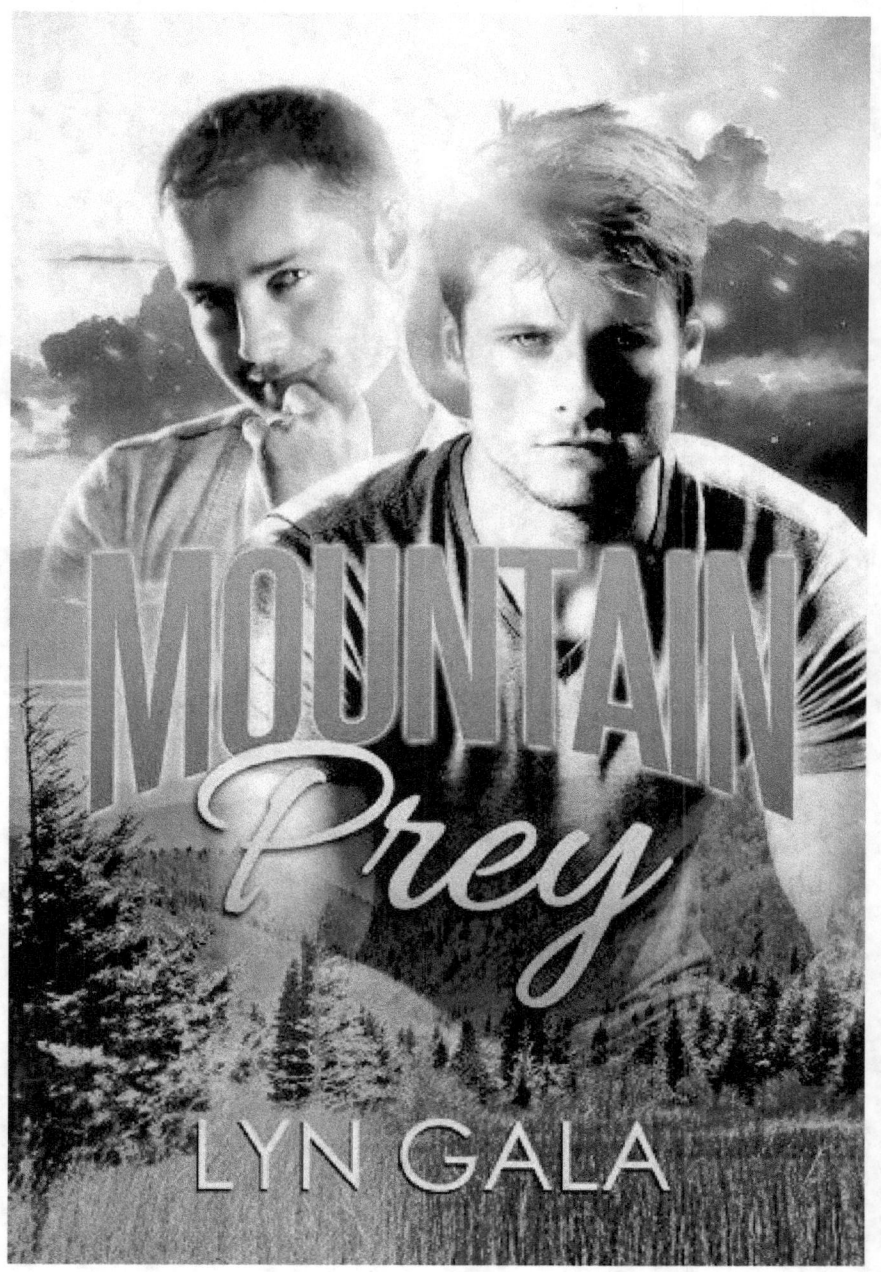

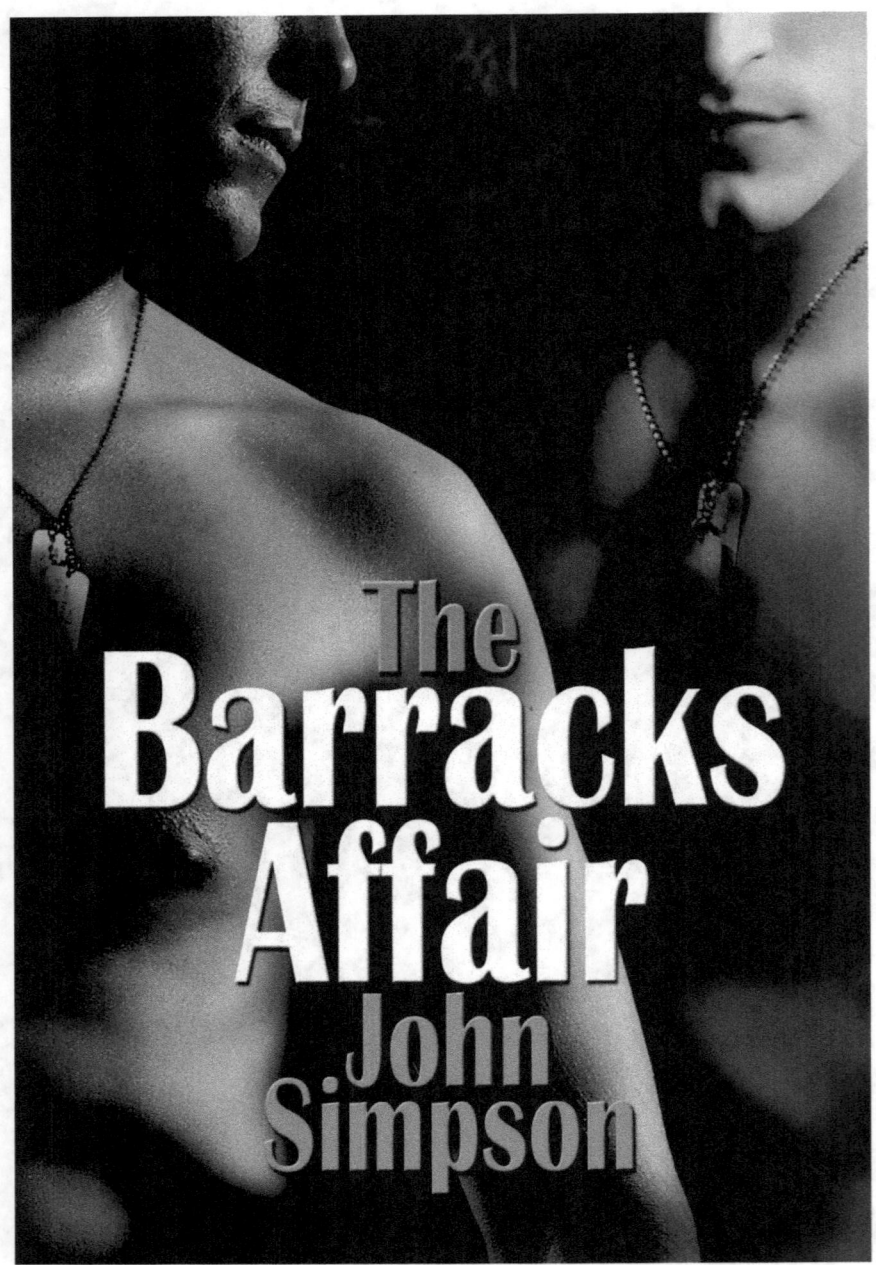